Radford Public Library
30 W. Main St.
Radford, VA 24141

MARY B. KEGLEY

****

FREE IN CHAINS

A Novel

KEGLEY BOOKS OF WYTHEVILLE, VIRGINIA
2002

D1118370

Copyright 2002 by Mary B. Kegley

MAY 3 0 2002

All rights reserved. No part of this book may be reproduced in any form or by any means, including placing any part of it on the Internet, except for the inclusion of brief quotations in a review, without permission in writing from the author, P.O. Box 134, Wytheville, VA 24382, mbkegley@AOL.com

Cover by Charles Phillippi
Cover Design by Stallard Studio

ISBN: 0-9641315-1-X

Library of Congress Catalog Control Number:
20022090558

Printed in United States of America by Walsworth
Publishing Company, Marceline, Missouri
Kegley Books, Wytheville, VA 24382

"Freedom is a natural right of all mankind."
"God of one blood created all nations, Africans not excepted."
Wythe County Deed Book 1, p 179, 1793

As in Biblical times "Rachel wept for her children" because they were not with her.

Dedicated to the descendants of Rachel Findlay wherever they may be.

Radford Public Library
30 W. Main St.
Radford, VA 24141

ACKNOWLEDGMENTS

There is no way to completely thank everyone who has assisted me in the completion of this my first novel. First, I have to be thankful that the clerks of the courts of Wythe and Powhatan counties have preserved the records of Rachel Findlay and some of her family. Without the records this story would not have been dreamed of and without documentation no one would have believed it.

The authors of the many books I have read about Negro and Indian slavery, both fiction and nonfiction, have been extremely helpful. Every one of them brought ideas I could use in my story. Thanks especially to those whose names appear in the bibliography at the end of the book.

There were many people who read the manuscript and made helpful suggestions. Sol Stein saw the potential for the story and used his pen to bring many defects to my attention. Beverly Repass Hoch and her husband, Frank, checked for punctuation and gave suggestions for misplaced dialogue and other defects. John Johnson, a researcher and author of local black history, gave me ideas of the language and grammar more suitable to the Negroes in the story. My daughter Susan marked up the first hundred pages and gave me more ideas than I had ever thought about.

My friend Charles Phillippi, director of the Settlers Museum, Atkins, Virginia, urged me on, argued with me about certain scenes, and gave of his time and effort to see that I made progress on the manuscript. He gave me permission to use the names he chose for the Indian characters, White Cloud and Fox Boy, and referred me to numerous books on the Catawba Indian Nation. In addition, he is a notable, prize-winning artist, and drew a picture of Rachel as he saw her. It appears on the cover.

George Kegley, former editor of the business section of the *Roanoke Times* and editor of the journal for the historical society in Roanoke, also read the many pages of the manuscript and made recommendations. William (Bill) T. Buchanan Jr. with his archeological and historical background, was extremely helpful in pointing out that certain words, colors and materials used in the clothing and certain foods were not available for use in the time period of the novel. He sent me rushing to the dictionaries to see if other words were out of place. Part of the story of Rachel Findlay would have been missing if it had not been for Robert Young Clay, who had gathered information about his family and about Rachel's daughter Jenny, who obtained her freedom in Madison County, Alabama. I appreciate being able to use his research for the novel. *Thanks* to all of you for your support and suggestions.

This novel would probably never have been published if it were not for my editor and friend, Sherry Hawthorne, who gave her expertise to every line and directed my path away from so many writing errors. I can only try to express my deep appreciation for all of her work even though I have not taken every tidbit of advice she offered I realize that your work is of the highest quality. Thanks, Sherry.

When the final draft was completed four more experts came to my assistance, read the novel and gave me their comments for the back cover. They were Brent Tarter, Ardelia Palmer, and Russ and Corinne Earnest. Once more, my friend, Shirley Grose prepared the pages for the printer. She worked tirelessly, putting in more than twenty-four hours, to be sure that the results would look professional. When it came time for the cover, experts at Stallard Studio combined art with photography and produced a very special and appealing cover by computer. Many thanks to all of you.

Mary B. Kegley

Chapter 1

THE TERRIBLE PLAN

"We won't see you no more. The Clays are sending us away."

"Law, what you talking about Rachel?" asked Grandmama Chance. Her voice cracked like a piece of ice in the summer's lemonade.

Rachel started to cry. Little Judy ran to her mother and whimpered. Grandmama's cloth, and her needle and thread wrapped in its folds, fell to the dirt floor. Grandmama Chance pulled herself out of the straight chair by the window and hobbled across the cabin floor with her arms outstretched. The three huddled together for several minutes, rocking back and forth, before Rachel spoke.

"I heard the marse say he don't want me and Judy here no more."

"Oh no. You ain't being sold, are you?" sobbed Chance.

"No, just sent away somewhere far, far away."

"Do you know where?"

"No, but I know we're going somewhere."

"That happens to slaves, Rachel. We know that. We already lost Aunt Judy, and cousin Hannah, and I's scared for your brother Samuel too. And you was gone for three years. 'Course, it seemed like a hundred."

Grandmama Chance patted the long black hair hanging down their backs and squeezed Rachel and Judy gently. "I was so glad Mitchell brung you back to us."

"Me too," sighed Rachel. "But I reckon going away is different this time. I'm really free and shouldn't be going nowhere I don't want to go."

"Uh huh, and just remember that. You and Judy is free."

"But we ain't got no papers."

"Not yet, you ain't, but they'll come from Williamsburg any day now. For you, and Judy, and Samuel, and me. When they come, we'll find you."

"Maybe we should run away now, run to somewhere I can be free."

Grandmama let Rachel lead her back to her chair and handed her sewing to her. "Don't know where that will be, Rachel. Now, dry your eyes and go to Marse William and see what this is all about."

When Rachel crossed the path and entered the big house, she heard loud voices coming from Clay's office. She stopped, peeked around the diningroom door and listened. William Clay was pacing back and forth, nodding his head and waving his hands in agitation. His son, Mitchell, sat quietly. After several minutes the gray head stopped nodding and William sat down at his mahogany desk.

"I told you before we could expect to hear any time. The time has come, and you must take Rachel and Judy and leave immediately," said William. "If you don't, they will be gone from here, gone as free people."

"Father," said Mitchell, "I can be ready tomorrow. I have been planning a trip to New River for some time. What shall I tell Rachel and Judy—or anyone else for that matter?"

"Never mind about telling the slaves or the neighbors.

I'll take care of that. Tell Rachel she's going to Mecklenburg or Kentucky—it won't matter which—to help with planting the crop."

"We talked before about the New River. There's good land out there on the frontier. I might just try my luck there," said Mitchell.

"Good idea. Just remember that these two will be your Negro slaves, not Indian slaves like the court is trying to tell us."

"I guess if some of our relatives hadn't gone to Williamsburg and testified against us, I wouldn't have to leave now."

"That's true. Damn it!"

Mitchell smoothed his blond hair and stood up. "I'll bet that Chance, Rachel and all in the slave quarters are a-waitin' the freedom news."

"Yes, they are. You must pack and get away from here before they receive the papers. I will not suffer the loss of any more of my slaves, even if they are of Indian blood. The sooner you're on the road, the better."

Rachel rattled the pewter plates and knocked them against the railing on the walnut buffet.

"Is that you, Rachel?" asked Mitchell.

Rachel came into the office and Mitchell reseated himself opposite the desk, drumming his fingers on the arm of his chair.

"Rachel, you and Judy are going on a little trip with Mitchell. You will be his slaves now and you will leave in the morning," said William.

"Yes sir, Marse."

"You go and fix up some clothes for you and Judy and

3

be ready at dawn tomorrow."

"Will I be comin' back here?" asked Rachel.

"Probably not for a long time," said William.

"But you know in a few days I be freed. They'll send the papers from Williamsburg."

"You never mind about being free. And don't talk about no papers neither."

He turned to Mitchell.

"You know, son, I'm sure that I am doing the right thing. Any young wench who can bear children is worth a lot of money, and a healthy child like Judy will be able to have children of her own in a few years. Let me think now, Rachel is nineteen and Judy is six. Yes, that's right. Her mother, Nan, would have been about fifty if she hadn't been poisoned, and let's see, Grandmama Chance must be about eighty, I would suspect."

"That's about right, Father."

William took his account book from the desk drawer, dipped his quill pen in the ink pot and wrote the words as he said them out loud to Mitchell and Rachel,

"May 1773, To Mitchell Clay, my son, one Negro wench named Rachel, age 19 and her daughter, Judy, age 6. Value $800 and $200. One horse $100, and two horses for trip to New River, $175."

On a blank piece of paper, William wrote the same words again and handed it to Mitchell. "Now remember, this is your record of ownership. Yes, I am doing the right thing, giving you part of your inheritance now. And you seem so fond of Rachel and the little one."

4

"Thank you, Father," said Mitchell, folding the paper and putting it in his pocket.

"Now, son, go pack your tools, some food, clothes, blankets and everything you might need for the trip. And, Rachel, you get along outa' here and get some things ready for you and Judy."

Rachel raced out of the house and across the yard and into the cabin.

"Oh, Grandmama, it's true, we won't be coming back. Marse Clay just said so."

"Oh, no, Rachel. No, no." Grandmama Chance could not say another word. She stumbled into the chair and put her head down on the table and sobbed. "And just as you was about to be free."

Rachel patted Grandmama on the shoulder and wrapped her arms around her neck.

"Please don't cry, please. Come on, help me pack up a few things for the trip. If I have to go, I have to go. No choice. We never have a choice."

Rachel reached for her dark blue dress hanging on the wall, folded it carefully and laid it on the wooden table.

"Grandmama, tell me one more time what it was like when you first come here. Please." Rachel had heard it all before, but wanted it told again so she could remember forever.

Grandmama struggled to her feet, picked up the white apron that Rachel had dropped on the floor and began in a trembling voice. "Rachel, it was a fright for me and Fox Boy. We knowed nothing of the words. The only one we could talk to was each other. I was called White Cloud—"

"And my Pappy James was called Fox Boy. Is that right?"

"Uh huh, he was. Marse Henry Clay, you know,

5

Mitchell's grandfather, he gave us new names. He said he found me by chance on the road so my name would be Chance."

Grandmama picked up Judy's two little dresses from the chair and added them to the pile on the table. "And Bess was here, and about a dozen other slaves. She helped me get used to this place, and larned me words like *whip, work, tobaccy, field, big house, Marse, Missus,* and the like.

"Did you work in the big house?" asked Rachel.

"At first I was in the fields, but I was no good at that tobaccy work, so I got to be in the house with the Missus. And Fox Boy, your Pappy James, the same. Only he work with that big buck, York, in the blacksmith shop. He was big and strong."

"Did you have a brown dress like mine?" asked Rachel. She folded the only other dress she had and placed it on the pile.

"Just one or two like that, no blue one, just brown."

Rachel opened the little wooden box near the foot of the bed. She pulled out some stockings for Judy and herself and passed them to Grandmama.

"I never had no stockings at all," said Grandmama.

Rachel reached to the bottom and pulled out two red shawls. She held them to her face.

"You made these for Judy and me. I'll think of you every time I sees them and know that you loved us enough to make these pretties for us."

Rachel crossed the room and hugged her Grandmama, crushing the shawls between them. "Thank you."

"Better not pack them. It'll be cool in the morning and with no coat you might need to have them around your shoulders," said Chance as she returned to her chair.

6

Rachel put the shawls on the bed. "Guess we'll need the blankets from the bed. I'll pack them in the morning."

"How you git to be with Marse William?" asked Judy, who was watching every move.

"I walk all the way from the Catawber Nation in South Carolina, a long, long ways. Marse Henry Clay, Marse William's father, captured us both and made us walk, well, maybe I should say, run."

"Run?" asked Judy.

"Yes, run. We was tied to the horses with a rope around our waists and when the horse trotted, we trotted, or else we got dragged on the ground. And our feet hurt all the time. We didn't have no shoes. And we couldn't get free."

"What was Henry Clay doin' there in Carolina?"

"Back in them days, him and Peter Womack was called Indian traders. They spent a lot of time among the southern tribes. He brought beads, cloth, axes, bells, pins, needles, and mirrors, and all kinds of things. When ole Marse Henry came to the Catawber, he got pottery and baskets from the women and then deer skins from the men. But they wasn't s'posed to take no people."

Chance closed her eyes and shook her head. "You know, Rachel, I near drowned in the river, some big river with the water so high we had to swim across. If it hadn't been for your Pappy James I woulda drowned."

"Didn't you live on a river?" asked Rachel.

"Yes, we was called the River People, Catawber. That means River People. We fish, get water for our horses, and I play at the river bank a lot of times."

Chance stirred from the chair and supported herself with her cane. "Before the sun sets, walk with me to the graveyard. I want you to say goodbye to your mama, and I want to talk to your Pappy James."

With Rachel on one side and Judy on the other, the three ambled down the sandy road and at the edge of the woods sat on the ground near the sunken graves, marked with small wooden markers.

"Here's your grandpappy, Pappy James," said Chance pointing her gnarled finger to the spot. "I call him Fox Boy. He was a fine Catawber brave. He was you mama's pappy, and your Aunt Judy's and Aunt Aggie's. Thomas was his'n too."

Chance inched to the right and settled at the grassy spot where Nan had been laid to rest years ago. "Now there's your mama, Nan. Her life ended when you was a baby."

"I think you told me once she was poisoned."

"That's what we think, Rachel. Marse Clay brought Doctor Findlay. She was so sick. He did everything he could. He said he thought it was arsenic poisoning."

"Who did that awful thing?" asked Rachel.

"We ain't sure but three Negro boys was hanging around a lot and one was jealous of the others. They got in a fight over Nan. Next thing we knowed she was sick."

"But then you was like my mama, wasn't you?"

"Yes, I was and still am. And you have this darlin' little one over here," said Chance reaching for Judy. "You two and your brother, Samuel, are all I got. Your Aunt Judy was taken away, and now you two will be gone too."

"Where's Samuel now?"

"Samuel's over at the next plantation and when he gets free he is going to git him a wagon and do wagoning."

Chance reached for the edge of her apron and wiped away the tears. "Help me up, it's time to go. Say goodbye to your mama."

8

Rachel and Judy mumbled their goodbyes to someone they never knew. Grandmama Chance whispered her native words to Fox Boy, her strong Catawba brave.

At dawn the cabin doors opened and more than twenty slaves, some black, some mulatto, some Indian, gathered in the yard. Negro Peter held the packhorses and tightened the straps on the loads. Rachel and Judy held onto Grandmama. Chance tried to wipe the tears away but they fell so fast she could only wash her face with the sleeve of her dress.

"Don't forget, Rachel," said Chance, "You are free even without the papers. Our lawyer told us that the General Court will decide today or tomorrow in our favor. The court done it in many other cases."

"Why didn't you get free before now?" asked Judy.

"I knowed I couldn't find my way back to the tribe. I was with Fox Boy, and all my children was here together. But now it's different. I wanna die a free person. And I want you and your mama to be free."

Rachel shivered and tears dripped off of her high cheekbones into the dusty road. *What if I never see my grandmama again? I don't know where I am going to be, but I know it is a long ways away. What if I never return to Swift Creek?* The thought paralyzed her and she stopped near the cabin door.

"I heard Marse say that we might go to plant crops in Mecklenburg, or that we might go to Kentucky." She turned to Grandmama Chance and continued. "I don't know where those places are, or how far away."

"Didn't you say Mitchell was talking about the New River."

9

"I don't know where that place is neither. If Samuel was to look for me and Judy, where would he look?" Rachel dried her tears with the back of her hand, stomped her foot and pointed toward the big house. "One thing I knows for sure, Marse William Clay don't want us to be free. Going away was the Clays' scheme to keep us all in slavery. And there ain't nothing I can do about it."

"Mitchell, son, you best be goin' now."

Mitchell moved to the door of the big house at dawn. He turned to his father, and shook his hand. "I'll be leaving now. Everything is ready, except I left my tobaccy on the desk." Mitchell retreated to the office.

William stood on the porch silently smoking his pipe. He knew of his father's trips to South Carolina. Father Henry and Peter Womack were energetic travelers and noted traders, so he'd heard. They spent much time visiting the Indian nations in the South. He figured it was about 1712 or thereabouts when Chance came home with him. The trip had been a long one, eighteen months, his mother had said. The traders had actually taken their trade goods beyond South Carolina.

William remembered his father talking about the trip and bringing back the beautiful young Indian girl he named Chance and an Indian boy he named James. They became part of the Negro, mulatto and Indian slave family at the Clay plantation. Clay moved to the chair on the porch and lit his pipe again. He had hoped that none of his slaves would ever file in the court for their freedom.

The smoke circled William's head as he thought of the others. After the death of old Henry, Rachel's brother, Samuel, went to live with brother Thomas Clay. Old Judy

10

and Hannah were pledged for a debt and taken to some place he could not recall. Mitchell brought Rachel and Judy back home from Mecklenberg to Swift Creek, about three years ago.

William watched Rachel, Judy and Chance standing in the early morning light. He knew that many slaves of Indian descent in the neighborhood had filed for their freedom and easily obtained it. That's what made him angry. The courts were convinced that the slaves were held under false imprisonment. Hundreds of them knew that their mothers and grandmothers were never legally enslaved. One time, though, that was possible, but not if the Indians came into Virginia after 1705. And Chance had come in after that time. Rachel knew, and William knew, that they were entitled to be free. Samuel and little Judy would also be free, maybe today, maybe tomorrow. Chance had waited near three years for the court to decide. They thought they would be free forever.

"Not if I can help it, not if I can help it," muttered William. He broke off a piece of his clay pipe and threw it across the porch railing into the patch of daffodils.

"Rachel, did you bring your clothes?" shouted Mitchell from the top step. "And some things for Judy too? You know I told you to have everything ready."

"Yes sir, Marse Mitchell, I got them ready." She returned to the slave quarters, dragging her feet as she went up the three steps and disappeared behind the closed door.

When she returned she had her red shawl over her shoulders, and the one for Judy in her arms. She held the remaining clothes, wrapped in a blanket roll tied with a leather strap. Her right hand curled around the walking

11

stick. She knew that the trip ahead was not going to be all riding. She came to the horses. Everyone gathered around, eyes brimming with tears. They said their farewells and murmured words of encouragement.

Rachel scrambled up on the gray horse, and Mitchell put Judy in front of her. Judy was crying softly.

"We's together. Don't cry now." Rachel tried to wipe away the tears from the sad little face. "And we'll be with Mitchell, not some stranger."

"I don't want to go."

"I know, I don't neither. It is a day we will not forget. Something terrible is happening to us."

Judy and Rachel turned to watch the family, their family, fading in the distance.

Chance stumbled up the cabin steps, and closed the door with a bang. *I will not forget this day. Rachel and Judy gone, and my dream for them gone. Their right to freedom gone too. I dreamed of release from slavery and release from the whip. All gone, all gone.*

Chance settled into her chair and pounded her fists on the table and began shouting. "I hate you, hate you, hate the whole Clay family. You split my family in two again. I hate you."

Chance raised her bloody hands and hammered the table one more time. "I know of the beatings, the drudgery, and the endless work of slavery. Nothing will ever be the same at Swift Creek. I wish I was dead."

Chapter 2

THE TRIP TO THE FRONTIER: 1773

Mitchell had decided to follow the road south to the Appomattox River and to stop at the Amelia Courthouse first. Then their journey would be westerly. Eventually he would stop in New London in Bedford County where he had visited before. From there they would stop at the Town of Fincastle. There he was sure that he could find out about the New River land and present conditions.

After several days of enjoyable riding, the blue mountains of Western Virginia came into view. Their smooth, round peaks were beginning to turn lime green with spring growth. At a distance they looked purple and blue, tinged with shades of green.

On the other side of the mountains there were pleasant valleys, and more mountains could be seen in the haze in the distance. They would soon be on the road to New River. At each of the tavern houses where they stopped, Mitchell asked for information about the New River people, the settlements, the land, and any detail he could get. He knew this would be helpful when he came closer to the place he had determined would be a good place to settle. It would be so far away from Swift Creek no one would know that

Rachel or Judy had Indian blood, and they would be recognized only as his Negro slaves.

The news on the frontier was encouraging. Mitchell heard that many settlers had arrived from Pennsylvania and Maryland and more were coming in every day. The land was plentiful, the soil rich, and the timber tall. The number of springs seemed to be unlimited and water in the creeks ran swift and clear. Every pioneer who wanted land could buy on easy terms at a good rate. A new land, a new challenge, and a new existence lay ahead of Mitchell Clay and his prize possessions, Rachel and Judy. In the meantime he could surely find a place to live, at least temporarily.

One foggy morning on the Great Road near Fincastle, a blue-eyed, black-haired stranger rode along side Mitchell and his slaves and began a conversation.

"Where ya' going, friend?" asked the Irishman.

"Goin' to the New River to settle," said Mitchell.

"I heard they is Indians out that way." The suggestion came with an Irish brogue. "I heard all is quiet now, but doubt that will last."

"And you, where you going?" asked Mitchell.

"Goin' to a spot no one has taken. Gonna get some cattle and horses, and plant a little Indian corn and maybe some day I will have slaves like you."

"Don't they plant tobacco out here?"

"Don't think so. Not cotton neither. Just Indian corn."

"Have ya' any kinfolks out this way?" asked Mitchell.

"Not yet, but more are comin' any time, comin' out of Pennsylvania. Land's too expensive up there."

"Do you think the Catholic Church will find you way out here? You're Irish ain't ya?"

"We're Presbyterians—you know, Protestant people.

14

Don't you know nothin'?" asked the Irishman, bristling.

"Guess not," said Mitchell sheepishly.

"Well, the old governor of Virginia, what's his name, maybe Goose or Gooch, or something like that. He said we could have our own churches out here. The only reason was he wanted someone to protect all those Englishmen in eastern Virginia from the savages who live beyond the mountains."

"Sounds like a governor. He can sit pretty in Williamsburg, or sometimes even stay in England and still run this place, or he thinks he can, anyway."

Joining them at the spring near the town was a group of people speaking a language that Mitchell did not recognize. He learned that they were speaking German and were from the Rhine country. Noted for being good farmers and eager immigrants, they too were traveling into the New River area.

When the travelers arrived in the Town of Fincastle, they went up the hill to the new courthouse, past the new log houses to the local tavern next to the jail. The innkeepers had good food and drink, and it seemed that the merchants and blacksmiths had plenty of work.

Mitchell took it all in. He would soon have to make a decision. A few more miles and the New River would be in sight. Other travelers gave him advice on which way to go, where the best land was, and each, of course, had their own ideas. Now that Mitchell was on his own, he could finally make his own decisions. No Father to tell him what to do.

Three weeks after their departure, Rachel, Judy and Mitchell came to New River, only to find that many of the most suitable places had been taken by others. It was here that they learned that there was some good river bottom land on the Bluestone River, a branch of the New, a day's journey beyond the settlement. The next day they found their way to a place called Clover Bottom.

True to its name, it was covered with clover. Mitchell removed his black hat and looked in every direction. Along the river banks the land was flat with a few large rocks. It stretched as far as he could see. It was better than he imagined. A few hundred yards from the river, the fields were flanked with large trees. Mitchell noticed a clearing in the woods, and he found a big spring nearby. Before dark he set about building a lean-to.

"Marse Mitchell, where is the cabin for us?" asked Judy.

"We'll all be together here in this lean-to 'til we can build a cabin. It only takes twenty-eight trees to make a one-room log cabin, or that's what the innkeeper told me. So tomorrow we start cutting down trees."

"What 'bout a garden?" asked Judy. "Is we goin' to have a garden?"

"Yes, we will do that too. You and me have to clear a little ground, plant the Indian corn, and maybe some pumpkins."

Rachel and Mitchell Clay had never done such hard work, but they knew they had to get a crop in or they wouldn't survive the winter. Mitchell and Rachel worked side by side trimming the limbs from felled trees and with Judy's help had made brush piles to burn later. Mitchell and his horse worked the logs into a pile at the edge of the field. Somebody would have to show him how to build a log cabin. When the ground was prepared they put in the corn and a few pumpkin seeds and rounded up the hills.

Mitchell made a trip to the ferry to get supplies. On one of his trips, he bought Rachel a cow. She named her

Queenie and milked her twice a day. In the summer evenings after Judy was asleep, Rachel and Mitchell often sat on one of the logs talking quietly.

"It's so peaceful here. Hope you like it like I do, Rachel."

"It's so far away from Grandmama Chance and everyone at Swift Creek. Law, how I miss 'em."

"But Rachel, you know I will always look after you and Judy. I want you to know I will never sell you, never. You have my word."

"It's different out here. Not many people have slaves. Not like at your pappy's house."

"We grew up together, Rachel. I promise to be with you always."

Mitchell moved closer to Rachel, putting his arm around her waist, pulling her close to him. "You know you are my wench, don't you?"

Rachel did not answer.

In the fall, Rachel and Judy helped Mitchell pick the corn and the pumpkins. They found some chestnuts in the woods not far away, and she and Judy filled their wooden buckets more than once. Sometimes they caught fish from the river, and often Mitchell brought a rabbit home for their dinner. Deer and turkey were plentiful too.

When they had enough logs to build a little cabin, some of the neighbors came and helped finish their little house. The three of them moved inside and settled down to winter before the stone fireplace.

Chapter 3

THE SALE: 1774

John Draper, a tall lanky frontiersman, seated astride a black horse, moved through the brush and into the open, studying the grandeur of the river scene. In the distance he spotted the little cabin and turned in that direction.

Draper approached the young man chopping wood near the cabin door and introduced himself, lifting his black hat slightly.

The young man said, "My name's Clay, Mitchell Clay. Draper, you say? Seems I heard that name before. Isn't there a Draper's Meadow?"

"Aye, that's true. Named for me. Lived there one time, back in the wartime. Them Indians came in there and burned everything. Not much left of that place now. Took my sister and her children, killed my widowed mother and my son, and wounded my wife, Bettie, and took her away to the nation on the Ohio."

His voice was harsh with bitterness as he continued.

"Those damn savages killed Colonel Patton too, and wounded a lot of others. And there was nothing I could do. Nothing."

"I'm sorry. Where was you when this happened?"

"Me and William Ingles, my brother-in-law, were in

19

the field without our guns, and all we could do was watch as ten or more of them came in and burned everything and spread the white man's blood around."

"Did your wife get back home?"

"Aye, had to pay a ransom for her and after six long years I got her back. My sister walked back from the Ohio but hasn't been the same since. She and her husband run Ingles Ferry on the New River. As for me, I moved to the Peak Knob Mountain. Couldn't go back to the meadows. Just couldn't."

Mitchell dipped some water from the bubbling spring with the gourd and handed it to his visitor. "Don't dwell on it now. It's over and done with," said Mitchell.

Draper slurped the refreshment and wiped his chin as the water spread over his wool shirt. "Thanks. Over and done with. Yes."

"What are you doin' up this a way?" asked Mitchell.

"I was here during the war and scouted out places on the Bluestone looking for Indians. I got a warrant for my service, a thousand acres, and this seemed to be the right place to choose the land."

"But this is my land," explained Mitchell, waving his arm toward the Clover Bottom.

"Don't think so, Mr. Clay. I came down river to see about this very piece of land. I have my warrant and need a survey next. I told the surveyor when I was here before where I wanted the lines to run. It looks like you're trespassing on my land," said Draper in a matter-of-fact tone.

Mitchell grabbed the gourd from Draper's hand and threw it on the ground. "What do you mean? I filed for this land last month and expect to git a survey any day now," he said, his voice growing louder.

"What I'm telling you is that I hold a warrant for it and

the surveyor will be here soon. I own this land and you are trespassing and I want you out of here right now."

Mitchell stiffened. "But we've been here over a year. We've cleared land, built a cabin, planted a crop." Mitchell's voice trembled as he looked over the improvements he had made.

"That may be, Mr. Clay, but this is my land. Now clear out. Out." said Draper. His voice was icy hard.

Mitchell started for the cabin when the door opened and Rachel and Judy appeared.

"Who's here, Mitchell?" asked Rachel.

"This here's John Draper. Says he owns this land," said Mitchell in a gruff tone.

"Them yours?" asked Draper as he studied the two figures on the doorstep.

"Yeah, they're mine."

Draper edged closer, and gave Rachel a long look, his blue eyes investigating her body from head to foot. He saw a beautiful brown-skinned woman, a woman apparently with child. Rachel took a step back and stared at the steps. She started to close the door but Draper stopped her.

"You two sure would make a great addition to my slave family. Got three men and I've had them for a long time. Need some women there. And Bettie sure could use some help."

Draper wondered what Clay would take for them. He had never seen such beautiful black eyes.

"Where did you get these two?" asked Draper.

"My father gave them to me just before I left eastern Virginia."

Draper turned his head to look again at Rachel and Judy. "You two could come and live with me."

Rachel made no answer.

21

"Maybe we can make a deal." Mitchell avoided looking at Rachel as he spoke. He took Draper's elbow and edged him away from the cabin. "I'd hate to lose all the work I've done here. How much do you want for your land?"

"You thinking of buying my claim?" asked Draper.

"Maybe. Maybe a trade would be more like it."

Draper studied Clay's face. Did he want to sell Rachel and Judy? Did he want to find a wife somewhere? Did he really want the land?

"I'll tell you what, Mr. Clay, if you give me the wench and her youngun' right now I'll sign over the whole thousand acres," said Draper. "But it's got to be done right now." Draper waved the title at Mitchell.

Mitchell reached out his hand to shake on it and said, "You got a deal."

Rachel heard the words, trade, sell, deal, and only last night Mitchell had promised not to sell her. Especially now that she was with child. None of the Clays had sold their slaves, just bought them and kept them for family. She listened in horror. At first when she told Clay about the new life inside her belly, she was sure Clay wouldn't sell her. Would he now trade her for the land? Was that any different from selling her? Now she felt an awful dread. She wanted to stop up her ears. She wanted to run away. She wanted to die. This was worse than any whipping, worse than being dead and gone forever.

Rachel heard the man on horseback say, "Get your stuff, wench. You've been sold. You're coming with me."

She looked at Mitchell Clay. Tears slowly rolled down

22

her cheeks. Her hands clasped her belly. "Don't do this, Mitchell."

"Sold? Wait a minute!" shouted Clay. "Not so fast."

Rachel let out a sigh, held her breath, and waited. Mitchell turned his back to Rachel and walked away. "We need to make this here trade legal-like, Draper," said Mitchell, pulling Draper aside. "I need you to sign over the land on your title bond, and I s'pose you want a bill of sale for the Negroes."

"Yes, that's right. But we need to find some witnesses and someone who can write the papers."

"I heard William Ingles is over at the Harman's on 'The Horseshoe' on New River. They could be the witnesses and help us get the papers in order," Clay volunteered.

"Well, it's still early, we could ride over there now. Or do you want to wait until tomorrow?" asked Draper.

"Let's go right now. Rachel, gather up your things for you and Judy, saddle the horses, and we will be on the way."

Rachel ran from the cabin to the shed, put her head up against the stall and cried. She raised her clenched fist and pounded on the stall until her hand was numb.

Why hadn't Samuel come to rescue her? Should she tell this tall black-haired man that she was free? Who would ever believe a slave? Besides, Mitchell had that paper from his father if there were any problems. And she had no papers, nowhere to go. If she spoke up she would be whipped.

She gathered up her few possessions from the cabin, put on her red shawl and brought her child to the two men and the horses. She stood staring at the ground waiting for one of them to tell her what to do next.

"Get up, Rachel, and I'll lift Judy so she can sit in front," said Clay. "We have a wee bit of a ride so we can fix the papers and then you and Judy can go and live with Draper. I'll tie your things on the back here."

Tears welled up again in Rachel's eyes. Her hands touched her belly and she looked into his blue eyes and said, "You promised. You promised."

Rachel watched as Clay turned away, mounted his own horse and led the group as they moved out of the river bottom and toward the south. The morning sun was now overhead and the early cherry trees salted the hillside with their white blossoms. A few dogwoods had burst forth and were mingled with the other trees just beginning to turn from winter brown to emerald green. It would have been a beautiful day, but Rachel knew it was ugly, the ugliest she had ever seen.

When they stopped at a bubbling spring along the way, they took time too eat a few bites of bread Rachel had packed. Another three hours and Rachel was at "The Horseshoe" where several of the local citizens had gathered. Two men—she later identified them as Valentine and Jacob Harman—were unloading skins and furs and were showing them to their neighbors and the Northern traders.

"William, are you here anywhere? William Ingles!" Draper called out.

It was Ingles' wife, Mary, who answered. "Oh, John, how wonderful to see you. William is across the river but will return shortly. Come in, come in, and tell me the latest news of Bettie and the children. We have not seen each other for months it seems."

"What a nice surprise to see you, sister Mary. Are you here visiting the Harmans?"

"Yes, I decided to come along with William just for a day or two. We return to the ferry tomorrow."

They entered Harman's log house, and Catharine Harman and Mary stirred up the coals in the fireplace and set out the tin cups. Rachel and Judy sat on the steps at the cabin door, as John and Mitchell stepped inside. John stretched his long legs around the rungs of the chair and tilted back against the cabin wall. Mitchell sat at one end of the wooden table.

"Made a good deal today, Mary," said Draper. "Got me two wenches, and a good chance of a third one. I've traded my thousand acres I had for serving as a lieutenant in the late war. Probably more practical too."

"Didn't you think about settling up there on Bluestone?" asked Mary.

"I thought about it, but I am well settled at the Mountain and probably would never move to Clover Bottom anyhow. Besides, those nigger men of mine need some women." Draper smiled. Mary poured the tea and Catherine offered the bread to the travelers.

"And I got a good deal, too," said Mitchell. "Got me some good land and now I can go look for a wife." Mitchell pushed the fresh-baked bread into his mouth and continued talking with his mouth full. "Now I can have a real family."

"Guess the wench and her child will need something too," said Catharine.

"Yes," said Mary, fixing a small serving for each of them. "Mr. Clay, you take it to them."

"If the horses need water take them to the little trough Jacob made out near the shed," said Catharine.

Mitchell moved outside, passed the bowls to Rachel and Judy without a word and without looking at either of them.

Rachel's voice dropped to a whisper. "You promised,

25

Mitchell. You promised not to sell me and Judy."

Mitchell ignored her. He went down the lane to greet William Ingles, Valentine and Jacob Harman, as they crossed the river bottom and approached the Harman cabin. They greeted each other and entered the cabin, passing Rachel and Judy on the steps.

Draper announced that it was time to tend to business.

"We need your help, William. And yours, Valentine and Jacob," said Mitchell." I have exchanged the Negro woman and her child for Draper's interest in the land on Clover Bottom. Need the papers drawn up."

"We can do that," said William. "Let me find some paper, the inkpot and quill. Adam Wall can write it and we three can be the witnesses."

When the four gathered at the table Adam began to write.

> *To whom it may concern. Know ye that I Mitchell Clay for and in consideration of the sum of one hundred and twenty pounds current money to me in hand paid by John Draper (the receipt whereof I do hereby acknowledge) have bargained and sold & by these presents do bargain and sell to John Draper his heirs and assigns a Negro Woman named Rachel aged 20 years or thereabouts and a Negro girl name Jude age 7 years or thereabouts, the title of which Negroes I and my heirs will for ever warrant & defend to the said John Draper & his heirs and assigns against the claim of all persons whatsoever. Witness my hand and seal this 25 April 1774.*

Mitchell picked up the quill, dipped it in the inkpot and made his X in the space under the words "his mark." Adam added the word "Seal" encompassed by an off-center circle and the words, *Signed and sealed and delivered in the presence of* —. Then Ingles took his turn, signed his name W. Ingles with the letter W joining with the flourish of the I in Ingles. Jacob Harman signed next followed by Valentine Harman.

Draper took his papers from his pocket, found the title bond for his land, turned it over and wrote

> *I hereby release all my right title and interest in 1,000 acres on Clover Bottom on the Blue Stone River, a branch of New River to Mitchell Clay.*

He signed his name. *Jno. Draper.*

The papers exchanged hands, and although the bill of sale indicated money had actually been paid, Clay and Draper had reached an agreement as to the value of the two Negroes and the release of interest in the tract of land. Now Rachel and Judy, or Jude as Adam wrote it, were the property of Draper and the thousand acres were Clay's forever.

"Thank you, gentlemen," said John. "Now, William, I have one more favor to ask."

"What's that?" asked William.

"I need to borrow one of your horses so Rachel and the child can be taken to my house. Do you have an extra one over here? I'll be back next week and bring the horse to you then. Can you spare one horse for a week?"

"Certainly can, dear friend, you can have the black mare."

"Fine, fine," said Draper. "Let's get started for the valley. We will stop somewhere on the way tonight and be home tomorrow."

"I will get the mare." William disappeared toward the barn.

Rachel, with Judy riding in front of her, was on the mare in a few minutes with their few belongings fastened behind. She turned and looked at Mitchell Clay. She clenched her teeth. She said nothing. He wiped his nose with the fringe of his hunting shirt and slapped his leg.

"Goodbye, Pappy Mitchell," said Judy, waving one hand and wiping tears with the other.

Chapter 4

THE SUMMER OF 1774

Bettie Draper was standing at the front door of the two-story log house nestled at the foot of the mountain where she and John had been living for about ten years. Two of her children were carrying water from the nearby spring. One of the Negroes was plowing the field to the east, and cattle and horses were grazing in the valley to the west.

"Bettie," said John, his face beaming as he rode up, "I brought you some presents. This here is Rachel, and the little one is called Judy."

"John, surely not. You know I—" She stopped in mid-sentence and looked at Rachel again.

"Are you with child?"

"Yessum. I am."

"Where did you get the money for these slaves?" asked Bettie, shaking her head.

"Traded my land for them. You know, the tract on the Bluestone."

"John, where are we going to put them?"

"In the slave cabins, over yonder. With Will and Peter and Caesar. They'll make room. Peter, are you there?" hollered John.

"Yes, Marse," said Peter, looking at Rachel as he came

from the first little cabin.

"Find a place for these two," said Draper, pushing Rachel toward the cabin.

"I know you will find them useful," said Draper. He put his arm around his wife and walked toward their house.

"I'm sure that's so, but you know I am not in favor of holding people in slavery. I never liked being treated like a slave to that old Indian chief in Chillicothe, and I don't want anyone else to go through what I did."

"But, Bettie," interrupted John.

Bettie continued. "Six years of slavery was too much for me. One day was too much. Whipped, yes. Starved, yes. Humiliated, yes. Chained, yes. I know what slavery is, even if I am a white woman. John, how could you do this?"

Bettie pulled away, mumbling to herself. "Men can do anything they want to. Women don't have a thing to say about it." She ran up the steps, leaving John scratching his head.

Rachel, Peter and Judy were soon joined by Will and Caesar. Judy curled up on the only bed in the cabin and closed her eyes. Peter took Rachel's few things and put them on the small table near the door. Rachel laid her red shawl on the chair.

"You tired?" asked Peter.

"Sure am," said Rachel. "Every bone in my body is aching and with this baby growing inside I can't breathe too well neither."

"Will, go get her some water from the bucket outside. And, Caesar, can you find her something to eat?"

"Yes, indeed," they said in unison.

"You say your name's Rachel? And this here's Judy?"

"Yes, and you Peter?"

"That's right and I'll help you, best I can. Now you and Judy can have this cabin, and me and the others will be next door. We don't have no extra bed, but I can make one for the little girl in a day or two."

"Thank you," said Rachel, covering Judy with her blanket.

After Rachel had a little corn bread and some water they moved out to the steps of the cabin. Everyone gathered around.

"Where'd Marse Draper find you beautiful people?" asked Peter.

Rachel lowered her head, her eyes closing. Then she smiled as she looked at Peter. "Over Mitchell Clay's. He traded a piece of land for me and Judy. Him and me worked hard on that land, and now I'm to work here for the missus and the marse."

"We sure worked hard here the las' three years. We did all the plowing, all the corn planting and all the haymaking. The marse, he's never here."

"We cleared the stumps from the fields too," added Will.

"We does all the work, and if we don't git it done when he wants it or just right, he takes out the whip and hit us across our backs," said Caesar. "This old gray head has done seen too much of that."

"And we's scared all the time, of him sure 'nough, but we also heard Injuns might come again to burn out the settlers," said Peter.

Caesar got up and limped across the yard, pacing in front of the cabin, his bare feet stirring up the dust.

"Yes sir, we's heard them fellas in Caintuck that was measurin' out the land had to come home. Them Injuns don't like the white folks takin' their land," added Caesar.

"And the marse has been going to muster helping train

31

the militia. They's going to be called out soon," said Peter.

"What's that mean?" asked Rachel.

"It means that on those days, all the growed men of the neighborhood meet with their captain. They practice drilling, they learn to use their knives and guns, how to take orders, and how to march," said Will.

"Lot's a-drinking going on too. And fight, boy, they loves to fight." Caesar laughed. "I have seen some sights when I went to the muster grounds."

"Things are bad 'round here," Peter said. "Those white folks sure are scared. Many of them done gone back east. Left their land and everythin' else. But Marse Draper, he says he ain't going nowhere."

"What's we gonna do if them Injuns comes here?" asked Rachel.

"Guess we all go to the fort that they's building down near Ingles Ferry. Missus Bettie and her family and all of us, but the marse, he'll be going to fight," said Peter.

"That's right. He don't like Injuns none," added Will. "When the marse was a youngun his pappy died in the woods somewhere out here. He said it was Injuns. And they killed his mama, his child, and his neighbors. And took his wife. No wonder he hates them."

"And the Injuns hated all of the white men, and when the war closed in '63, and the English won, they was full of anger. Ain't got rid of it yet," said Peter.

"Those Shawnee didn't like the white folk taking their hunting grounds away. Too many settlers came in here," said Will.

"Do you think they will come after us here?" asked Rachel.

"They will, Rachel, they will. Over at muster the soldiers were talking and they say that the Injuns watch us all the time. They see us building cabins, planting crops, and more people coming every day. They don't like that," said Caesar.

"I thought the Injuns made a treaty setting the boundaries. That's what Marse Clay told me," said Rachel.

"Didn't do no good. Too many settlers wanted the land. They just kept coming in, inviting their friends and kin to come and jine them, and nothing was the same," said Peter.

"How's this going to end?" asked Rachel.

"There'll be no peace until we kill them all."

"Or they kill all us," said Rachel, shaking her head. She disappeared into her new cabin home.

As the summer of 1774 wore on, John Draper learned that the Shawnee Towns on the Ohio were the center for the marauding parties who often visited the Virginia frontier. They soon became the terror of the English border, and their attacks were more frequent as their resentment grew. The western rivers, New River, Holston, Clinch and Powell, wherever white men had settled, were the targets of the Shawnee.

John Draper stood by the fading embers in the fireplace smoking his pipe. He interrupted the whirring of Bettie's spindle.

"Got my orders, Bettie. Just got word from Colonel William Preston. He tells me to get my men together and prepare for a little expedition. Looks like I'll be leaving tomorrow."

"Why are you getting orders from Preston?"

"Well, he got his orders from Governor Dunmore and Colonel Andrew Lewis was ordered to raise troops too.

33

They plan to meet on the Ohio later on, up there where the New or Kanawha River comes in."

"And will Colonel Preston be with you?" asked Bettie.

"Not sure about that, but he has to give the orders, contact the captains and the majors, and get the men ready for the trip. Did you know when he is in the field he wears a silver gorget around his neck, so we can see where he is? But he don't always go in search of Indians. He sends the captains and their men. In the meantime, the settlers over on the Bluestone have seen signs of Indians, and I must go," said John.

"Is he calling out other troops?

"Yes, because Preston just discovered that the Valley of Virginia from Staunton to the Kentucky line is in what he calls a military frenzy. And we will all soon be in the midst of war."

"But you aren't a captain," said Bettie.

"I know I'm just a lieutenant, but I'm volunteering right now and going to join James Robertson to search for Indians. They've been sighted down the river. I'm taking about a dozen men with me. Later we'll all be going with Lewis."

Bettie looked up with troubled eyes. "I heard from Mrs. Ramsey there aren't many families left around here. And up as far as Reed Creek the land is deserted. Did you know that, John?"

"Yes, Bettie, I'm afraid so."

"What are we to do here with you gone?"

"I want you to pack up those seven children of ours and take the slaves with you and go to the fort over at Bell's Meadows. It's not far from William's ferry on the river. You've been there many times, and William will direct you from there. As for me, I am going in the other direction."

When Lieutenant Draper arrived on August first with his thirteen men, he found Robertson and his men had built a log fort at Culbertson's Bottom on the river. They were waiting there for the troops to assemble.

"Seen any signs today?" asked Draper when he reported to Robertson.

"Welcome, Lieutenant. Yes, indeed, this very morning we saw signs that the Indians had been here, probably near nightfall. Also, Jones over yonder thought he saw some of them in his neighborhood."

"How many men are here?" asked Draper.

"With yours, I reckon about thirty-three of us."

"What's this I hear about no ammunition and little food?"

"That's true. We have little of either. I have repeatedly asked for supplies from Colonel Preston, but none have come as yet. We'll just have to do the best we can. I am ordering most of the men to head out in the morning to search for Indians, and in fact every morning and to return here every night. Set off about sunrise."

"Yes sir."

For the next few weeks, Draper and his thirteen men, joined by seven others from the area, made regular trips, sorties, the military called them. They set off each day at sunrise toward Clover Bottom and the Bluestone River. They found burned houses, scattered livestock, abandoned war clubs, rumors of scalpings from the displaced settlers, and footprints of the enemy everywhere they went. There was no question but that the community was in danger. But no one had seen an Indian to kill.

35

Back at the fort at Bell's Meadows, Bettie, and her seven children, Rachel, Judy and the other slaves, decided to risk returning to the foot of Peak Knob or, as Bettie called it, Draper Mountain. They had been several weeks at the fort with other women and children of the New River area. There had been no news of attacks in recent days and all seemed to be quiet. No one had seen or heard of an Indian in the area. So they went home.

When they got to the Mountain the Negroes took turns as lookouts, never going far from the house. Bettie barred the door each night and offered Rachel and Judy a place to sleep on the floor in the loft. Every day they watched for the enemy and hoped that instead they would see John galloping down the road toward the house.

Twenty-two days after they came home, John Draper rejoined his family, only to learn that Colonel William Preston had called for immediate enlistments for Dunmore's expedition.

On the day John Draper returned, Rachel told Bettie that it was time to give birth. In spite of having little Judy, the fear of the pain was still with her. And that was just the beginning. She was all alone and so far from her family. No midwives out here, and no Grandmama Chance to help her. Why wasn't she back home on Swift Creek? Why hadn't Samuel come with her papers?

She was grateful for Bettie. It seemed to Rachel that Bettie thought of her as a woman and not as a slave now. She brought cold damp cloths to mop the sweat from her face. All night long she comforted her in the tiny cabin. Finally just as the sky lightened, and with one last scream, Rachel delivered a son. And Bettie was there to wrap him

36

in a little blanket. She handed him to Rachel as she left the room.

Rachel cuddled her baby and sang a little song. In between the soft words she sometimes raised her voice and declared, "You gonna be free, little one. You gonna be free, jus' the same as I am free. Grandmama Chance told us we's free. So, we's free."

No one heard her except the little one, shining like a new copper penny. Then tears came to her cheeks dropping like raindrops on a spring day.

Bettie went to the desk and entered the baby's name in the household ledger: "Robbin, son of Negro Rachel, born September 15, 1774, one blanket." Here was her record for the future when someday the Drapers would have to pay tax on the Negroes they owned. And here was a record of her little gift for the new baby.

The Draper children visited Rachel in the cabin. They gawked at the new copper-colored face being held by Rachel. Judy patted the blanket but the Draper boys, George and John, Jr., were interested only for a moment. The two little Draper girls, Mary and Elizabeth, held Robbin's little fingers and talked to him until their brother Silas came and brushed them out of the way. He touched the baby's straight black hair and patted his cheek. Little Nancy started to cry for attention, and at the same moment, Bettie's last child, James, born just a few months before Rachel's arrival, mingled his cries with his little sister's.

Ever since her arrival, Rachel had helped the oldest boys with chores. But she also looked after the babies, Bettie's and hers. She loved to sew and made clothes for all of the children. She often sat by the fire with Bettie, both spinning their wool into yarn and their flax into thread. John had promised a loom and a loom house so Rachel could begin weaving for the family. But other matters had to come first. Matters of war.

Chapter 5

POINT PLEASANT

In early September Colonel Preston ordered the companies to march toward Point Pleasant. John Draper enlisted with Captain Walter Crockett's Company as the first lieutenant and marched with his company and about fifty of his friends and neighbors. They stopped at William Thompson's plantation on Back Creek to the east, rested a day or two, and then crossed the mountain. After many days traveling to the northeast, they came to the camp at Fort Union on the Big Levels of the Greenbrier River. Here they were joined by about two hundred more from all parts of Southwest Virginia.

Draper left his tent and began to search the crowd for his sergeant. He passed dozens of tents spread out around the big spring. Some soldiers were sleeping, some talking, and others drinking. Some were watering the horses, others butchering beeves for the next meals. All were waiting for tomorrow's leg of their journey, one hundred and forty miles to the meeting place where the Kanawha and Ohio rivers came together, not far from the Shawnee Towns.

Sergeant Wood, from Crockett's Company, was sitting on the ground, looking solemn. Draper asked, "What's this I hear about supplies?"

"Everything is in short supply. Blankets, hunting shirts, flour, lead, powder, and canvas for tents. We don't have enough to go around. Not enough for me anyhow."

"More will come in soon, don't worry. You won't starve and you won't freeze. Now go tell the rest of the men."

Three weeks later, the army reached the mouth of the Elk River. Draper noticed that the river was smooth and calm, and free from rocks and rapids. He approached the camp and saw some men making canoes and others unloading sacks of flour. Soldiers were watering horses, hundreds of them. And hundreds of men were milling around as they waited for orders.

"Where's the scouts?" Draper asked Captain Crockett.

"They were sent on ahead to search for Indians. We don't want to be surprised as we move up to Point Pleasant."

"What are my orders, Captain?"

"Get your men to help load the canoes. Put in the kettles, the flour, and other supplies. Keep the loads coming. You can keep about twenty men with you and I'll take the rest and march on to the Point."

"Yes, sir. And are we meeting Colonel Andrew Lewis at the Point?"

"Yes, we should have about a thousand soldiers in all, and from the latest count we have five hundred pack horses and over fifty-four thousand pounds of flour. On the hoof we have about a hundred head of cattle. You remember that long line, a couple of miles or more, coming across the mountain?"

"Yes sir. And those cattle-drivers chasing them through the woods," said Draper.

"Yes, and the camp followers, those young women, chasing the men. And some deserting along the way," said

Captain Crockett, laughing.

"All that drinking and shooting off guns without good reason. And us so short of ammunition."

"The sutler surely never minded the orders he got about providing liquor to the soldiers."

"No, he didn't."

"How far we got to go yet?" asked Draper.

"About five days journey I would think, and we should be at Point Pleasant."

When Draper reached the camp, he saw a long line of tents spread along the river's edge. After his men found their assigned spaces, they soon joined the soldiers who were splashing in the river, washing their sore feet and their dirty clothes. On the following day, everyone in camp gathered for a sermon. Scouts were sent out, hunters had gone to find meat, guards were on duty, and as the stars appeared in the October sky, all seemed to be in quiet readiness for the soldiers to attack the Indians in the morning.

On the morning of the tenth, Draper was rudely awakened by shouts of his men, echoing yells and screams of others nearby.

"Shots fired! Hunter's been killed! Shots fired!" Draper was on his feet at once and looking to the north of their encampment he saw the scouts and guards running into the camp screaming, "Shawnee coming, Shawnee coming!"

"Attack, attack! Attack those savages! On your feet, on your feet!" shouted Draper as he slung his rifle over his shoulder and his tomahawk to his hip.

Two lines of soldiers marched away from the camp at the river's edge just as the sun came up. Colonel Charles

Lewis led the right and Colonel William Fleming the left as the two lines led the attack. Draper and his men fell into the line.

Draper saw the enemy coming, armed with rifles, shotguns and tomahawks. The savages fired relentlessly, and Draper could hear the shattering of bones, the screams of the wounded and the dying. He fired back. Smoke everywhere. Confusion everywhere.

"Attack, attack!" shouted Draper.

He moved forward. He saw the dying colonels, privates and sergeants. William Fowler, one of his friends, fell by his side, most of his face missing. Draper loaded, fired, retreated to the rear, reloaded, came to the front and fired again. The body of a young warrior was so close that Draper's gun was swept from his hands. He struck with his tomahawk and killed again. His hunting shirt was covered with Indian blood. William Hill, one of his own men, stumbled back and his blood flowed over the grass and Draper's boots. Draper heard the groans of the wounded, heard the whistling of the balls and the shouts and hideous cries of the Shawnee, who continued to attack, all seven hundred of them. Not just for an hour, but for twelve long hours, ending only when the sun began to set.

When the smoke cleared, Draper saw the bodies of Indian chiefs and young braves strewn across the fields. There were white soldiers, young and old. Scalps were missing. Faces were contorted in agony. Bodies floated in the Ohio, near where more than seventy Indian rafts were found. Doctors themselves were suffering from their own wounds and help for the others was limited. Their cries would last for days.

Sounds of Battle were still ringing in Draper's ears. He could see blood, see wounds, see his friends screaming in

42

death, see the Shawnee dying, see death everywhere.

Somehow Draper had escaped injury, and when the battle was over he returned to his campsite, collapsed exhausted on the ground and slept. An hour later he suddenly stood up, calling to his fellow soldiers, "Attack, attack! The enemy is here!" But all was quiet. He had seen the enemy in his nightmare.

This war held neither honor, pleasure, nor profit, only death and destruction. Yet the men at the camp seemed to think they had been successful in defeating the Shawnee. When the enemy retreated into the night, the officers were already planning their next step. They wanted to cross the Ohio and burn the Indian villages.

On October 11, Draper sat down at the camp at Point Pleasant to write to his wife, Bettie. He wanted her to know about the battle which had taken place the day before and that he had survived. He took the piece of paper, dipped the pen and began his story.

> *Dearest Bettie,*
> *You will be glad to know that the battle with the Shawnee Indians is over, and I have survived without a scratch. Thanks be to God. Never have I seen such chaos and such distress as here on the field where many of our fine friends passed into the land beyond, and others are so injured that they cry constantly with the pain of their wounds. Many more will die I fear, as there are many wounded, few medicines and bad doctors. And little of anything to eat.*
> *When we left the camp at Union, there were 500 pack horses loaded with 54,000 pounds of flour, followed by about 100 beeves leading the*

way. We marched about fifteen to twenty miles a day, and camped the best we could each night. The supply waggons brought us some tents, cloth to make some more, and a short supply of powder and ammunition. I was glad I brought my own blanket because they too are scarce.

Some of the men were employed building canoes which were used to carry the flour and other supplies to the Point. The pack horses did not go past the mouth of Elk River and many of our riding horses were worn out and left behind. The river to the Ohio was quite calm and easy traveling, not like the New River in places we know and love.

When we arrived at the Point there were about 800 or 1,000 militiamen assembled, and such a pleasant place before the horrible scene began. We pitched our tents along the bank. We left about 200 as a rear guard.

Before dawn on the 10th there were 700-800 (some say no more than 500) of the savages ready to attack. They were mostly of the Shawnee tribe, who treated our families in such a cruel and inhumane way. I was anxious to engage them in battle and our plan was to attack that day. But we were greatly surprised when one of the hunters sounded the alarm early in the morning, and before we could organize our line the savages were upon us. They had come in the dark of night so they would be ready for the early morning attack. They crossed the Ohio in 70 rafts which they hid along the bank of the river, and waited for the daylight. The battle was fierce for several hours, and some guns were still firing at dusk. The slaughter on both sides was horrendous. We claimed scalps of many of the noted warriors who were leaders of the tribe, and feel that they have been vanquished forever. Some of us will probably cross the river and burn their villages, so we do not know when we will be home.

I have seen Mitchell Clay, as well as Zekiel and David Clay who marched with us, although in a different company. None of them were injured. They asked kindly about Rachel and Judy. Colonel Charles Lewis was severely wounded in the action and died shortly after, and Dr. William Fleming was severely wounded, but may live. Several of our captains and many privates died in the attack. The count is incomplete but about 150 were either killed or wounded.

I have been very anxious about you, the children and the Negroes, and especially Rachel and Judy. It is my hope that you have taken control and have ordered them to help you rescue the crops in the field, and have them obey you at all times. Every one of the men here has the same concerns about their families, because we heard about the scalpings, robberies, the stolen cattle, missing horses, and their cruelty to the settlers on the Clinch and Holston. It is my prayer that you have protected yourself well, and know that I love you and the children very much and long to return to you soon. I will try to write again

*and let you know what the plans are about our
return.*

With my love and deep affection, Yours,
JOHN
Per Mr. Brander

When Mr. Brander delivered the letter on his way to
Reed Creek, Bettie thought it was from Captain Crockett
telling her John was dead. She tore open the letter, wiped a
tear from her eye, and read briefly. "Thanks be to God.
John was not injured," she whispered.

Bettie had continued barring doors, keeping a close
watch on the children when outside, and demanding that
Rachel never leave them alone. The Negroes had gathered
in the crops and tended the cattle and horses. Although
everyone was afraid of what might happen, they had seen
no signs of Indians in their neighborhood.

October passed into November and November into early
December with no other letters from John. Bettie thought
the worst, but tried to keep her feelings to herself for the
sake of the children.

The first snow arrived, concealing the pines on the
mountaintop with several inches of sparkling cover. Rachel
was preparing soup at the stone fireplace. Judy and the
Draper children were playing quietly nearby. The horses
in the field sounded restless, neighing and snorting.

"Maybe they do not like the snow," said Rachel as she
walked to the tiny window. She saw three men trudging
through the snow and approaching the house.

"Somebody comin', three of 'em!" shouted Rachel.

46

"Rachel, quickly now. Take the children and go up the stairs. Be very quiet until we find out who it is. Hurry," said Bettie. She pushed the children up the stairs and took the rifle off the rack over the fireplace.

Bettie looked out the window. The closer the men came, the more she thought that they looked familiar.

"Maybe it's John, maybe it is!" said Bettie. She reached up to her head and smoothed her hair, straightened her apron, and put her face against the windowpane, setting the rifle near the door.

Now the men were within a few feet of the door.

"Yes, it's John! Children, children, it is your father! Rachel, bring them down. It is safe."

When the door opened John hurried inside, took Bettie in his arms and swung her around the room. "I am home. So glad to come home to you and the children."

John reached for the children, hugging them and kissing them and holding his baby in his arms. Rachel stirred the soup and hurried around the room preparing the table and the meal.

"These two fellas at the door were in my company," said John. "You know Joseph Crockett and Josiah Ramsey. They need some food too. They are on their way to Reed Creek. We have had low rations and some days we had nothing to eat. Rachel, find us some more bowls."

"Yes sir, Marse."

"And get us some of Bettie's good bread and if we have any, a little whiskey would be good."

"Oh, yes sir," answered Rachel.

Bettie helped John off with his coat, revealing his slender body where the flesh had disappeared over the last few

47

months. Tears came to her eyes.

Joseph and Josiah joined the family at the table.

"I reckon it's the best food we've had since we left, ma'am," said Joseph. "It is wonderful, wonderful to know we survived that terrible ordeal. Mighty fine food. Thank you."

Josiah nodded his agreement and added two words, "Wonderful, wonderful."

When the meal ended, the men picked up the chairs and moved them to the fireplace where they smoked their pipes in the warmth of the glowing flames.

"Haven't been this warm since we left in September," said Joseph. He rubbed his hands together as he stood by the hearth.

"Children, come now. Your father wants to talk to us. Rachel, you and Judy come close to hear what your master has to say."

John puffed on his pipe, the smoke swirling around his black hair, and when all was quiet, he began to speak.

"Bettie, I could not write you again. I had no paper, and there were so many trying to write home that no one had paper to spare. I am sorry, I know you were worried. I wrote you after the battle."

"Yes, John, I looked for a letter every day."

"Well, I will never forget the horrible scene, and I do not want to remind you again of those pitiful wounded men. We helped tend the wounded, buried the dead, and many of us slept on the ground without a shelter over our heads."

Joseph and Josiah nodded and shivered. "Aye, that's true."

"Our next assignment was to cross the Ohio and destroy the Indian villages. About two hundred of us manned canoes and rafts and completed the mission in a day or two. We burned their corn, their homes and everything.

"It was a terrible scene," added Crockett, "but now maybe those Indians will leave us alone."

"We knew that the march home was going to be worse than going out to the Point because we had so little food. The weather was getting worse, and many of us were weakened by our trip and our stay at the Point. But I thought about sister Mary who bravely made her way home at about the same time of year, eating nuts and herbs and little else, and knowing she survived the ordeal I knew we could too. We found a rabbit or two and a turkey so had some nourishment but, Bettie, nothing like the feast we had here today."

Bettie smiled and nodded.

"Tell us, Bettie, what is the news from here?" asked John.

"The rumors are that there will be war with the English. Many of the counties are drawing up resolutions to support the idea that we don't like to be told what to do by the English. We want some say about our own lives. Some of the hotheads think that we would rather die than give in to the English."

"Damn it! If it isn't Indians, now it's the English. No peace to be had around here."

"The county had a request from the Continental Congress to give their thoughts about those English."

"Yes. There was talk of that when I left. Has anyone done anything for Fincastle County?"

"Not likely," said Bettie. "All the men have been at the Point fighting. The justices of the court are the ones to do it. I think they'll plan a meeting when all the men get home. Are the others on their way?"

49

"Yes, ma'am," replied Joseph. "The camp was in the process of breaking up. Fresh horses were brought in for those that weren't able to walk. Everyone wanted to be home before the new year."

"That's true," added Josiah.

The evening wore on with children nodding and ready to sleep. Rachel took the children to bed and left Bettie and the men talking by the fire.

"It is truly a blessing having you home, John," said Bettie. He reached for her hand and held it so tight it might have been a trap.

"Thank you, Bettie. Now these fellas here have to leave for Reed Creek. Their families will be waiting."

Chapter 6

REVOLUTION

The early days of January 1775 were bitter cold, with high wind and blankets of snow everywhere. The logs in the fireplace sizzled and seemed to burn all too quickly. About the end of the month, word came to the Drapers that the Fincastle County Justices had drafted and passed their resolutions and that they had been forwarded to the Continental Congress in Philadelphia as requested. The consensus of those who drafted the local resolutions was that England should no longer tell the people of Southwest Virginia what to do.

John and Bettie sat near their stone fireplace discussing the news and how it would affect their family. Bettie was busy spinning and John was smoking his pipe.

"John, what do you make of all of this talk?" asked Bettie.

"Bettie, I'm sure that war is on the horizon. If it's not the Indians, it's the English. We cannot decide anything by sending resolutions to anyone, anywhere. Some right here in the New River Valley are set against these ideas," said John.

"Anyone we know?"

"The talk is that Captain Burk and his company are

refusing to be part of the conspiracy as he calls it. He and his men favor the King, or have those Tory sentiments."

"But they wouldn't fight against you and your men, would they?"

"Surely they would, Bettie. Their beliefs are just as strong as ours. They see us as being disloyal to the King. They think we are the ones who have committed treason. Maybe they are right."

"But we aren't really mad at the King, are we? I thought it was because of some of the laws that parliament passed."

"You're right. But it's difficult to separate them. We have lots of individual liberties now, living so far from England as we are. It takes months to get orders from the Mother Country to Williamsburg and weeks for the news to reach us here. Sometimes, we have to act on our own."

"Those Tories are so headstrong and outspoken. They shout 'Hurrah for King George' at every opportunity," said Bettie. "And I suppose they will be tried soon."

"Yes, they will. And we will be at war and ready to fight for what we believe in," said John. He reached in his pocket and pulled out his copy of the Fincastle Resolutions.

"The last lines of our resolutions say it all, I think." He began to read.

> *"But if no pacifick measures shall be proposed or adopted by Great Britain, and our enemies will attempt to dragoon us out of those inestimable privileges which we are entitled to as subjects, and to reduce us to a state of slavery, we declare, that we are deliberately and resolutely determined never to surrender them to any power upon earth, but at the expense of*

our lives. These are our real, though unpolished
sentiments, of liberty and loyalty, and in them
we are resolved to live and die."

"My, that certainly is strong language. Are we really prepared to defend our liberty by dying?"

"I think you will find that those who see the government of England as depriving us of our rights and liberties are willing to fight at all costs for what is right." John stirred up the fire and added another log as he continued.

"We will fight for what is due to us as residents of this remote region where we have so faithfully defended the land from those savages, and at great risk. We defend liberty every day, with a threat of death not far behind. Remember our recent engagement at the Point?"

In the slave quarters, Peter poked at the fire, stirred up the coals, and when the flame rose from the ashes, he added another log. He tilted his chair against the wall. Judy was clinging to his knee. He patted her head. Little Robbin was asleep on one of the beds. Peter looked at Rachel sitting at the table busy with her sewing spread out over her swollen belly. He smiled.

"What you smiling at?" Rachel asked.

"I know I is a happy man. The children and you, Rachel, make me happy. I am so glad you came to stay at Draper's. And soon you'll have my baby. I think I will name him Tom."

Rachel laughed and continued with her sewing. "You know, Peter, we know about the King across the ocean, and the people in Virginia who were determined to be free. Maybe all of us can be free too."

53

"Maybe, but do you think that all this new talk of liberty for the white folks will mean we gets our freedom too?" asked Peter.

"Don't know," said Rachel. "You know I told you before, I am free, my grandmama Chance was an Injun woman."

"That's what you say," Peter said. "But if you is free, why you still here and a slave of Marse Draper?"

"My brother, Samuel, me and Judy went to court for our freedom three years ago and before I could get word of it, I was brought to the New River where I knowed nobody, and had no family or friends."

"Why you didn't run away?"

"No place to run. No Samuel to help me. I knows I is free, but the worst of it is I ain't got no money, can't travel nowheres except with the marse, and don't know nobody to talk to about it," said Rachel.

"Can't you go back to that court and tell them what happened?"

"It's a long, long ways from here. Maybe three or four hundred miles. You know, at Williamsburg."

"Then find a court closer by."

"There's one over at the lead mines, but I have to get there first. Nobody will let me go no place." Rachel pounded her clenched fist on the wooden table, knocking the tin cups to the floor. The baby stirred and Judy crossed the room to comfort him.

"I be free one day, really free, and these children too. Even yours," said Rachel as she picked up the cups and set them on the table with a bang. "I heard Marse Draper say that the Shawnee Injuns were likely to be trouble again. And some folks on one side of England and others opposite, the marse thought that war was coming again. With war, how can we talk of freedom? We'll have to wait our time."

"If those white folks wants their own liberty perhaps they will help us git ours," said Peter. "Not every one of those white folks wants us to be slaves."

"You're right, Peter. Missus Bettie for one. The only good about it," added Rachel, "is we git some food and a roof over our heads."

"But we's work hard, we's help the marse, and git no pay. Don't git that much to eat neither. He whips us when he gits angry and chains us to the springhouse wall. Who wants to stay here with the likes of that going on?"

Rachel touched the marks on her left cheek not yet healed from the stroke of the last whipping. Her back was covered with raw sores where Draper left his marks. And what had she done to deserve it? She dropped a plate full of food on the floor.

"I don't see how we can do any better right now. If we left here, where would we go? How would we git any place without gitting caught? It'd just mean one more whipping for me. And you too, if you went with me. I've got younguns to worry about. I feel like a possum trapped up the tree. But I am thinking of telling the missus and maybe she'll help us," said Rachel.

"Why would she do that?"

"Well, she got took by the Shawnee Injuns and kept for six years. It was like being a slave to that old Injun chief. Maybe she would see how it is for us."

"Why you wanna be free anyway?"

Rachel stood up, threw her shoulders back and stuck out her chest. "First of all I'm an Injun, not a Negro by law, and ain't supposed to be no slave neither. That's the first thing. I is different from you, Peter. You is a slave,

Radford Public Library
30 W. Main St.
Radford, VA 24141

have no reason to think you will ever be free, but is different, and I knows that freedom will mean a lot to me and my family. I could work for myself, earn my own way, and so could my younguns, and that's just for a start."

At the bedside she patted Judy on the head, picked up the sleeping baby and hugged him close to her apron. "I could have my own money, go where I wanna go and stay as long as I wanna. I could go back to Swift Creek to see Grandmama Chance."

Rachel tried to tone her voice to a lower level, and took a deep breath. She straightened her back like a broomstick and began again. "Nobody could beat me, brand me, or sell me or my children. I could marry and have my husband and my family with me forever. And I could live wherever I wanna."

She turned her back on Peter and put the baby on the bed. Rachel's shoulders began to shake. In a trembling voice she added, "I could celebrate any time I wanna, I could learn to read and write, and I could be a real person. That's my dream. And my dream of freedom won't go away."

"Don't let it go away, Rachel." Peter shook his head and decided she was only daydreaming and that as far as he knew there was no way any black person could ever be free. Oh yes, he did hear that if he served his marse especially well, saved his life, or something like that, the marse might, just might, free him. But Peter never even thought about it. For him he knew it was impossible. But Rachel she was a strong woman, a very strong woman, and he hoped her story was true.

Peter reached for her hand and squeezed it. Then turned her around and enclosed her in his arms. "You know I loves ya' gal. Let me hold you and love you."

56

They sat by the fire holding each other, watching the light dim and the flame crackle. Judy was snuggled next to Robbin and was sleeping with her arms around him. Soon Rachel and Peter climbed into the bed and entwined their bodies, feeling the passion and the excitement. In their short time together, Rachel knew no chains, no heartache, no longing for freedom. She knew she was loved.

In 1776 it became clear there was no compromise coming from England. King George declared the colonies in rebellion. George Washington had been chosen leader of the navy and the army. The British hired the Hessian troops to come to America to assist them in quelling the rebellion. Men like Thomas Paine attacked the monarchy, and Thomas Jefferson's cherished words, "life, liberty, and the pursuit of happiness," echoed through the colonies. Loyalty to the king was now classified as treason. Soon the cases would be heard in Southwest Virginia, at the new county seat, Fort Chiswell.

At the old fort an Irishman named James McGavock had set up his store and trading center, built an ordinary and was responsible for getting the courthouse and jail constructed. The first court meeting was held there in January 1777, and John Draper was there.

"Good morning, Will," said Draper to his brother-in-law William Ingles. "I hear you are now colonel of our Montgomery County militia."

"Yes, I am. And you will notice that Will Preston is our county lieutenant and James Robertson, lieutenant colonel and Walter Crockett, our major. It's good to have our friends as military authorities on the county level."

"I believe I am to be confirmed as captain today," said John. "Is that right?

"Yes, and several others with you. The men will meet at muster next week, but you will be sworn in today. Come along inside. The court is now sitting."

Preston, Ingles, Robertson, Crockett and Draper and a dozen or more others raised their hands and repeated after the clerk their promises to defend American liberty and to renounce and refuse allegiance to George the Third, King of Great Britain. Theirs was true allegiance to the Commonwealth of Virginia, as a "free and independent state." And so Draper received his commission.

The justices were appointed and took their oaths of office. Soon they were sworn to uphold their allegiance to the Commonwealth of Virginia and promised to conduct the Montgomery County court sessions in a legal manner.

One of their new duties was to list every male over sixteen from the various militia companies of the county and obtain their oaths of allegiance. As it turned out, many of the residents refused to take the oath and were considered to be enemies of the state. These men were to be disarmed, were not allowed to hold office, and could not sit on the juries or acquire land. County Lieutenant Preston was in charge of seeing that the Tories or Loyalists were arrested and disarmed, not an easy task. Preston soon learned that many of his neighbors were loyal to the king and that most of them were in Thomas Burk's militia company, where only four or five were in support of the American cause. He swore to find them, see them tried and hanged, if necessary.

At the September Court in 1777, Draper was again at the courthouse when Jacob Kettering, a miller by trade and a resident of Reed Creek, was tried and found guilty for declaring himself a friend of the king. He was sent to jail in Staunton the following January.

On the same day Laurence Burkholder was convicted and fined ten pounds. He was to post bond for his good behavior for twelve months.

"What do you think, William?" asked Captain Draper of his brother-in-law. "Do you think that now we shall have some peace around here with Kettering and Burkholder taken care of?"

"There are too many of them, I fear. The rumors are that the country is sold out to France, and neither those German-speaking settlers nor the Scotch-Irish are much in favor of that. There's said to be over four thousand of those damn rascals in Montgomery County alone."

"Did you hear anything about a Tory named Griffith or Griffy?" asked John.

"Yes, I did, and I think he is the ringleader but we can't prove it yet. But we will, we will."

"Maybe we will know more at the next court. In the meantime, be careful of yourself and your family, Will. I hope Mary is feeling better these days," added John.

"Mary is so melancholy. She doesn't want to be with any of us. It is hard to see her so uneasy and so distant when she was once such a happy woman. I do believe she has not recovered from her ordeal of twenty years ago."

"Please tell her we send out best regards and love. We will come to visit you soon, if Bettie is able. Ask Mary to come to the valley to see us and spend some time with Bettie if she will. "

"She will not go anywhere, I fear," said Will.

"I suppose you know that I am ordered out to the Blue-stone to look for Indians. I hear they have been again seen in that neighborhood, and I thought we had solved that problem at the Point."

"Well, nothing is really ever solved by war. Someone else just picks up the same ideas and goes on from there. I fear we will be fighting on three fronts this time—the Indians here in the southwest part of the Virginia, the Tories all around us, and the English, probably in North Carolina and eastern Virginia. It will be much more difficult than the Point."

"I hate to tell Bettie that I will be gone from home again. We have seven children, and she is not well. Thank goodness she has Rachel and my three Negro men to help her. By the way, Rachel is expecting another child soon."

"How many children does Rachel have?"

"This will make three since she joined us. Rachel had a boy last time and named him Tom. She's taken up with our man Peter and we had a little ceremony for them, you know, a jump over the broomstick kind of thing. It was Bettie's idea."

John took his horse by the reins and lifted himself into the saddle and rode off, waving at William as he went.

"Hello!" shouted John when he arrived at home. "Where is everyone?"

Draper's oldest son George, now about eleven years old, answered.

"Father, Rachel is having her baby. Mother is helping her."

"That's fine," answered John. He sat at the kitchen table and ate some corn bread then, settled by the fire with his pipe.

"Is there going to be a war?" asked George.

"Yes, I think so. The news from the courthouse seems

60

to be that Indians may be after us, but also the English and the Tories. The Tories are the ones of our neighbors who sympathize with the English."

"Father, will you have to go to war?" asked George in a worried tone.

"Yes, in fact I must leave in a few days to go on the Bluestone to look for Indians, like before when I went to the Point."

"Is war really bad?" asked George.

"Yes, son, it is really bad. So many good people are injured or killed. And it doesn't seem to solve anything."

"If it is so bad, then why do you go to war?"

"Because we must protect ourselves from all the evils that are against us, and we hope that we will be the winners. But no one really wins in war."

Their discussion was interrupted by a baby's cry. "The baby's here!" shouted George. The other children came running, and before long Bettie came in from the slave quarters and brought a baby girl for all to see.

"This is Nan," said Bettie. "Rachel is naming her for her mother. Everyone is fine."

Everyone looked at little Nan, held her tiny fingers, admired her straight black hair, and peaked beneath the blanket their mother had given to Rachel for the new baby. That night another name was entered in the ledger: "Nan, a daughter of Rachel, a Negro wench, born September 28, 1777. One blanket."

The next morning John took his rifle and powder horn from their resting place over the fireplace and his hunting shirt from the back of the cabin door. Bettie was sitting by the fire holding James in her lap.

61

"I'm sorry Bettie, but I must rendezvous with my men this morning. We will march to Bluestone to look for Indians. Our tour will last about a month or so, and then I will return," offered John helplessly.

"Oh, John, I am so tired of war. I am sorry you have to go, and I will count days until your return. Please be careful." She rose from the chair, put James on the floor and came to stand close to her husband. He reached for her and held her closely for several minutes, saying nothing.

Captain John Draper and his men spent two months on the Bluestone River guarding the new forts recently constructed, scouting for enemy Indians, and providing some protection for the settlers. Shortly after that tour he and his company spent six months guarding the frontier and searching out and skirmishing with the Shawnee Indians.

At home the court continued to hear evidence of treason in Montgomery County. Confessions were obtained by deposition where neighbor was tattling on neighbor. The great fear of 1779 and 1780 was the loss of the lead mines, only eight or nine miles from the fort. The Tories continued their attempts to take over this strategic location and were defeated each time in their efforts.

Before long the call came for support of the troops in North Carolina against the British and the Tories who had congregated there. Captain John Draper and his men and others with their companies of militia were among those called to duty, a month at a time.

The captain wondered if he could go through a war again. His nightmares and memories of Point Pleasant still lingered. Now again he would see the enemy die. He would hear the moans and screams of the wounded. When the battle was over he would see the bodies spread over the fields and smell the blood poured out on the grass. Sounds, smells, and memories. And nightmares! He was invariably screaming, "Attack, attack! It is the enemy!" And he was waking up in the camp, getting up and marching outside his tent, earnestly watching for the enemy until one of his men would come and bring him back to his camp cot. John Draper was determined never to go to war again. But night after night in his nightmares, he did.

Chapter 7

1781

During the years of war Bettie and Rachel worked together, each of them caring for their children, worrying about the war, fearing for their lives on a daily basis, and keeping the farm going the best they could. Rachel helped to feed cattle, sheep, and chickens, loaded up the crops, drove the wagons and, with the help of Peter, Will and Caesar, killed and dressed hogs each fall. They planted a big garden, gathered the beans, corn, and cabbages. They picked apples from the orchard and wandered in the mountain for chestnuts. They made cider, dried apples, and milked cows. The children helped pick wild strawberries and blueberries in season and gathered the eggs they found in the boxes in the barn. Peter often found honey in the bee trees on his walks in the woods. Flax seeds were sewn and when the crop was ready Rachel, Judy, and sometimes the Draper children, would take turns with the flax brake, the hackles, and the spinning wheel. Peter would shear the sheep and everyone helped gather the wool into the tow sacks.

At the house they mended clothes, made new ones for the children, and took turns making the bread and cooking the meals. Will tried to make simple leather shoes for the children, and Peter made beds for his little ones.

The war dragged on, but the October morning was bright and silent at Draper Mountain. Peter and Rachel were ready to begin their day. Rachel touched Peter on the arm and stopped him outside the Draper house.

"I reckon I am ready, Peter," said Rachel.

"Ready for what?" asked Peter.

"I feel close to Missus Bettie. I want to share my dream of freedom with her. I've pondered over it and I am ready." Rachel looked at Peter and waited for him to say something. Peter hesitated, looked to the house, looked to the ground, looked back at the cabin.

"You sure, gal? That is a big step. I don't want to lose you." Peter touched her gently on the cheek.

"She won't send me off. She'll understand, I knows she will. I want to see brother Samuel. I want those papers that show I'm free. But Samuel hasn't come. Samuel can't find me."

"Well, if'n you reckon it's the thing to do, then do it."

Rachel smiled and touched his arm as he headed to the barn. She went into the Draper house looking for Bettie. After the morning chores were done, both women sat at the spinning wheels before the fire.

Rachel drew a deep breath.

"Missus, I knows you was captured by Shawnee Injuns and taken away. I knows that was bad for you because you couldn't leave and come home for a long time, or so I hear."

"Yes, Rachel, it was a terrible experience. I missed John so much and I wanted to come back to Virginia and the New River, but I couldn't leave. I prayed every day that

66

John would ransom me. I felt trapped."

"What's a ransom?" asked Rachel.

"Why, that's when someone gives money or goods in exchange for the person's freedom. The Indians liked yard goods, you know the ones bright red and blue, to make shirts, and they usually wanted something to drink, and some beads, and bells, and the like. And John finally was able to ransom me. But I was sent to be with an Indian chief, to be his slave. And I stayed there six long years."

"Do you s'pose I could be ransomed?" asked Rachel.

Bettie turned her head sharply and looked Rachel in the eye."I don't know, Rachel. Why did you ask?"

"Well, when I was sixteen and Judy was three, my older brother, Samuel, and my grandmama, we filed for our freedom in Williamsburg. Before I got word, Marse Clay brung me out here and before I knowed it had sold me to Marse Draper."

"How could that be, Rachel? From all I have heard no Negro could be free at that time, in the 1770s, for any reason unless they had saved their marse's life or something like that."

"No ma'am, that's not it. You see my grandmama was an Injun woman who was captured, just like you was, only a white man took her and brought her to Virginia. She coulda been free if she had got herself a lawyer right away, but now when she's old, I knows she's free. I knows this is 'cause no Injun woman or her children or grandchildren should have been held as slaves."

Shock filled Bettie's heart and soul. Was Rachel lying? Was she dreaming about all of this? Was there a possibility that she might be entitled to her freedom by law? Surely John would know if that were true or not. But Bettie looked at Rachel and could plainly see the shiny copper skin, the long, straight, crow-colored hair, and the features of a beautiful Indian woman.

"Rachel, I am not sure what to say. If you are entitled to your freedom, how is it that you are Mr. Draper's slave?"

"Well, I heerd Marse Clay tell the marse that I was a Negro wench and I think that's what he put on the paper when he sold me. But Marse Clay knowed I had filed a freedom suit and would soon get my freedom and he and his father planned to send me away before the word came."

"How did you get your freedom?"

"I come from an Injun woman, my grandmama, whose name was Chance. She was captured by Marse Clay's grandpappy in the South. She come from the Catawber tribe. My brother, Samuel, was s'posed to bring me the papers, but guess he can't find me."

"That is an amazing story. I don't think we can use ransom in this case, but let me think about it. My heart tells me that slavery is wrong, and I realized this especially after being held so long myself. I just must find a way to help you. But Mr. Draper will not like it so let me see if I can think of a way without telling him right now. If I tell him he will be angry with both of us."

Rachel reached for Bettie, withdrew her hand and turned back to the spinning wheel. "Thank you, Missus. Now at least someone other than Peter knows my story."

Bettie wanted to give Rachel some assistance if the story was true. Probably just a lie. How could she help her anyway? Rachel would need some money, but now the money was worth nothing. She might need a lawyer, but she could not get one for Rachel without explaining to John what this was all about. Did she know anyone else who could help her? Someone at the courthouse could help if she made limited inquiries. She knew it would take time, and she knew that it would be difficult to persuade anyone that the story was true. No one had ever talked about such a thing. Of course, if Mr. Mitchell Clay knew, then perhaps others would know too. But she had decided one thing. Rachel should be free if she was legally free.

What would John think? Or do? Of course he would be against it in every way. He bought and paid for Rachel and Judy and now there were other children to think about. Clay had certainly deceived John, if the story was true. And if John lost Rachel and Judy he would be a loser, not only of labor, but the land he had traded for the two women. And if Rachel got free, Bettie would have no helpers. What a dilemma! Maybe, after all, it was best to let things be.

When Captain John returned from war, his wrinkled, unshaven face set his eyes in hollow boxes, and the family often found him staring and glaring into space. Here Captain John relived his engagements with the Indians and the Tories, screaming and sobbing as he marched back and forth in the yard. His mind had taken him back to those wartime days. His nightmares were full of wartime violence and there seemed to be no let-up day or night. He would never be the same. And Bettie did not tell him about Rachel. The Revolution had not ended and the captain was called again to come to North Carolina to fight Tories.

A few weeks later, Peter, Rachel, Bettie and some of the children set out for Fort Chiswell to visit the trading post and to take corn to be ground at McGavock's Mill. Now was Bettie's opportunity to ask some questions.

When Bettie, sitting in her side saddle and dressed in her best clothes, reached the Great Road, dust was flying in every direction, and looking to the east there seemed to be a large company of horses and wagons heading in her direction.

"Peter, get that wagon moving so we can get in front of the crowd. You children in the wagon, hold tight as we move along quickly. Cover your faces with your handkerchief if you need too."

Peter slapped the reins against the backs of the black horses, and they responded with a fast pace, leaving the dust in the distance. Soon they had rounded the bend, forded Reed Creek, and came into the fort. Peter left Bettie, Rachel, and the children to visit the store, and he took the wagon over the hill to the mill. He had a few vegetables he wanted to trade but would tend to the corn first.

"Good morning, Mr. McGavock, sir." Bettie greeted the trading post owner with a smile. "There seems to be a lot of excitement around here today. What's going on?"

McGavock looked up, nodded to Bettie, noticed Rachel and the children, and in his best Irish welcome greeted Bettie warmly. "My dear, it is an approaching wagon train. They tell us there are about five hundred people on their way to Kentucky. They are from Spotsylvania County."

"Five hundred people! What a large group that will be camping on your grounds tonight. Will you be able to accommodate them?"

"Yes, to some extent. As you say, they will be camping, and they do have their wagons. They can use the water from the spring, and we have some extra corn, lead, and powder, and the post is well stocked with other necessaries. But I fear those people will be greatly distressed to learn that they will have to trade in the wagons for pack horses."

"What do you mean?" asked Bettie.

"Well, the wagon road goes about another hundred miles, but after that they will find only a single trail suitable for horses and not wagons."

"But they could turn in those wagons when they get to the end of the good road, couldn't they?" asked Bettie.

"No, we have the last trading center of any kind for the next hundred miles. We are trying now to gather in enough horses for them so they can go on their way. We have sent word out to the neighbors that we need horses and will give good prices for them. We found out about a week ago that these folks were coming here, so we have many horses penned up over on that hillside." McGavock pointed to the golden hill to the west.

"Who is leading this wagon train?" asked Bettie, continuing her series of questions.

"They say he is a Baptist preacher by the name of Craig. He just got out of prison a few months ago because he was preaching the Baptist religion. When he got out, he decided to go to Kentucky, and I understand everyone in his church decided to go too. And some neighbors and friends besides." McGavock turned to greet another friend, and Bettie and Rachel moved off to look at the yard goods nearby.

"Rachel," said Bettie in a whisper. "This may be the chance I have been waiting for. I hope I can talk to someone on the train, the preacher perhaps, and see what can he knows about cases like yours."

"Thank you, Missus. I'll take the little ones and go look for the wagons."

"Yes, and when they come in, come and get me."

Free in Chains

At the mill, Peter unloaded the bags of corn from the wagon. When he finished he stood near the race and waited. He watched the water swish by on its way to Reed Creek, and heard the wheel slowly grinding, grinding, the stones turning and crushing the corn, throwing the meal into tow-linen sacks. He knew it would take some time, so he sat on one of the fieldstones near the wagon and waited, and admired the red of the maples, the yellow of the poplars surrounding the mill.

When the second wagon approached, Peter didn't recognize the copper-skinned driver. Some white master had a new man, thought Peter. The stranger came to join him and began the conversation.

"Howdy, name is Samuel Findlay. I come from the east, well all over the place I s'pose, cuz I drives this here wagon everywhere. And it's mine!" added Samuel.

"How can that be?" asked Peter.

"I'm a free man, a free man," bragged Sam. He pushed his hands through his heavy head of straight black hair.

"Naw, ya' ain't," argued Peter.

"Uh huh. I really and truly is. I been free since 1773. Among those first cases ever brung in Virginia. Me, my sister and her daughter and my grandmama were on the same papers."

Samuel reached in his pocket and pulled out a paper carefully wrapped in sheepskin, but as far as Peter was concerned it could have been a deed, a will, a letter, or a note, because he could not read it. Still, he was curious.

"Can't read none. So, tell me about it," said Peter.

"Well, 'twas like this. My grandmama was captured in South Carolina and brung here, well, not right here, but to Virginia as a slave. She didn't know it, but the law back then said she should have been free and not a slave."

72

"My mother was her daughter, and she could have been free too, but died too young. It was us, Grandmama Chance, and her grandchildren that know'd what we had to do before it was too late."

"Don't make no sense to me," said Peter. "Why would anybody say you was free?"

"Well, we went to the General Court in Williamsburg, and we got our freedom. We got it." Samuel shook the paper in front of Peter's face.

"Went to court? Had a lawyer? And how could he tell the court that you was free?" said Peter, scratching his head.

"Well, we was from an Injun. My grandmama was an Injun from South Carolina."

"Wait a minute! You say's your grandmama was Injun?" asked Peter.

"Yes, in the Catawber tribe, her name there in South Carolina was White Cloud."

"How'd she git here?"

"Injun trader named Clay took her and a boy named James and brung them back to Chesterfield County, way over in eastern part of Virginia."

Peter gulped. He raised his hand to his head and muttered a few words to himself. He studied the handsome man with the Indian complexion. He saw the high cheek bones, the long nose, and copper skin. Sure did look more Indian than Negro.

"What's the matter?" asked Samuel.

"I knows a woman, a slave woman, who says her grandmama was an Injun from the Cataber tribe. I didn't believe her story, but she told me she really is or should be free, 'cause she's her granddaughter."

Samuel wiped his brow. Before he could get his words together, the McGavock's mill hand, Thomas Ramsey, called.

"Get those bags out of here, Peter. And you, yes you, get up here and get your load next," shouted Ramsey.

"We have to talk later. What's your name?"

"It's Peter, and I's Captain Draper's slave, just up the road a piece." But he knew he was not heard; only Ramsey's voice could be heard hollering again, "Get along now." The horses lurched, the wagon creaked and the wheels turned slowly under the heavy load, moving up the hill toward the trading post. Peter looked back as the free man was heaving sacks to the miller.

Maybe Rachel was not telling a tall tale after all, thought Peter. But I have to find Samuel again. I must find him for Rachel.

Samuel Findlay could only wait for his corn. He could hardly believe what he had heard. Who could that woman be? Someone else out here from the Catawbers? He rubbed his back and stretched and began to think about the quirks of fate that brought him to this place.

Yes, he did get his freedom in 1773. And he had chosen the name Findlay, naming himself for the old doctor that was so kind to his mother, Nan, as she lay dying at Clay's. He had worked for a wage in Manchester for five years until he had enough money to get his own wagon. Then he was in business for himself acting as a contractor for the army. They needed wagoners during the war to transport goods to the lead mines on New River and to bring back loads of lead for the army. And to carry goods anywhere and everywhere the army might be. Because he looked more like an Indian than a Negro did, he became one of the most trusted free man in the city. Seldom was he questioned or stopped. Only two or three times was he asked for his papers.

For three years he had been criss-crossing the state, doing business for Virginia. Now 1781 found him at Fort Chiswell, where he had come to get the corn ground at the mill. He had left the lead mines earlier that morning loaded with corn and with a list of supplies that were needed there. The state had transported Negroes to the mines recently to work the lead, and as the workers processed the lead Samuel was one of ten wagoners waiting to transport the finished product to the army in eastern Virginia. But the lead was not ready, at least not enough for ten wagons, and no one was willing to travel alone in wartime.

A couple of months ago it began to rain and it rained for weeks. The small streams climbed over their banks and the river rose till it flooded the pastures, carrying the mills and livestock away. Buildings were torn from their foundations. The mill at the mines, at the mouth of Mine Mill Creek, was lifted up, twisted into sticks of wood, and the debris carried downstream by the raging river. With no place to grind the corn, the superintendent of the mines sent Samuel with the load to use McGavock's mill. And so he sat and waited.

I must talk to Peter some more. Maybe I can find out who this person is. It surely sounds like it might be Rachel, but that would be such a miracle, and besides everybody in Powhatan County said she had gone to Kentucky. No, someone said she was in Mecklenburg and someone else said Pittsylvania County. Grandmama Chance thought she would be on the New River. Nobody really knew. Samuel concluded it was probably not her.

75

The first of the covered wagons rolled onto the hilltop, McGavock directing their location. Soon they had spread out in circular formation over several fields and hillsides. Bettie and Rachel watched in amazement. Never had they ever seen such a number of wagons, nor so many people. It was not long before their leader came to McGavock with outstretched hand, and said, "My name is Craig, Lewis Craig. Thank you for your help out there with the wagons. Now I have to have more help."

"What is it?" McGavock asked, offering his hand.

"We have dozens of little children with us, and some of them are sick with a fever. We need someone to nurse them, to help us with them. Could a doctor help? Or some of the womenfolk? Our women have been up for days with them and are near exhaustion."

"Of course, of course," said McGavock. "We don't have a doctor anywhere near here right now, but several of the women in the neighborhood are good with medicines and such. Mrs. McGavock will know what to do."

Seeing Bettie and Rachel close by, McGavock turned to them and introduced Bettie to Craig, then asked, "Could you go up to the house and fetch Mrs. McGavock? And if you two can stay awhile and help, we would be obliged."

Bettie and Rachel turned to each other and nodded and then went up the hill to the house.

"Mary McGavock, where are you?" shouted Bettie from the front door of the log house. The aroma of bread and meat came from the log kitchen out back.

"Guess that's where she is," said Bettie in a whispered voice.

The two women went to the kitchen and found Mary with her hands covered in flour. She was kneading more bread for the big oven nearby.

76

"Bettie, Bettie Draper, come in," said Mary. "Excuse the dusty hands, but I am trying to get some extra bread made for the travelers. I see they have arrived."

"Yes, Mary, it is good to see you, but James sent me up here to tell you that there are a lot of sick younguns in the wagons. They need someone to help with the sickness on the wagon train. Can you help, or is there someone else close by we can get?"

"Well, if I could get away from this bread making, I could go and then there are some others we can send for. What seems to be going on?"

"I understand the children have fevers and have had them for several days. The mothers are exhausted."

"Does your girl know how to make bread?" asked Mary. "If she does, then we could leave her in charge of the oven, and we could go and see about them younguns."

"Rachel, you know what to do." Mary and Rachel traded places, Mary wiped her hands on her apron and reached for a big wrap-around apron for Bettie so she could cover her pretty clothes. The two left Rachel in charge of bread.

On their way to the store they saw Peter and his wagon coming to a stop nearby. Bettie summoned him and asked if he could go and find some of the other women. Mistress McGavock would give him directions. With that Peter followed the road down the hill, urged the horses on with his whip and was soon on the Carolina Road to the south. He knew where to go.

Back at the store, Reverend Craig, full of bluster and importance, showed them the way to the wagons where the sickest children lay. Mary went to one wagon and Craig and Bettie to another.

"Reverend, before I go in there, I need to ask an important question. Please forgive me for delaying this visit to the children, but I must know the answer and you are the only one I know who can help me."

"Go on, Mrs. Draper. What is it?"

"Well, I have heard, but am not sure I am hearing right, that there were some people of Indian extraction who were held in slavery. Did you ever hear of that?"

"Why yes, my dear, there were several cases not too long ago. They brought cases in the General Court in Williamsburg, claiming they were descendants of Indians held illegally in slavery. Is that what you mean?"

"I guess so, yes, that's it. But did they ever become free?" asked Bettie.

"Yes, the ones I heard about did."

"What if someone was moved away before they knew they were free, what could be done then?"

"What do you mean, Mrs. Draper?" asked Craig.

"Well, suppose, just suppose, that the marse did not want them to be free and sent them away from the eastern part of the state to some place else, maybe even Kentucky, and sold them as Negroes and they are enslaved. What then?"

"I don't really know. Never heard of that. But suppose they would have to get a lawyer to look into it. I know the others brought suit with the help of a lawyer and all for free too. They claimed they were paupers, and with no money, the court gave them a lawyer free."

"Thank you," said Bettie, and the two went inside the nearest wagon to see what could be done for the children.

"This is Mrs. Draper. She is here to help you," said Craig. "I will go to the next wagon to see if Mrs. McGavock needs me, and we will soon have more help. We sent Peter for some more women over near the mines."

When Bettie climbed inside the white tent covering, she knew that the two little children she saw huddled together under the dark coverlets were seriously ill. Beads of sweat were sparkling on their foreheads and their hair was wet and plastered to their scalps. The mother had been awake too long. Her eyes dropped and her motions were routine, wringing out the white rag in the basin of spring water and wiping the little faces of her children. None of it seemed to do any good. Their skin was hot like a coal in the fireplace, and the moaning continued intermittently, giving Bettie the idea that they were out of their minds with some strange and terrible disease.

Bettie took over. She told the mother to sleep on the pallet next to the children while she did the mopping, wiping, and comforting of the two little ones. The night would soon be too cool to take anyone outside. Meanwhile, Mary McGavock was doing the same thing in the next wagon. Reverend Craig was trying his best to comfort those without help, announcing that soon others would be coming to assist them. Mumbling personal prayers as he went, Craig had made the full circle of the wagon lot.

James McGavock realized that every one who could do anything would be called upon to help. He had Bettie's and Rachel's children going to the spring for water and filling a larger pail which McGavock's servants carried to the wagons. Over and over again they dipped clear cool spring water for the sick. Rachel finished the bread and proudly delivered the golden brown loaves to the store for McGavock to sell to the new arrivals. Back and forth she went to the kitchen bringing an armload each time. When all of the loaves were at the trading post Rachel turned to help at the wagons. Long into the night the women continued their care of the sick. There was no medicine to give, only cool water to ease the fever. Only comforting words for the little ones. Near dark Peter came with some of the Sanders women, the Newells, and the Herberts. More would follow tomorrow.

In late afternoon, Samuel Findlay had reloaded his wagon with the bags of corn meal and had begun his journey to the lead mines about eight miles away, not knowing where his next assignment would take him. When he arrived at the mines there was much excitement about the sickness on the wagon train, and the women, young and old, had gathered at the furnace to await their transportation to Fort Chiswell. Colonel Lynch ordered Samuel to empty the wagon promptly, throw in some blankets for the women to sit on and return immediately to the wagons at Fort Chiswell.

When the women arrived, Mary McGavock and Bettie Draper invited them to join them in the circle of wagons and assigned each of them sick children to help. Now there were about thirty with what appeared to be the same illness. The next morning they were no better, but at least the mothers had been able to take a few hours of sleep and prepared for the day ahead. Some of the children were covered with red spots.

The men met with McGavock and his servants and began to trade in their wagons. Samuel was asked to help, moving trunks and goods, blankets, food, water, guns, lead, flints. Gradually they loaded the packhorses. Two large baskets were put on either side of many of the animals, and the children, in spite of their sickness, were wrapped in blankets and made ready to travel. Peter lifted sick children into the baskets, and the older ones into the saddles with mothers, fathers, and older friends and relatives behind. McGavock was keeping the ledgers for each family, noting the kind of wagon, its condition and its price, the horses added to the family's inventory, and any goods purchased at the store. Each account was settled, not with money because it was worth nothing, but with trading what they had to spare for the necessaries. A chair here and there, a trunk too large to travel on horseback, a small table, a wooden bucket, pieces of a bed, a desk, and anything else to make the account even.

The condition of the families was pitiful but they would not stay longer. They wanted to be in Kentucky before Christmas, and an arduous journey was ahead. As each bundle was secured and each family member lifted into place, horses were lined up ready to cross the milldam and climb the next hill to the west. Before noon a train of five hundred people, some riding, some walking, and one hundred weighted-down horses moved out of the fort.

Bettie gathered her children, Rachel and her children, and Peter and they began the trip back to the foot of Draper Mountain to the east. Back at home Rachel and Bettie were busy preparing for the return of Marse Draper. The news came that Cornwallis had been defeated and everyone felt that surely the war was now over. Captain John would be expected to return with his militia company from North Carolina any time.

"Missus, you find out anything about freed people, while you was gone?" asked Rachel.

"Only this, Rachel, that Indians elsewhere in the colony

did receive their freedom, but that preacher Craig had never heard of anyone being sent away before they got their freedom. He said that the only way to find out what could be done was to find a lawyer to help."

"Thank you!" exclaimed Rachel. "Maybe the next time we go to Fort Chiswell and the courthouse you can help me find somebody."

"Maybe, I can do that. I do not want to bother your master with the problem, so we will do it between us when we can. Don't give up, Rachel. Being free will be more than a dream for you. It will be a reality and soon, very soon. I am determined that you will not suffer any longer. I thought about this a lot. I did not like being held as a prisoner and neither do you."

"Thank you," muttered Rachel. She went upstairs to put the marse's younger children to bed.

When Rachel returned to the slave quarters she found Judy and the other children, tired from the day's journey, stretched out on the mats on the wooden floor. All seemed quiet and peaceful. Then Peter came in swinging the feed bucket, put it in the corner and dropped into the wooden chair by the table. His head hung down, and his voice was soft and quiet.

"Oh, Rachel. I don't know how to tell you this. Something good and something bad happened over at the fort."

"What are you talking about?" asked Rachel.

"Well, I met a man who says he was a free man, a wagoner he was. Said he owned his own wagon and traveled all around the state. He showed me a piece a paper that showed that he was free. I couldn't read it none, but that's what he said anyhow."

"Yes," said Rachel. "When you gets free you have papers to prove it so you won't be captured and put in jail.

Where did he come from?"

"He came from the east, he says, and his grandmama was an Injun from the Catawber tribe, said her name was White Cloud."

"White Cloud!" screamed Rachel. "His grandmama was White Cloud?"

"Yes," stammered Peter. "What is it, Rachel?"

"My grandmama's name in Injun was White Cloud, but Marse Clay gave her the name Chance." Rachel dropped into the chair in disbelief.

"Where is this man? What's his name? Where can I find him?" Rachel's questions kept coming in rapid succession.

"I don't know where he is, that is the bad news. I only know his name was Samuel, and—."

"Did you say Samuel?"

"Yes, that's what he said his name was. Don't remember no other name, just Samuel."

"Peter, my brother's named Samuel. Where can I find him?"

"Don't know 'cause he left the fort about the time we come back here. I tried to tell him where I live, but the miller made us move on and I had no chance to tell him where I was. But I did tell him I knowed a woman who had an Injun grandmama. He seemed interested, but we couldn't talk any more. I wish I could help, Rachel. Now that you are mostly sure that was your brother, Mr. McGavock or someone at the fort might know where he was goin'."

Rachel shook her head, curled up her fingers and pounded both fists on the table.

"Will I ever be free? What do I mean, *free*? I AM free, free but still in chains. Free but still treated as a slave. Free but still doin' the bidding of the marse. Free but still sufferin' the whip's lash every time he's home. The trouble is that out here in the New River settlements nobody will never believe me. Nobody will believe I's already free."

Peter reached to comfort her, pulled her body to his chest. He reached for her hands, unfolding her stiffened fingers one at a time. He said nothing.

Two weeks had passed since their visit to the fort, and there was nothing new to give Rachel hope. But there wasn't a day that went by that she did not talk to Peter about her freedom. It was the only goal in her life, she decided. From now on she would work toward being free, really free. And Bettie would help her. It was in one of these moments of reverie that she heard rapid footsteps and then saw that it was young John Draper, running to the slave quarters, shouting as he crossed the muddy yard.

"Rachel, Rachel, come quick. It's mother! She's terribly sick."

Rachel ran to the big house and into the bedroom where she found Bettie writhing in the bed, tossing and turning, throwing her arms back and forth, her eyes rolled back into her head and her babble incomprehensible. Rachel had seen it before those children at the fort. Whatever it was she did not know, but it was not good.

"Get me some of the coldest water you can find, John. Your mama's awful sick. Send George to find Dr. Smith as soon as you can. I will need rags to wipe her face and I may need some help later to keep her in the bed. Go, go, quick as you can."

When John left the room Rachel pulled the covers back, smoothed them so that the blankets were even at the top and bottom, and moved the pillow under Bettie's head.

But it was damp and Bettie's hair was just as if she had come out of the creek. Rachel smoothed the dark strands away from her face and took her apron and wiped the back of her neck. She went to the trunk at the foot of the bed and found some sheeting and a pillow sham and replaced the wet casing on the pillow, then tore some of the sheeting into strips and began to dry Bettie's fevered body. Rachel knew it was bad. She mumbled over and over to herself, "Missus Bettie, Missus Bettie, does ya hear me? You gonna be all right, all right. Now Rachel's here to take care you." But Rachel was afraid.

John returned with the water and Rachel emptied some into the basin and put the rest in the porcelain pitcher. She wet one of the strips of sheeting and began to bathe and smooth Bettie's forehead. If she could just get her to cool down, she would be better, but that did not happen. For two days the delirium continued, and Rachel never left the bedside. The doctor came and sat for hours. He bled his patient and did his best to preserve the life that was fading away. The boys, John, George, Silas, and James, hovered at the foot of the bed, taking turns sitting on the old trunk nearby. The Draper girls, Elizabeth, Mary, and Nancy, cried near the fireplace and wondered if their mother would get well. And if their father would get home in time.

Captain John Draper came home early in November to find a freshly marked grave east of the house. He stood at the place of solitude and quiet and screamed. "Damn this war, anyway! I have lost my Bettie and I was away fighting Tories. It is all my fault. If I had been here this wouldn't have happened. Damn this war—damn it!" He picked up his rifle, flung it to his shoulder, straightened his back,

85

threw up his head and marched and marched until, hours later, he fell in the garden near the house, totally exhausted. When the children found him he was cold and covered with a light snow which had fallen after sunset. Gently they carried their father to the house and put him to bed without a word.

Draper mumbled to himself, "This is not a good way to celebrate the Cornwallis victory at Yorktown in 1781. I have lost the dearest person in the world—my beloved Bettie."

Chapter 8

THE HANGING

On August 6, 1782, John Draper was much improved and looking forward to visiting with his soldiers, his neighbors and friends who had gathered at Fort Chiswell for the court day. Rachel and several of the children rode the wagon driven by Peter, and John rode his own horse, with a bay colt tethered behind. Today, Peter was taking another load of corn to McGavock's mill to be ground. He had a few vegetables he hoped to sell, and the captain was looking for a good trade on the young colt.

On arrival John stepped into the courthouse, leaving Peter to unload at the mill. The others would be visiting with their acquaintances and trading at the store.

"All rise, all rise. Oyez, Oyez, the court will now come to order," chanted the bailiff. Nine Gentlemen Justices, James McGavock, James Byrn, William Doak, William Ward, Adam Dean, Robert Sayers, William Love, Samuel Ewing and William Davies, were on the bench. Draper knew them all.

"You may be seated," continued the bailiff.

"The first order of business," stated the clerk, "is swearing in of Benjamin Bailey. Please come forward, sir."

Bailey appeared before the nine, raised his right hand

and began repeating the oaths as given to him by the clerk.

"I, Benjamin Bailey, do solemnly swear that I will uphold the laws of the Commonwealth of Virginia, and administer justice to the best of my ability, so help me God." When finished he took the empty seat on the bench and became the tenth member of the court for the August session.

Draper listened as tithable lists were returned. *Let me think a minute. I will have to pay taxes on myself, my oldest son, about eighteen horses and probably forty head of cattle, and of course my dozen slaves.*

Next he heard that inventories and appraisements of estates were ordered to be recorded, and the will of John Haven was proved and the appraisers appointed. Leftover business from the war was included when James Beaver proved that he should be paid for 106 pounds of flour taken from him for the use of militia under Captain Love in 1780. On a sad note, the estate of Henry Francis, deceased, required counter securities. Oh yes, thought Draper, the widow and oldest son, John, were not too responsible. The men who signed on their bond needed some assurance that the administrators would handle the estate properly.

Draper's thoughts drifted back to the day Henry had been killed in North Carolina where he was serving as a captain of the militia with his men, most of them from Cripple Creek. His own young son, also in the company, saw what happened and his rifle was immediately brought to his shoulder and fired. The killer lay dead a few yards away, and Draper had seen it all. He began to shake as he relived the battle over and over again. All the memories of Point Pleasant came charging into his mind, the dead, the dying, the scalps missing, the cries of the wounded. Too much war. Too much death. Too much blood. Draper stepped outside. He did not want to remember.

"Hello, John," said his neighbor, Andrew Boyd, holding out his hand. "How are you?"

"Only fair, Andrew, only fair. The war, this terrible war, I can't get it out of my mind," said John. "It grows worse every day too. The prices are so high I can buy nothing, the money is worth nothing, and my place is going down hill daily. I have lost Bettie and now I hear that I am supposed to free my slaves so they can be free like the rest of us. I will soon have no one."

"John, that new law was passed which now gives us a way to free the slaves *if* we want to. I can make a deed and set the time limits, or I can do the same by will. But who wants to do that anyway?" asked Andrew.

"There is big talk among some of our neighbors about doing the right thing, you know, freeing our slaves," John added. "I don't know about you, Andrew, but I need every one of my Negroes, gotta get that farm going again. Bettie tried, but my fences are down, brush in the pasture, weeds in the fields, barn doors off, leaks in the roof. Damn war!"

"The slaves are also talking," said Andrew. "You know Joseph Baker, don't you? Well, his Negroes have been agitating for their freedom. He has told them in no uncertain terms he will never free any one of them. In fact he has been chaining them at night for fear they will escape, and he has whipped several for insisting on such talk when he has told them no."

"I know Joe Baker," said John. "Has a bad temper and a mean streak in him. I've seen him throw a fit. Wild man! And stubborn as a block of granite."

When they were ready to part, young John approached his father and Mr. Boyd, now a Gentleman Justice on the court.

"Good day, sir," said John, lifting his hat.

"Hello, John, you have my sympathy about your mother."

"Thank you, sir."

"I have come to ask about the church service over at the Boiling Spring. Will they be meeting this Sunday?"

"Yes, I believe so," said Boyd.

"Well, I plan to visit there and hope to take Miss Jane with me. You know Miss Jane Crockett."

"That's nice. Does your father plan to come with you?"

"I told him that Miss Jane's mother, you know, the Widow Crockett, would be glad to see him, to sit with him during service, and to provide the picnic after, but he just walks away when I say that."

"Well, the Widow Crockett is a nice lady, and so is Miss Jane. When Sunday comes he may change his mind."

On Sunday, the August morning began with a pink and blue sunrise and when young John got ready for church, he was surprised to see George, James and Silas and the girls all ready to go. Captain Draper insisted that they go to church, and at this time he would accompany them. Surely the Drapers would be fully represented in the Presbyterian congregation on this glorious morning. The ride to church was less than thirty minutes and the day so pleasant that the captain seemed to be in another world. On arriving at the little log church, he noticed that others were gathering in groups talking, some men under the trees, others next to the horses and the women by the front door of the log building. There were some of Nathaniel Welshire's children, Billy and Tommy Herbert, with their guardian,

Colonel Walter Crockett and his family, some of the Sanders families, and Colonel Lynch from the mines. The
Widow Crockett, her daughter Jane, and her three other
children arrived shortly and greetings were exchanged.

"It is going to be a lovely day for a picnic, isn't it, Captain?"

He only nodded his head bashfully. He was trying to
decide whether to sit with her or not. That was a real com-
mitment and he was not sure he was ready to make it. Son
John and young Jane exchanged secret looks and the two
wandered toward the church.

"Will we tell them today, John," she whispered. "Probably so, that is, if Father is in a good frame of mind. Some
days he is not himself, and I don't want him to think me
ungrateful or anything like that, but if we get married I
want to start a place of my own." He patted her hand. They
exchanged loving looks and waited.

The Widow Crockett, a woman of thirty-five years, was
an attractive, vivacious woman who could and did look
after herself. Her husband had been dead about ten years
and had left her with four children, now reaching adult-
hood. She had managed through the war and had brought
her children up in the best way, strong in their Christian
beliefs and strong in their politics. The neighbors heard
that she had not planned to remarry after the ten years had
passed because she realized she could manage herself, and
besides, the men were regularly away at war and could not
be relied on. She became an independent woman educat-
ing her children. She was known for ruling her Negroes
with an iron hand. The word was around the neighborhood that she was meaner than one hundred mules.

Her husband had arranged for purchase money so she
could buy slaves to help support her and the children after

his death. And she had done just that, Cato being a healthy buck about twenty and Cynthia a young girl of ten years at the time of purchase. Cato had learned the blacksmith trade while working for her deceased husband, Samuel, and he was never without work at the blacksmith's forge. Lately he had come to Draper Mountain to do similar work for the Drapers, and the rumor was that he had found Rachel's Judy, a beautiful young girl, and was attracted to her.

When the service began Captain John found his place beside the widow and her children. Jane smiled to herself. Maybe she would marry after all. It couldn't be that bad. He had plenty of land, and George had already married his sweetheart Barbara. Young John would marry her daughter, Jane, and the girls would soon be leaving home too. There would be room for her and her children and her two slaves. He might be a good husband. Well, that was in the future, thought Jane. I'll pray about it. She tried hard to concentrate on the scripture and the sermon.

Captain John was thinking that she was too pretty to be alone. Besides, George was gone, and he supposed Mary would leave him soon, as she would soon be eighteen. Elizabeth was only two years behind, and of course John was courting Miss Jane. There would be room for all of them without any additional work to the house. The Widow had slaves Cato and Cynthia, and that did not seem to be a problem either. Yes, he'd consider the Widow Crockett as a suitable mate. He'd think on it. He looked out through the small window to the east and the sun spread its rays over the cherry trees and blue mountains. He felt good.

The Welshman, Evan Williams, led the singing. Everyone joined in and when the last verse was heard, everyone moved outside to the grove where the horses were tied, and the wagons stilled. The blankets were soon spread and the baskets of food were opened. Families gathered together, said their thanks for the day and the food and promptly began the meal. After the meal the children played nearby. Captain John and Jane were in charge of packing the remnants away when young John and young Jane came to help. John could see that his father was in good spirits, probably because of the Widow Crockett and her friendliness. John took his chances and asked his father if he would approve his marriage to Miss Jane Crockett, daughter of the late Samuel and Jane Armstrong Crockett. Jane, watching anxiously, squeezed her mother's hand. The captain, who had seen the relationship blossom, readily agreed and volunteered the transfer of two hundred acres of the finest land in the valley to his son on the wedding day, or shortly thereafter.

"Thank you, Father. That is wonderful."

"When do you think you might be married?" asked the captain.

"Probably at Christmas time, if that is satisfactory to you, sir."

"Yes, indeed. That is a wonderful time. Congratulations and best wishes to you both," said the older man and reached for his son and held him close. Widow Crockett hugged her daughter and dabbed her eyes with her lace handkerchief.

When John and Jane moved away and walked toward the little meetinghouse branch, the captain moved toward the Widow Crockett.

"Would you like to see the boiling spring? It is down on the creek not far from here."

"That would be special, Captain Draper. Now that we're going to be relatives we really should celebrate." The widow extended her hand.

"You know that's how this little church got its name, from that Boiling Spring. The church has been here since 1769 when the Reverend Craig visited to collect money for the work of the Presbyterians. I remember that," said the captain.

Jane took his arm and the two strolled toward the bend in Reed Creek where the spring bubbled and boiled from the ground. They had not reached their destination when a horse galloped toward the church steps.

"Something's wrong," said the captain as they turned and hurried back to the church.

The captain hollered, "What is it?"

The young rider was Hugh Patrick, and his black horse was glistening with silver sweat.

"Sir, you must get away from here now. You and everyone else," shouted Hugh. "Joseph Baker has been killed, his head cut through with an axe."

Hugh took a breath and continued, "His two Negroes, Bob and Sam are 'spected and we're looking for them right now. They may come this way. They are dangerous and are sure to be headed east, away from here."

"We must get the families gathered up, the children are scattered along the creek," said the captain. "Hugh, could you ride down that way and tell them while I get the horses, wagons and carriages ready to go? Who knows where those bastards are!"

He turned to Jane and suggested she get the baskets of food and the blankets and hurry back to the church steps.

He went to the grove for the horses and as he went, shouted for the others to hurry along so they could leave together as soon as possible.

The day had come to an end with frightened people on every horse and in every wagon and carriage. There had been talk about Negroes wanting to be free and who were willing to fight for their freedom. The neighbors believed it was possible that an uprising might take place, but never expected that their neighbor would be murdered in cold blood. Captain John offered to accompany Jane and her family to Reed Creek, a few miles to the west, and suggested his son John travel with his brothers and sisters to their destination to the east.

Draper would soon learn the details. Word had spread throughout the area that Baker was missing. The sheriff and his deputies had gone to Baker's home, searching woods and stream, fearing the worst. Rumors were rampant that he and his slaves had argued about their freedom, and knowing Baker's temper everyone suspected trouble. The coroner had joined the search. Soon Baker's body was found in a cave not far from his log house. His axe-ridden head was scarred beyond recognition.

In the meantime, the deputies had galloped down the main road hoping to find Bob and Sam, the most obvious suspects. Late Sunday evening, they were discovered in a barn, their bodies bruised and bloody. They were put into irons and taken to the courthouse at Fort Chiswell. After questioning by some of the court's justices, they confessed to the crime and could only look to be hanged.

At the next court day, Captain John Draper brought his slaves to Fort Chiswell, where the two murderers were ordered to be hanged in front of the courthouse. The men of the crowd eagerly awaited the event but had ordered their wives to remain at home. But it was different for the Negroes. Most of the nearby slaveowners brought their own slaves, men, women and even the children, to the fort on this momentous occasion and directed them to stand close to the oak tree, the hanging tree, where the lives of Bob and Sam were to end. Each Negro was in chains, and all had been told by the master that if they had any idea of doing anything like that they too would suffer the same fate. Their legs trembled and their eyes blinked. Their voices were still for they knew death hovered over the fort.

Rachel and Judy and the children, and Peter, Will and Caesar were shackled and pushed to the front line. Once more, Rachel raged at her condition, standing in the field in chains with her children, knowing that she was a free person. And she could say nothing. It was inside that everything was hidden, had to be hidden, and inside where the rage of fire burned. As she watched, tears rolled down her cheeks. This time she could not reach the apron to wipe away the sadness and frustration.

Rachel watched the sheriff as he prepared the ropes. Bob, the first to feel the rope on his neck, was put on the back of the black stallion. Most of the crowd cheered. The sheriff smacked the horse on the rump and the body was left swinging. When the last of life's breath had faded from Bob's limp body, the sheriff hollered, "He's dead."

Cheers rose from the crowd. Again and again.

And this day they would do it again and again, for Sam, the next one ordered to die, did not die easily. When Sam mounted the horse, the crowd cheered, but when the rope broke and his body fell to the ground, there were hisses and boos. The sheriff had to find new rope, and quickly, for he knew the temper of the crowd. A deputy ran toward McGavock's trading post, two others held and shackled Sam awaiting the continuance of the event.

"Kill him, kill him," began the chant from the left of the oak tree. Soon the echo was picked up to the right and then to the rear. The sounds of "kill him, kill him" continued, growing ever louder. Captain Draper could see that the militia would have to do something. He found his lieutenant and gave orders to find any of the others who might be attending court and to hurry back to the big oak. Draper called on his friends and fellow soldiers to assist and to keep the people away from the tied and shackled Sam. The militiamen lined up and linked arm and arm to keep anyone in the crowd from breaking through. When the deputy returned with the new rope, a hush fell on the crowd. Watching carefully, they saw the new rope installed and adjusted and all was ready once more. Sam was dragged to the noose, and he was again in place. When the horse trotted toward the trading post, the body was left swinging on the rope, swinging and thrashing while the crowd waited and waited. Finally it was still and the sheriff announced, "Sam is dead."

Roars, cheers, hand-clapping, and waving of hats in the air ended the celebration. Only the cries of the children could be heard above the crowd's roar.

It was a frightening scene, and Rachel, Judy, Peter, Will and Caesar and the children felt a sickly dread but dared not show it.

When the captain approached, Rachel heard him say in a loud voice, "It's what those devils deserved, exactly what they deserved. And if the rope had broken again I know that there were many in the crowd who would have been

97

happy to stomp the murderer to a pulp. I would have done it myself."

When they returned to Draper's at the Mountain, Rachel and Peter held each other quietly and promised each other they would never resort to violence. But it was not long before their master did.

Rachel heard the gossip in the Negro community that the captain would soon have a wife, one Rachel feared she could not trust and would not like. If she did not get her freedom now, she might never be able to fulfill her dream. These were rumors, of course, but she did not like the thought of a new mistress at the Mountain. She knew too much about that skinny mean woman.

Chapter 9

THE WHIPPING AND THE WEDDING PLANS

During the weeks that followed, Rachel, again with child, knew she did not want to bear another slave child, another person that would be bound in slavery. She had not learned the name of any lawyer, Bettie was dead, and there seemed to be no one else to help her. She decided to take things into her own hands. Maybe the young master would help. She decided to risk asking the question. She found the younger John in a chair by the fireplace.

"Marse John, would you help me please," begged Rachel.

"What is it, Rachel?" answered John.

"I needs the name of a lawyer who can help me git my freedom. Do you know one?" she asked.

John put his papers on the nearby table and stood up.

"Rachel, what are you talking about? You know no lawyer can help you get free. The only way you can be free is if my father decides to free you in his will or by a deed. Don't you know that?" he answered impatiently.

"That's not the way it is, Marse John. I is free 'cause my grandmama was an Injun. All I need is a lawyer to help me."

"What do you mean, an Indian? I never heard that before."

"Well, it is true. My brother, Judy and me, and my Grandmama, we all got our freedom before we came out here, but Mr. Clay didn't want nobody to know. I knows he told a lie to your father and called us Negroes, when we ain't all."

"Now, Rachel, that can't be."

"Yes, Marse John, yes, tis."

"I will ask my father about this, for I am sure there is not a word of truth in what you say. And besides, father will never set you free." John turned to walk out the door.

"Don't tell him, please don't tell him," begged Rachel. "He will be mad with me and beat me. Please, I beg you."

Her pleas were ignored and now she was in serious trouble.

In no time at all, Captain Draper came marching across the muddy path to the slave quarters and pulled the door open.

"Rachel, what are you talking about? This Indian business surely can't be true. And for telling these lies I am putting you in the chains again. This time until you tell me that you have been lying and promise not to do that again. I don't want to hear another word about your being free. No more, do you hear? "

Whip in hand he slashed her across the back, reached for her hair, pulled her across the room, slashed again, dragged her down the two wooden steps, and pushed and prodded her to the stone springhouse. Inside on the left the chains were fastened to the wall. He pushed her against the wall and up to the metal pieces which he quickly slipped over her wrists. Before she knew it Captain Draper had slammed the door and disappeared into the night.

100

The place was damp and frigid. The water gurgled and lapped against the stones and the jugs, and a rat hurried across the dirt floor to the hole in the wall. Rachel's arms were soon aching and numb, her back throbbing and bleeding. And she knew that the punishment had only begun. She would get little food, be attached to the wall for days and this in spite of the fact she was soon to have another child.

Perhaps this was a good thing. Then her child would die and she could feel like she had accomplished the impossible by not bringing another slave into the world. But was that really true? "No!" she shouted to her unborn child. "You're not a slave, you is free, and I is free." The shout of defiance faded to wails of pain and sobs that could be heard to the slave quarters.

Before sunrise the next morning she heard a noise at the door. Turning her head slightly to the right she saw in the gloom a curly head and a black face. "Peter!"

"Rachel, Rachel," he whispered. "How you gittin' along?"

"Not good, Peter. My hands are numb. My fingers ain't got no feelin'. My back throbs from the lashes. I have been standin' here all night like this."

Peter came closer, smelling the dampness and the odor of urine. Seeing her distress, he held her closely and felt the new life kick him in the stomach. She flinched. Her back was raw. He backed away and reached inside his shirt to pull out some corn bread. With the little cup he dipped water from the far end of the springhouse and brought it to her.

"This is all I can find. But maybe better than nothing. I will try to come again when it's dark tonight." He held the cup and let her drink and held the corn bread so she could eat a few bites at a time.

"Thank you, Peter. I know Captain Draper won't bring me anything to eat and neither will young John. If it wasn't for you, I'd die right here."

"Let me wipe those places on your back. I have an old kerchief here and I will get some of that cool spring water. Hope that'll ease the pain." He moved to the water's edge at the far end of the springhouse, dampened the kerchief and lovingly bathed the wounds on her back.

"I best leave now," said Peter, "cuz it will be light soon. I don't want the marse to catch me here, for that won't help you at all." Peter slipped quietly out the door.

For five days and nights Peter opened the springhouse door, covered his nose with his handkerchief to keep from inhaling the odors of her body's excrements and brought what little food he could find and the little cup to collect the water. And his kerchief to bathe the wounds. And finally some lard to ease the pain. But nothing could ease the smell of the filth and muck Rachel had deposited on the springhouse floor.

Nancy, the captain's daughter, ambled toward the springhouse door and reluctantly went inside.

"Father sent me to undo the shackles. He says you can go to the quarters now. But he doesn't want to hear any more about freedom."

Rachel's arms were soon at her sides. She waddled toward the light at the doorway, supporting herself against the stone wall. She was blinded by the morning light and she took every step slowly and carefully.

"I'm not sure I can walk."

"I'll get Peter for you." Nancy ran calling his name as

she went toward the cabin.

Peter held Rachel around the waist, careful not to touch her back where the lash marks were still raw. Together they slowly went up the steps and into the cabin. Rachel sat at the table and tried to eat what Peter gave her. Her hands and arms were too weak to lift a piece of corn bread. Peter fed her and patted her on the cheek.

"It'll get better. Let me fix your back and git you a clean dress."

"Peter, thank you. You don't never let me down."

Only a few days after her release to the slave quarters, Rachel had a son and named him Peter. No mistress came with a blanket this time, but the master wrote in the ledger, under the heading "Peter and Rachel," the entry for the new baby: "Rachel, my Negro wench, this 30th day of September, 1782 had a male child named Peter." The first was Robbin, born in 1774, the next was Tom, then Nan for her mother, followed by Amelia, and the new boy called Peter, the fifth child born at Draper's, all carefully documented in the ledger.

Rachel was silent for weeks after little Peter's birth. Inside her head there was turmoil. Why should I have more slave children? Every one of them will be sold. Perhaps given away. Same thing. Gone from here. Gone from my eyes. Why am I so helpless? I will never be free. I have to face it. Don't want to face it. But what can I do? Samuel ain't never gonna find me. And now to add to my misery, old Marse Draper's seeing the Widow Crockett.

On October 15 Rachel brought her children to the Draper house as ordered. All the slaves were there. John

Draper and his son were standing at the fireplace as every-one came in the door.

"As you know, young John here is going to marry at Christmas time. I plan to do the same at the same time." The father put his arm around his son and smiled. "We've decided to celebrate together."

"Gonna get married here?" asked Rachel.

"Last night John and I sat around this fireplace trying to make that decision. We decided that probably the best place to have the wedding would be at Fort Chiswell."

"Places to stay, lots of space for the well-wishers and McGavock's tavern with good food and good whiskey," added the younger John.

"And room for all those Crocketts. We could fill the fort with them alone. I want my militia men to come too so there will be a crowd."

Peter looked uneasily at the two men. "Are we all to come there too?"

"Yes, everyone will come there. We need you and Will and the boys to handle the wagons and the horses, and Rachel, Judy and the others to help with the food. The children can help too."

"Goin' to have music?" asked Will.

"Yes, you and Caesar and Peter will be the music for the dance."

"Thank you, Marse," they mumbled as they went back to their cabins.

After all was quiet in the cabin and the children asleep for the night Rachel tapped Peter on the arm.

"Peter," she whispered. "You awake?"

"Yes, Rachel."

"I am trying to decide what to do, Peter. I cannot live like this, trapped like a rat in a corner. I suppose I could run away, or try to find me a lawyer, or make up my mind to accept my life in chains."

Taking a big breath, she let the words continue to tumble from her mouth. "If I run away, I would have to take the baby. I would have to find some money, or I could steal some, and then I would have to leave everybody at the Mountain. I heard the money is worth nothing now, and I couldn't leave little Peter behind. I can't leave my other children, nor my comfort and support over the years, you, my man Peter. Besides, if I left with the baby, we surely would die. And where would we go?"

Peter reached for her, drew her close, and held her. He tried to understand her suffering.

"I could try to find a lawyer, but that seems impossible. Marse Draper won't allow me to travel unless he is with me. I ain't been to the fort since Missus Bettie and me helped those travelers. And I don't know no lawyers, and even if I did I ain't sure they would know what I'm talking about. That preacher man didn't seem to know what to do about it."

"Maybe when we go to the fort for the wedding at Christmas time, there'll be a chance to talk to somebody there or find a lawyer," said Peter.

"I doubt that will be the time or place. The court won't be in session at that time, and only the friends and relatives of the Drapers and Crocketts will be there. I won't have no chance."

"The time will come, Rachel, the time will come," comforted Peter.

"That woman, Widow Crockett, has been the boss of Cato and Cynthia for more than ten years. Cato told Judy that she is so mean to them. If they disobey they're locked up for days."

"I hope Marse Draper won't let her be boss lady," said Peter.

"You know Marse Draper is over fifty years old, and he might not be around all the time. I hate to think what might happen then." Rachel sighed and pulled the quilt up over her head.

Peter could feel her body heave and heard the deep sobs. He knew tears were running down her cheeks. All he could do was hold her.

"Rachel, we'll get through this together. We will. You are a strong woman, and you can't give up your dream of freedom. You can't."

In the next few weeks Rachel was forced to make new shirts for the two Johns, to mend suits, to darn socks, and to go about her usual duties of cooking, weaving, and tending to the children. The boys needed jackets and vests for the wedding, and the girls insisted on new dresses, which she and Judy worked on daily. When Christmas week approached, she and Judy were making cakes and bread and preparing hams for the celebration.

In the loom house Rachel and Judy took turns making a coverlet for the marse's bed. They had spun the thread, dyed it indigo and beet red, and were working out the pattern from an earlier now-worn bed cover.

The plans had been made at the fort, but there was some question about the minister who would perform the service. Rachel had heard father and son discussing the choices at the table a few weeks earlier.

"John, my son, we must find a minister to marry us.

Have you heard anything about any Presbyterian preacher being in the area now?"

"No, Father," replied the younger John. "The last one I knew about was the Reverend John Brown, but he is not here any more. And Boiling Spring Church has no regular preacher. So where does that leave us?"

"One thing we need to do is have our brides-to-be have the banns posted to notify the community that there will be two weddings. The notices need to be put in public places, you know, like the courthouse, the tavern, and the mill. Anyway, we should have the banns at three places, and as we have no church services here now, this is the best we can do."

"Why do people do that anyway?" asked John.

"Well, it is to prevent illegal marriages. You know, if someone saw the notice, or heard the banns read in the church, they could speak up and say that the wedding should not take place because the groom is already married, for example."

"Father, I heard about that German preacher, what's his name, Schroeder, Shrader, or something like that. Did you hear what he did?"

"No, I didn't. What happened?"

"Well, he was invited over to the Hadley place to marry one of the boys and his German bride. Never asked any questions, but posted the banns at the water bucket, the fireplace and the front door, and claimed he had placed the banns in three public places. He immediately set about and married them. Last year the court heard the case against the Mr. Hadley for bigamy. It seemed he had a wife still living somewhere."

The two men chuckled as they thought about the water bucket and fireplace. "Guess we won't get that preacher to

107

marry us," said the younger John.

"Well, that leaves only one choice. There was a Church of England minister named Balmaine around the fort some time back. He was a chaplain for the troops, but old man McGavock liked him and invited him to stay around for awhile. If he is still there he would be just fine. He certainly is used to marrying the soldiers, and doing things properly," suggested Captain Draper.

"Great idea, Father. I will see to it tomorrow when I go to the fort. Do you want me to go on to the Crocketts up on Reed Creek and tell them what we have in mind?"

"Yes, you better do that after you find out if Balmaine is still around. Let the ladies set the time and then get back to Balmaine, if he is there. If he is not there, we can find someone else over near the mines, or possibly Edward Morgan would come up from Neck Creek and perform the ceremony."

Rachel learned a few days later that Alexander Balmaine had moved on to Winchester after his stay at the fort. Young John traveled to Morgan's who lived on Neck Creek, not too far from Ingles Ferry, to the east. Morgan agreed to perform the double ceremony on Christmas Eve. The ladies agreed to the date and to Morgan. They all knew him as one of the prominent Methodist preachers from the Holston to New River.

The few days before the ceremony, Captain Draper came to the slave quarters and, because it was a Christmas custom, rewarded them with an extra supply of meat and corn meal, and a small keg of whiskey. He let up on the work to be performed and gave them a few days to spend quietly before his celebration.

Rachel called her family together, Judy and her two little children, Lockey and Rhoda, her sons Tom and

Robbin and her girls Amelia, Nan, and her new little one, Peter. Her Peter, Will and Caesar, and Judy's Cato joined them. She had made little blankets for her grandchildren, an apple pie for her sons, little corn shuck dolls for her girls, and a new shirt for Peter. Will, Caesar and Cato were not forgotten and received walking sticks she had found in the nearby mountain. The ham, corn bread and potatoes were served with style, and whiskey for the grown folks added to the special event. Judy had learned to read but they had no book, so they told each other stories. Judy picked the Christmas story about the wise men and the star. They had heard it many times and when Judy forgot a few words here and there, Robbin and Peter joined in.

It was not long before Caesar pulled out his fiddle and Will his sticks and kettle, and all were dancing and singing to celebrate their Christmas. Peter and Rachel led the dance, Judy and Robbin stepped up to the middle of the floor, and before long everyone had joined them. It was a happy time, one the family enjoyed usually once a year. Happiness to Rachel was family.

Chapter 10

THE WEDDINGS

On December 23 Rachel took the best clothes of the Draper girls and boys and packed them in the small trunk. She took their warmest clothes from the wardrobe as they prepared for their trip to the fort. Rachel arranged Captain Draper's new shirts, his suit and his darned socks next. The finished coverlet was placed across the top.

Under the direction of young John and his brothers, Peter, Will and Caesar loaded the wagon with kegs of whiskey, cider, cooked hams, pies, cakes, breads, and cookies. Live chickens squawked as Peter tucked their cages into the wagon. He loaded the trunk last and gave everyone blankets and fur covers. A brick or two, heated in the coals at the fireplace, kept their feet warm. It was a pleasant day, sunny, cool but not cold. Rachel was in charge of much of the food, Peter was in control of the horses, while the Draper boys and girls were packed into the wagon. They soon led the way. Rachel, Judy and the children were huddled in the next wagon, promising to help at the wedding party. Will took the reins and their wagon began the trip from the Mountain to Fort Chiswell. Captain Draper rode his favorite horse, and young John joined him. The entourage left the Mountain in the early afternoon.

On their arrival at Fort Chiswell Peter and Will unloaded the wagons. They took the trunk to the inn with the girls. Caesar took the horses to the stable. The younger Draper boys tagged along. Peter unloaded his wagon at the McGavock kitchen, where much of the food would be kept until the right time. Rachel and Judy and the children found a place in the slave quarters and were joined later by Peter, Will and Caesar. The captain and his son found their way to the tavern dining room where they ordered some whiskey. McGavock welcomed them.

"Glad to see you, Captain, and you too, John, and here's the whiskey, the best ever made around these parts." McGavock bragged, as he passed the pints to the two men. They all laughed and as the Drapers raised their glasses they added, "Sure is, except for Draper whiskey."

"Well, tomorrow is your big day, isn't it?" asked McGavock.

"Yes, I suppose it is, for both of us. Can you imagine us both marrying into the same family?"

"I heard the Widow Crockett thinks you are a good catch. And her daughter is not far behind in thinking the same about young John. Those two are independent ladies though. Never saw the likes of those two in my life," added McGavock.

"Neither have we, and that's why we decided to marry them. Isn't that right, Father?"

"Certainly is."

"Have you seen Edward Morgan anywhere about?" asked the captain.

"He came in just a few minutes before you did. He's over at the trading post to get some things he needed."

"We will wander over that way directly and finalize the plans for tomorrow." The captain and his son took a few

112

more sips of the refreshment and left the tavern for the trading post.

Edward Morgan was in his thirties, red-headed, tall and with a thin narrow face. His gray eyes lit up as the Drapers walked into the post.

"Good evening, gentlemen." Morgan stretched out his freckled hand to the captain first and then to the son.

"Good evening, Reverend Morgan. Thanks for coming. What time are we having the ceremony tomorrow?" asked the captain.

"Well, the ladies seemed to think that about two o'clock would be best. It would give them time to finish preparing the food in the morning, and then everyone would have plenty of time to celebrate after."

"Good. Have you seen the ladies today?"

"No, Captain, not yet, but they live so close by I expect they might wait until the morning."

"I see," said the captain. "Tell me, Reverend, have you got a congregation yet?"

"I have been in the Holston River settlements for the last few months, but no luck there. I live up on Neck Creek, a branch of New River, and around there I see many who are interested. We have started a little church and I have about twenty members including two slaves."

"Slaves!" exclaimed the captain. "Why on earth are they church members?"

"The Lord loves us all, Draper. And the two there are devout members. They love to hear the word of God and are taking the message back to the slave quarters with them. It cannot help but make them all better people."

"Teach them too much, they will run away, or worse yet, they will see that we are killed. I don't believe in letting my people go to church. It is one thing for them to

113

hear the Word, but quite another to go to church."

"I understand you are not letting your people travel alone. Did you bring them here today?"

"I do not let them travel alone, and if they disobey they get locked in chains, and I have even had to give a whipping or two. Yes, they are here today, all of them. Rachel and Judy and their children and my three men, Peter, Will and Caesar. They will entertain us tomorrow with some music. Rachel and Judy will help with the cooking and serving. They have all those chickens to kill and to cook. That's all they are good for anyway."

"Now, Father," interrupted young John, "Those two women have looked after you every day since Mother died. Without them you would have been totally helpless, all of us would have been." The captain said nothing.

"How many slaves do you have, Captain?" asked Morgan.

"Right now, I suspect I have about a dozen. And when the Widow Crockett, I mean, Mrs. Draper, moves in, she will bring two more. With about forty head of cattle and about eighteen horses to look after, I can use them all. Of course, many of the children are too young to be much help yet."

"Did you hear that some of the slaves who served in the Revolution got their freedom for their service in the army?" asked Morgan.

"Freedom, freedom," said the captain, spewing his spit across the room. "Why should they have their freedom? It seems that's all they think about, freedom."

"Well, you know that the some of us Methodists don't believe in slavery at all, and those of us who have a slave or two are encouraged to set them free. You know you can do that now by a deed or even in your will, if you like."

"Well, I don't like, I will never set my Negroes free. They were never meant to be free. If they were, the good Lord would have seen to it." With that, Draper pulled on the back of his son's coat and urged him out of the trading post without another word to Morgan.

December 24 was another spectacular winter day. An early morning silver blanket of frost disappeared by noon. Little or no wind, and a bright sun. It would be a good day for the weddings.

Rachel and Judy started early. The chickens were killed, plucked and ready for cooking. Vegetables were prepared, and pies warmed by the fireplace. The kettle hanging on the iron arm over the fire was steaming. Cynthia and Cato joined them with hams, turkeys, and some venison, telling Rachel that the Widow Crockett and her daughter had arrived. Rachel did not see the two women, but heard them as they walked toward the fort.

"What they going over there for?" asked Rachel.

"Going to find a place for the wedding, for the crowd, and later for the dance, I suppose," answered Cynthia.

"And tomorrow you'll be coming to the Mountain with us."

"Yes, I s'pose so. I know Cato be 'specially happy about that so now he'll be with Judy more. Before, he had a long way to travel to visit her unless he could come to shoe the horses or sharpen tools."

"Yes, Judy's fond of Cato. And they have two little children, with more to come, I am sure," beamed Rachel. "That'll be the good part of having your mistress come to the Mountain. The bad part will be having her there at all."

"Why you say that?" asked Cynthia.

"Well, I hear tell she is a mean, bossy lady, and I expect

115

she'll try to tell me what to do. I don't think we'll get along very well. My marse's bad enough, won't let me go nowhere's without him and whips me for the least little thing. I don't think I can stand two of them."

"I reckon you got that right. She's very particular, that Widow Crockett. She does the same thing, don't let us go far without her, and whips us too for the least little thing. I thought of running away lots of times, but don't know where I'd go."

Rachel smiled to herself. *I am not the only one unhappy with a life of slavery. But Cynthia don't have the same hope of freedom as I do. Because I am already free—well, mostly—well, not really, but if only—*

The crowd gathered about two o'clock, probably fifty or sixty of the relatives, friends and acquaintances of the two families. Some of the militiamen who served with the captain filled the back row and were pleased to see their leader again. The slaves were standing behind the soldiers. Soon a hush came over the gathering as the two couples and the Reverend Morgan appeared.

Mrs. Crockett had a gray muslin dress, with matching hat and gloves. Her daughter, Jane, had chosen a blue silk dress and white gloves. They walked together to the front of the room where the two men and the Reverend Edward Morgan were waiting. The Reverend Morgan opened his book and began the ceremony. Each man presented his bride with a small gold ring, and each woman promised to love, cherish, honor and obey. When the pronouncement was made that John Draper, Sr., and Jane Crockett, Sr., were married there was a cheer from the back of the room and a scrambling of militia to meet the couple at the end of the room, holding muskets, rifles, and swords. They formed an arch over their heads with the swords and waited for the couple to pass through.

The younger John and his new wife waited to hear the words, "You are now man and wife," and then retreated to the back of the room, with friends and relatives smiling and nodding. Both couples disappeared to the outside and were soon followed by the guests. The tavern was set up for toasts to the two couples, and soon the place was crowded.

Rachel, Judy and Cynthia brought the food to the large room at the fort where the meal would be waiting. The chickens had been cooked, the turkey, ham and bread sliced. Large covered dishes held the corn, potatoes, green beans, and carrots. Pies, cakes, and other sweets were on a side table and at the end of the long line of food was a white cake waiting to be cut.

Gradually, the guests found their way back to the room at the fort and spread out to the makeshift tables recently assembled. The Drapers' whiskey and cider barrels were brought to the room and opened for all to enjoy. There were many toasts and lots of conversation and laughter. The cake was cut by the captain and his wife first, and the second cut was made by the younger couple. Each guest received a small piece of cake. Some took their portion home, others ate the cake there. Rachel served the cake and Judy and Cynthia helped guests at the tables. Finally, they all cleaned up and moved the tables to the side. Everyone seemed to be ready for dancing. Rachel carried some of the dishes to the tavern.

When she walked in, she saw Edward Morgan and Mrs. McGavock standing near the door.

"I do not approve of dancing," said Morgan. "Could you direct me to a room?"

"Oh, yes, right up the stairs inside here, and to the right

at the top of the stairs."

"Thank you, Mrs. McGavock."

As Morgan started to the stairway several of the militiamen grabbed him and asked him to dance. There was no sound of music anywhere, but they had been drinking and knew the music would soon follow. They laughed and cursed when Morgan refused, and insisted he dance with them. The drunken ruffians dragged him across the floor. Finally, they let him go long enough to gather his saddlebags and greatcoat and start his climb upstairs. One dark-haired, black-eyed young soldier grabbed him once more and pulled him back to the bottom of the stairs. Others joined in. After repeated refusals to dance, and repeated attempts to go upstairs, Morgan was finally let go, a scrape on his face dropping his blood on the pine floors.

Rachel heard the commotion and came closer to see what was happening. She was stopped when the blonde-headed sergeant pulled her back and hollered, "Get out of the way, wench. You are not to bother us. We are celebrating and we want the preacher man to dance with us. He says he doesn't dance, but we will make him dance."

Rachel hovered in the corner but was relieved to see that Morgan had successfully disappeared up the stairway. After more laughter and more drinking, three of the soldiers went upstairs and asked Morgan again to dance. Rachel ran from the tavern, searching for the captain, the only one she knew that could keep order.

"Marse, sir, please come," pleaded Rachel. "Some of the soldiers are hitting Mr. Morgan and trying to make him dance."

Draper motioned to his son John and the two hurried across the hill to the tavern. They could hear noise above and dashed up the stairs.

118

"Good God, sergeant, can't you keep your men under control? Leave this poor man alone!" shouted the captain.

"Morgan, you all right?" asked young John.

"These devils jumped on me, set my hair afire and then pissed on me. They are the most vulgar human beings I have ever seen." Morgan touched the back of his head and realized his skin had been burned and much of his red hair was singed. Some was matted in his hands.

"Get out of here! Get out!" shouted the captain. "I am going to get the sheriff and have you arrested for assaulting the preacher. Now get downstairs this minute."

The three men gradually backed out of the room and down the stairs. Draper knew them from his militia company and remembered he had had trouble with them before, especially when they had too much to drink. But this was beyond celebration and they knew it. When the Drapers came downstairs they saw Rachel waiting for news of the preacher.

"Rachel," said the captain. "Go get some water from the spring and some clean rags and see if you can help Mr. Morgan. His head is burned in places and needs attention, and he has a cut on his face."

"Yes, Marse," answered Rachel. She left, bucket in hand, for the springhouse. On her return she gathered the clean rags and carried a pitcher full of water up the stairs, knocked on the door, and asked to come in.

"Yes, come in, Rachel. I need your help."

When Rachel entered she could see the damage that had been done. Mr. Morgan was sitting on the edge of the bed in his long underwear. The pillow had been blackened by the fire and had gathered large clumps of his red hair. She gently dabbed at the back of his head, cleaning off the ashes, and gradually picked out the loosened hairs. There

119

were several burned places she gave particular attention to. Finally she had done all she could, except try to find some salve or herb somewhere which would ease the pain. She cleaned off the patch on his face where his blood had dried.

"Sir, I know it must hurt. Could I bring you a little glass of whiskey? It might help ease the pain."

"That would ease it a little. Thank you, Rachel."

When Rachel returned with the mug of whiskey, Morgan was dressed and had decided to come downstairs and sit by the fire. Rachel found clean bedding and changed the bed before joining him at the fireplace.

"What else can I do for you, sir?" asked Rachel.

"Rachel, if it wasn't for you, those fools would have killed me. Thank you for getting the captain. Only he could tell those devils what to do. Now what can I do for you?"

Rachel thought a moment and then decided that even if preacher Craig did not know about Indian slavery, maybe this preacher would know.

"I wonder, I hope," she stammered. "I hope you can help me get my freedom."

"Get your freedom?" asked Morgan. "What does that mean? You know only Draper can free you—and he can do it by will or by an emancipation deed."

"That's not it. I know he would never free me. But, you see, I'm free, in truth I'm free, but I don't know how to get from under these chains."

"What do you mean, you are free?" asked Morgan.

"Well, my grandmama was an Injun brought into Virginia at the time no Injun was to be kept in slavery. But she was anyhow. We, our family, learned we could sue for our

120

freedom, and my grandmama got a lawyer to fix the papers for her, my brother Samuel, and me, and for my daughter Judy. Before I could find out what happened in the court, my marse gave me to his son. He brung me to New River with Judy. Then he sold us as Negro slaves and never told anyone we were of Injun descent. Now I'm trying to find a lawyer who knows about such things. I want one who can bring the case here. He'll have to help me git some evidence from those who know us in Powhatan County where I lived before."

"Rachel, I never heard of such a case. I am sorry."

"If you ever do," offered Rachel, "let me know. Or help me find a lawyer who knows about these things. I'm sure I was freed back there in the 1770s, and the Drapers won't listen to me. Every time they hear me talk about it, they whip me and chain me to the wall in the springhouse."

"I am sorry, Rachel. No person should be treated that way. I do not believe in slavery. I will try to find out about such things. Sometime later I will be at the court turning in my list of marriages for the year and I will try to remember to ask about your predicament."

"Thank you, sir. Can I get you another bit of whiskey?"

"Yes, Rachel, one more to take upstairs. Now that the soldiers are gone I feel safe. You have helped me a great deal, and I thank you again for getting the captain here in such a hurry."

Rachel filled the mug once more and watched as Morgan climbed the stairs to his bedroom. She turned and walked out the door and down the few steps, across the hill where the sound of music drew her in.

Maybe Peter was right. There was someone to help her at the fort. Mr. Morgan was a good man who didn't believe in slavery. Maybe he would find a lawyer for her.

Rachel smiled to herself and hurried to tell Peter.

After the two weddings, the Draper household continued celebrating marriages and births. George Draper was
the next to marry and move to his own farm a few miles
from the Mountain. Mary had found David Love for her
life's companion in 1784, and two years later Elizabeth
married Joseph Montgomery. Young John, with Jane
Crockett as his wife, had settled on the tract of land promised by his father.

John, Jr., and his Jane had a son Samuel, about the same
time the captain and his Jane had a daughter Alice, whom
they called Ally. Another daughter, Rhoda, arrived five
years later in the captain's household, after several losses.
In 1792 the captain's daughter, Nancy, married Samuel
Patton, the son of Captain Henry Patton who lived on the
Thorn Spring tract a few miles to the east.

Young John and his wife Jane had a son, Joseph, who
arrived on Christmas Day 1794. No one could have been
happier than that young couple. Joseph was named for
Jane's brother, a captain in the local militia.

Rachel's family was growing too. Judy, Robbin, Tom,
and Nan, Amelia and Peter were followed by Sarah, David,
Polly, Peggy, and Jenny, the last born in 1795.

And as Rachel feared, her children were given away.
At the time of his wedding, George Draper got one of Judy
and Cato's little girls. Elizabeth Draper got Sarah; Silas
Draper got Robbin and Tom, who would later belong to
John, who also got Peter the younger. Later he would get
David and Peggy. The old captain kept Rachel and Judy
and the rest of her children, soon to number seven. When
Nancy Draper married Samuel Patton, she moved to be
near her husband's family and took with her Rachel's

daughter Polly. Miss Alice Draper soon got Jenny, and later Milly, a child of Judy's, and Melinda and Eliza, two of her grandchildren. When Rhoda Draper married Thomas Huey, she got Amelia and Nan (or Ann as she called her) and two of Judy's children, promised by her father, Captain Draper.

Rachel's offspring were scattered and she felt betrayed. There had been no opportunity to travel to Fort Chiswell or anywhere else since the wedding. The elder Jane Crockett Draper saw to that. Rachel was not free and more than twenty years had gone by. Her hopes and dreams were now just ghostly mirages. She feared her children and grandchildren would never be free, unless she could find a lawyer and get into the court. But there was no one to help.

Peter began to believe that Rachel wouldn't gain her freedom; it seemed to him that she had given up. There was no more talk around the fireplace, no more talk in the fields, no more talk in front of the Drapers. He could see the lines of despair and age on a once beautiful face. Her step wasn't as sprightly and sometimes he noticed a slump to her once proud and strong shoulders. She no longer was a young woman with strong Indian features, but a large yellow woman and a mother of eleven children. And the chains were ever present. The slightest incident provoked the Drapers enough to send her to the springhouse and to the chains on the wall.

Chapter 11

SAMUEL FINDLAY IN HENRY COUNTY: 1788

Samuel Findlay and his wagon continued their travels across Virginia. The war was over but supplies were needed everywhere. Thousands of people were on the move to Kentucky, and they were in need of salt, lead, corn, barrels, trunks, boxes, rope, iron, books, medicines, dry goods, chairs, candles, ovens, whiskey, rum, and wines, among other necessaries. In addition, inns had become more numerous as local citizens prepared to cater to the travelers, and the need for goods to be transported increased. Samuel was never idle.

In March 1788 Samuel had a load of goods from Richmond for Henry County, Virginia, down near the North Carolina line. When he arrived at the county seat there appeared to be a lot of commotion around the courthouse and he stopped to see. Many Negroes were gathered at the side and white men were on the steps talking in loud angry voices. He mingled with the Negroes, asking as he went, "What is it? What has happened?"

"Today was a trial of an Injun woman, called Hannah Fender or Findlay," whispered a tall black man close to Samuel.

"What'd she do? Kill somebody?" asked Samuel.

"No, no, no," was the reply. "She got her freedom today. She sued her Marse John Marr, and won her case. Even got forty shillings to boot."

"You sure of that?" asked Samuel. He could hardly believe it, but whoever this person was, he was going to celebrate with her. "Where's she now?"

"Over there by that wagon, the big brown woman in the bright blue dress. She's talking to her marse, well, her former marse, and some of the neighbors. Why you want to know?"

"Because I'm a free Negro and I want to congratulate her. I was freed by the courts in 1773, fifteen years ago now, and I want to give her hope for the future. Thanks for tellin' me."

Samuel pushed his way to the street and to the wagon where he saw a woman with long black hair, copper-colored skin and a big smile. The white marse had moved away and others came to talk to her and offer their congratulations. Samuel edged closer. His first close-up vision of Hannah was startling, for there was the picture of his Aunt Judy.

"Hannah!" he shouted as he pushed others aside to reach her side. "My name's Samuel Findlay from Powhatan County. You look like my Aunt Judy. Who are you?"

Hannah held out her trembling arms and tears flooded her eyes. "You," she said, "you my cousin Samuel."

The two embraced for a long time, rocking back and forth to look at each other every few seconds. Neither could believe what they saw.

"I was brought here by some of the Clays long time ago. After my lawyer filed my suit papers my marse had to let me go to Powhatan to get my evidence. You know, the depositions for the court," explained Hannah.

126

"I don't know how it is done now, but sounds to me like it is the same as when Grandmama Chance, Rachel, Judy, and me went to the court in Williamsburg." He hugged her again, and added, "So happy for you this day, so happy. Great things are ahead for you. As for me I have been very fortunate, own my own wagon and do my own work. No marse for me!"

"We need to talk more. Some of the neighbors have given me a place to stay, a little cabin on their place. Can you follow us out there? We leave in a few minutes to celebrate more."

"I will be right behind you, Hannah." Samuel returned to his wagon and lined it up with the others on the main street.

The celebration continued to the morning hours. Singing, dancing, and blacks and whites joined in this special event. When they were finally alone, Hannah and Samuel continued their conversation.

"My marse beat me, locked me up, and was a cruel man. I knowed I had to be free. I know that my Grandmama Chance and my mother Judy was supposed to be free, not free Negroes, but free Injuns. When some of the church-goin' ladies 'round here heard my story, they agreed to help me. They asked one of their lawyer friends to hear me, and finally he was convinced that he could present enough evidence that we could have the case heard. That is how it got started," offered Hannah.

"What you find in Powhatan? I have been gone ever since I was freed so haven't seen any of them except on a short visit. I went to Grandmama Chance's grave over there

127

near Swift Creek," said Samuel. "Grandmama Chance finally got her freedom, but died soon after. You know she was an old, old woman then."

"Well, the old Clays are almost gone. Some moved to Mecklenburg, some to Pittsylvania and Bedford so I hear. Some of the older women were the ones who helped me. They remembered Mama, and Grandmama Chance, and they remembered that Rachel, you and some others had got your freedom based on the same evidence I needed for my case. Old Mrs. Clay, she is now Lucy Marshall, she remembered Mama and Chance, and knowed old Henry Clay give Mama to the younger Henry Clay."

"How long it take you to git your freedom?" asked Samuel.

"Many years 'cause no one on the court want to hear the case. Mr. Marr, my marse, had friends there, and nobody was goin' to vote against him. But my lawyer put the case to higher court and even then it took three or four years. My last deposition was taken of Lucy Marshall in October about two years ago."

"But, now I'm free, free, free!" shouted Hannah, standing up and raising her hands to the rooftop. Samuel picked her up and swung her around the room, half dancing, half prancing. It was a memorable day.

Then Hannah remembered. "Where is Rachel and Judy? Tell me about them."

"I don't know," said Samuel. "I ain't seen or heard from them since Mitchell Clay took them West, but a strange thing happened a few years ago at Fort Chiswell, in Montgomery County. You probably heard of that fort, but anyhow, I was there with a load of corn to be ground at the mill and met a Negro man called Peter. I told him about being free and he didn't believe me, but said he had heard of a woman he knew who had talked of being an Injun slave and her grandmama come from the Catawber tribe, you know, like us."

"Was she there somewhere?" asked Hannah.

"Don't know but it sure did sound like Rachel. Peter said her grandmother's name was White Cloud, and you know Grandmama Chance went by that name in the Injun Nation. But before I could find out where she was, Peter was made to leave and I had to tend to other things, too, and our paths haven't met since."

"I heard Rachel went to Kentucky. Leastways that's what they told me up in Powhatan."

"Yes, I did too, so I thought that Peter must be talking about some other person. But the more I think about it, the more I feel like I got to go back up there and look for Peter or maybe Rachel herself, or at least find out about this other person who it might be."

"Well, somebody in Powhatan thought she had gone with Judy to Mecklenburg County, some others say it was the New River somewhere. Others hear it was Pittyslvania County. Guess nobody really know," said Hannah. "You be goin' there soon again?" she asked.

"I don't know, never know much ahead where I be goin'. But I do go to all parts of Virginia. Maybe some day I'll be back there."

Where you going from here, Hannah, or you stayin' here? asked Samuel.

"Right now I'm stayin' here. I been promised work by some of these same ladies and they are willing to pay me for what I do. I'm an excellent seamstress, I can spin and weave. I know the proper way to do laundry. I cook well too and I can keep a house as good as any person, black or white, in these parts or anywhere else." She was bragging

129

but she also knew that she would survive, could save money, could travel to the North if she wished.

The next morning Samuel set out again to deliver his goods in Powhatan County. Then he would be at his old home and maybe someone there would know about Rachel.

Chapter 12

ANDREW BOYD'S: 1800

Draper's neighbor, Andrew Boyd, had a substantial two-story log house and several outbuildings on Little Pine Run, not many miles from the Mountain. The Boyds and Drapers had been friends for many years. The Boyds had often visited in the Draper home, and Drapers were welcome guests in Boyd's home.

The Boyd slaves did most of the work, leaving Boyd free to educate his children, serve as a justice on the court, speculate in land and spend time with neighbors and friends. He knew that there was a great deal of anxiety among the slave owners in the community. They were fearful there would be an uprising against them by their black servants. Reins were tightened and the watch was increased for any evidence of disobedience or conspiracy. After the death of Bob and Sam at Fort Chiswell there seemed to be little evidence of hostility on the part of the local slave population, but the fear of such an attack haunted many slaveholders just the same.

On the night of June 25, 1800, just at dark, an orange glow filled the western sky. It is too late for the sunset, thought Andrew Boyd, as he stirred from his chair and looked out the window. There within a few feet of the springhouse was a huge fire spreading flames dozens of feet into the summer air.

"The barn! It's the barn!" yelled Boyd. "Help. Fire! Fire!"

The boys came running from their beds, the Negroes from their slave quarters, and before long a line of buckets had been set up between the springhouse and the fire. Horses were pulled from their stalls and the cows and calves driven into the field.

"It's no use," admitted Boyd. "The barn is gone to the ground." Indeed, the timbers had fallen in, causing sparks to fly in every direction, like shooting stars from heaven.

"Watch those other buildings!" shouted Boyd. "Don't let it catch over there." The Negroes, with shovels, sacks, buckets and rags, dug at the dirt, beat the ground and threw water on the spots where the sparks had caught. Over and over the work was repeated. Finally, the flames relented, and the smoke swirled around the shed, the kitchen, the loom house and the stable.

When the smoldering ruins had died to a puff of smoke, Boyd called everyone together and asked, "I want to know how did this get started? Which one of you set this fire?"

There was no answer. The dozen slaves shifted from one foot to the other and waited.

"I know one of you set this fire!" shouted Boyd. "If I ever find out which one of you did this you will die like Bob and Sam, swinging from the hanging tree."

There was still no answer. Finally, Boyd announced, "If we can get the logs, the lumber, and the shingles we will rebuild. *You* will rebuild it."

On an exquisite October morning the wagons and teams began to arrive. The children were riding amidst tools, timber, shingles and logs. Laughter rang across the Little Pine Run site at Andrew Boyd's, where men of the community were already at work. Rachel looked in one direction and saw the timbers laid out on the ground with pulleys and ropes, waiting to be hoisted. In the other direction she saw the ladders and the men at the top, looking like giant birds in the sky. She saw the tables spread with food, buckets of water from the spring and the animals in the field nearby. As she moved toward the kitchen she heard the chatter of the women around the tables, the bleating of the sheep in the field, the song of the hammers and the laughter and squeals of the children, black and white, as they ran in circles playing games. The air filled with the smell of home-cooked bread.

In the log kitchen, Rachel and Judy joined Melinda and Susannah from Boyds. They were busy making the bread, preparing the meat, peeling the vegetables, and making the pies. They would soon have fifty hungry people to feed.

"Rachel, I ain't seen you for many years. You been sick?" asked Melinda.

"Sick at heart and a prisoner," complained Rachel. "The mistress don't allow me to go to town or much of anywhere. Guess she thinks I'll run away." Crazy idea, thought Rachel. Where would she go?

"How come you here today then?" Susannah asked.

"Well, you know, the Drapers and the Boyds are good friends, and I reckon they thought I could be of some help here in the kitchen with so many people to feed. In fact, all of us came here today, even my little grandchildren. My little daughter Jenny, Peter, Will and Caesar come here too. I hear when the work is done they plan to have a frolic, and Caesar will play his fiddle for everybody to dance."

"You know, the neighbors are really frightened. They think we'll rise up and kill all the white folks. We ain't been to town lately either. Marse Boyd goes often to court and takes his sons with him and they do the buyin' and then have a wagoner bring the goods here later," sighed Susannah.

"That's right," said Melinda. "Our men folk ain't allowed to go no place neither. James has a wife over at the Sayers place and can't get to see her, 'lessen he sneaks away. She might get here today, 'cause all the neighbors and their slaves seem to be coming to help Marse Boyd.

"They probably heard about the dangerous happenings in Richmond and places in the east," continued Melinda. "That man named Gabriel, you know Prosser's slave, he had great plans to rise up against some of them white folks and kill them."

"I heard that too," said Rachel. "He was Prosser's blacksmith, wasn't he?"

"Yes, and was all of twenty-four years old," added Susannah. " A giant of a man too."

"But he was in trouble with the law before, wasn't he?" asked Rachel.

"Yes, caught him pig stealing. Not such a bad thing, we all have to do it to stay alive." Melinda giggled and the others nodded their heads. They all knew about pig stealing.

"How'd he get catched?" asked Judy, removing the bread from the oven and setting it on the table.

"I heard the overseer catched three of them. They got to fussin' and Gabriel jumped on him and bit his ear off, so's I heard." Susannah grimaced, touched her own ears and walked to the fireplace, swung out the crane and stirred the vegetables in the iron pot.

"Yes," added Melinda. "One got the thirty-nine lashes on his bare back. I see the scars from that and it don't look good."

"What happened to Gabriel?" asked Rachel.

"Everybody thought he would be hung right then, but he got a choice if he could recite a Bible verse. You know that benefit of clergy. If he did that then he only had to be burnt on his hand in open court. And that's what he did, he recited and the jailer burnt his hand." Melinda nodded her head and repeated, "And that's what he did."

"How you know that?" asked Judy.

"I hear Marse Boyd and Draper talking about it. That's what they say."

Melinda rolled out the pie crust and began to make apple pies. Judy cut the apples and piled them into a wooden bowl and as fast she did Melinda gathered them into the pastry.

"Then what happen?" asked Judy.

"Well, I hear the overseer was afraid he be killed and so poor Gabriel was arrested and put in jail till his marse bonded him for his good behavior."

"I bet Gabriel was mad."

"Yes, and wanted his true freedom—

Rachel interrupted. "Yes, true freedom, that's what I wants too."

Susannah came in the kitchen door with four headless chickens hanging by her side. Their feathers were piled outside the door. She cut them and put the pieces on the table. Susannah began again.

"You know, Gabriel hired out as a blacksmith, but he got little of the money. Most went to his marse."

"Nothing special about that," said Judy. "My Cato's a

blacksmith and he hires out in the neighborhood too. We know about that. Do all the work and gets little."

"I can see why Gabriel wants to take revenge on all of them white folks." Rachel pounded on the dough, shaped the biscuits and slammed them on the baking pan. She wiped her floured hands on her apron and added another white streak to her black hair as she talked.

"What I hear was, Gabriel talked up the killings with his trusted friends and word soon got around, even to several other counties around Richmond."

Susannah said, "I hear too that they planned to take guns from the capitol and swords, sickles, knives, muskets and so forth from their marses."

"Yes," said Melinda. "And Gabriel talked to many at the tobacco storehouses and backstreet taverns when he come to Richmond on Saturdays. Everyone of them wanted true freedom."

"What happened to them?" asked Judy as she started another basket of apples.

"Well, August 30 was to be the big night. Only thing was, it stormed and walls of water brung the plan to a stop. Bridges washed away and just a handful of men got to the city. They planned to go ahead the next day, but another slave give the secret away."

"And," added Susannah, "the militia got called out. They arrested a lot of folks, put guards at the courthouses, jails and the capitol."

"Is it the truth that some of them were hung?"

"I heard there was thirty or forty in jail, and many, maybe twenty or so, had already been hung. But not Gabriel," said Susannah.

"Oh, they will catch him sure enough. He ain't got no place to hide. Too many people know him and sooner or later somebody will report his hiding place."

"I could run away and hide for awhile, even thought about it," said Rachel, "but where would I go? They would catch me, bring me back, chain me to the wall, starve me, beat me. Besides I would have to leave Peter, my children, and my grandchildren."

"It would take some money too," added Melinda. "I don't know about you, but I have so little."

"I have been saving money for years, for the day I might need it to get my freedom. It takes a long spell. I sells a few chickens, a few sacks of beans, and a few ears of corn, and Peter, he work a little for some of the neighbors, but it seems hopeless."

Rachel could dream of freedom, but today she had more definite plans, plans which might take her further along the trail to freedom. It was her only chance in months and months to talk to someone from the court. Yes, Andrew Boyd, Gentlemen Justice, would be her only opportunity to find an attorney and get her case started. She felt like an old, old woman. Too old for her forty-seven years. If she didn't act soon, nothing could be done for her family. As for her, it was really too late now—not too late to be free but too late to enjoy a life of her own, a life where she could earn her own money, a life where she could see that her children and grandchildren learned to read and write, and a life where she could live wherever she wanted to. It was too late to escape the chains. If only she could succeed, then her children and grandchildren might have a chance for a new life. With that in mind as her new goal, she brushed the flour off of her hands onto her apron and slipped out the door toward the gathering outside.

As she walked across the grass, she raised her head high, searched in every direction for Marse Boyd. Finally, a gray-haired man on a cane came from the log house and picked his way down the lane to the barn lot. She intercepted him before he reached the others.

"Marse Boyd, sir," she began, "I'm Draper's Rachel. I hear you was on the court as a Gentlemen Justice, and if I can I would like to ask you a question."

Boyd, short of breath, was glad for the interruption and he leaned heavily on his cane and listened.

"Sir, my Grandmama was an Injun from the Catawber nation, and I understands I have a case for the court to hear, you know, a freedom case. I was brung out here by Marse Mitchell Clay, you know, over on the river. He sold me to Marse Draper, and signed the papers so I would be listed as a Negro slave and—"

"Now girl, enough of that. You are a nigger and that's that. The only way you will ever be free is if Draper frees you. Don't you know that?"

"No, no, that's not it. I should be free 'cuz of my Injun grandmama. I heard that others like me got their freedom by filing suit," she added in desperation.

"Girl, your telling me is not enough. If you are in the court, you must be able to prove this silly idea of yours. Besides, I am good friends with Draper and I could never bring your case into the court, you know that. You need a lawyer to help you, and I am not a lawyer."

"I know I need a lawyer and he wouldn't cost me nothin' either. 'Cause the new law says so! Besides that, Drapers would have to promise not to keep me from getting my witnesses," said Rachel.

"A free lawyer?" Boyd laughed at her. "Indeed, a free lawyer?"

"Where can I find a lawyer? I can't get to town 'cause Mrs. Draper won't let me go there. How can I find one?"

138

"Girl, the lawyers are usually at the courthouse on court day, but I don't know which ones will be there for the next court, or any court for that matter. I think you better get rid of your idea of filing suit. I cannot, in fact I will not, help you. Now be gone! Be gone, I say." Boyd limped away and Rachel lowered her head and stumbled across the yard toward the kitchen.

"I reckon there's some lawyer out there knows what to do. I know I is free 'cause my Grandmama Chance was an Injun. Grandmama Chance told me," mumbled Rachel to herself.

Her determination faded. Her life would be the same as before. Follow orders, say nothing, do all the work, have no time for herself and her family, and never go nowhere. And then there were the whippings, the hunger, the days of isolation and imprisonment shackled to the wall. If it wasn't for her children and grandchildren, she would die.

Samuel Findlay rolled out of Evansham at daybreak, his wagon loaded with goods, barrels, bales, wooden chests and boxes, and his team fresh for the morning ride. With the new towns like Evansham and Christiansburg, there was a great demand for carpenters, painters, house-joiners, wagon makers, brick masons, furniture makers, and merchants. He was transporting goods to the stores to meet the demand of the new citizens. They needed lumber, nails, wagon wheels, iron pots, bricks, tools of all kinds, paint, and that was just the beginning. The merchants needed inventory and supplies for the families. He often brought calico, damask, linens, cottons, needles, pins, and thimbles for the seamstresses. Last week he delivered coffee, all-spice, medicines, guns, flints, bells, brushes, pewter dishes,

139

silver teaspoons, porcelain plates and even China cups and saucers. Yesterday he brought to Evansham some baskets, shawls, school books, ovens, sad irons, knives and forks, candlesticks, combs, scissors and trunks. To the innkeepers he delivered whiskey, brandy, rum and several kinds of wine.

The wagon shook and tilted. The horses found the road was rough, the ruts deep and the ditches filled with water. Stumps were evident here and there, not just on the side of the road but in the middle too. The overseers of the road had more work to do since the recent rains. The creaking of the wheels and the slapping of the harness against the backs of the grays were the melodies of the road. And just ahead, Samuel saw Fort Chiswell where he had visited so many years before.

When was that? He thought awhile. It was during the Revolutionary War, about 1781 or 1782. Too many years for him to remember. And that's where he heard the name Rachel. Now it was much too late to ask the questions about her.

At McGavock's store at the fort Samuel unloaded wine, bolts of yard goods, some nails and dishes for the store, now operated by old McGavock's son, Jamie. He could see that the log courthouse and jail were in need of many repairs and were no longer used. The McGavock house was no longer inhabited by the Irishman and his family, for he had moved to Max Meadows several years before. Two of his sons had moved to Nashville in Tennessee where they were among the early settlers. Other children had married and settled nearby.

The mill was now quiet and probably would not operate again. Its heyday had passed. Samuel looked around at the site and realized too that the palisade had been torn

140

down, log by log, and the once busy hillside now was a ghost of its former self. A few years had made a difference. As the grays came off the hill and headed east, the wagon rattled along the muddy road, with Samuel whistling to himself.

The next stop was Robert Graham's whose two sons had begun a mercantile business and needed supplies. After unloading a few barrels, a chest or two and some boxes, Samuel asked directions.

"My next stop is Gentlemen Boyd's, that is, Andrew Boyd's. How do I get there?"

"Only a couple more miles east of here, just off the Great Road. His is a big two-story log house facing east. You won't have trouble finding it today, for every wagon, horse, man, woman and child of the neighborhood is going there to build a new barn. Stay on the main road about five miles more. Then follow the crowd," offered Graham.

"Guess that's why that Marshall's store in Evansham was so anxious for me to deliver the goods today, 'cause of the barn raisin'. Maybe I can stay over there. By then my wagon will be nearly empty and tomorrow I will be goin' back to eastern Virginia. I might even be able to find another load to carry east."

Samuel clicked his tongue and the grays picked up their feet and headed east once more. It was not difficult to find Boyd's, as Graham had promised. He found his way in behind the other wagons and moved slowly along with the crowd. The wagon rocked from side to side, as the ruts grew deeper here and there. His load shifted to the right and back to the left and settled back into position. Surely it would be safe until he could find Mr. Boyd.

Finally, he pulled up in between the kitchen and the springhouse. He turned the wagon around and began to back the horses up into the open space near the loom house. The wagon tilted to the left through the ruts and over the rocks. The load shifted. In a desperate attempt to protect the load and his team, he urged the horses to the right. The load shifted back, but this time the barrels came too far to the right, and the wagon overturned. Samuel jumped, the horses bucked and reared up. The barrels rolled off, the chest and wooden boxes followed and Samuel was pinned under them.

His groans and cries for help brought men, women and children running to his side. Some Negro released the grays, others moved the boxes and barrels, and the women offered immediate suggestions for his care. But Samuel could not move. He knew his leg was injured and probably broken. His life's work seemed to be at an end. The wagon and goods lay in a heap at his feet.

Seeing the commotion, Justice Boyd hobbled toward the springhouse. His son, Thomas, helped him across the field and suggested that they stop for a rest, but they continued. When Thomas had his first view of the scene, he knew there was a cause for alarm. He had taken his medical training with Dr. Smith and knew what must be done. He took charge as the others backed away.

"My name is Thomas Boyd, and I'm a doctor. What's hurting you, boy?

"Sir, it's my leg, my right leg. It feels like I might have broke it when I jump off the wagon."

"Let me see, now," said Thomas as he examined the leg. "Yes, I believe that it may be broken. First thing we do is fix it so you cannot move it."

He motioned to Negro Susan and her son, Jim. "Get me some sticks and some sheets to wrap around." They hurried off and the doctor continued his examination.

142

"You have no wound, and it is not a bad break, but with the swelling I must wrap it up and you, boy, will be on your back for awhile. Then later I can fix it so you can walk on it while still wrapped up. But now, where is your marse?"

"There is no marse, sir. I'm a free person, a free person of color because my Grandmama was an Injun. Here, look in my pocket and find that paper that tells all."

Boyd stared in disbelief. Free, he thought, free and from an Indian! Probably wasn't true, but he reached in the pocket and pulled out a piece of yellowed paper whose edges had been tattered and whose outside had accumulated years of dirt from being so long in the pocket.

Thomas unfolded the paper and read,

> *This is to certify that Samuel Findlay is a free person of color, having received his freedom from Henry Clay of Powhatan County, Virginia, on May 4, 1773, at the General Court in Williamsburg, where it was decided that he was descended through his maternal line from an Indian who arrived in Virginia after 1705 and that he had been illegally held in slavery.*

Doctor Thomas returned the paper to the dirty pocket and took the sticks provided and wrapped the sheeting around the leg at various places, stabilizing the injury. He pulled blankets from the wagon and with help of the bystanders placed Samuel on his blankets near the kitchen.

"I'll be back soon with some laudanum for the pain," said the doctor and walked toward his father's house. Others began to gather up the broken boxes, pushed the barrels aside, and with twenty or so hands, they set the wagon right side up. The horses had been taken to the field and left to graze. The harness was returned to the wagon, and all was pulled to a space near the loom house. The accident scene was restored to normal. The doctor moved on to the barn looking for his father, but met him halfway.

"Father, we may have some problems here. That nigger over there says he is not a nigger at all, but a free person of color. What do you make of that?"

"They talk big but seldom are free. Probably trying to escape to the North or somewhere else."

Andrew Boyd viewed the scene with distaste. Troublesome niggers were not what he wanted. He and Thomas came to Samuel's side, and the old man glared at him from his standing position, overpowering and in a foul humor.

"What are you doing here, nigger?" asked Boyd in a demanding tone.

"Sir, I was delivering goods to Mr. Andrew Boyd, the Gentlemen Justice of Wythe County, and when I was turning the wagon it upset."

"What did you bring me? Was it some of the whiskey and wine I ordered? Did you have some flour on there? And how about nails? We need nails today."

"Yes, sir, all of them things was on the wagon, and all are delivered. I didn't see any spillage on the ground, so the sprits must be intact. The nails is in them smaller barrels, and the flour is in them big barrels. Nothing broke open when it tipped. Mr. Marshall in Evansham asked me to deliver the goods to you."

"Very well, I'll get someone over here to move these things to their places. Now boy, we need to let your marse know what has happened."

"Don't have no marse, sir. I'm a free man. That's 'cause I'm descended from an Injun grandmama. Got freedom

144

from the court in Williamsburg."

"That's what I told you, Father. He claims to be free, and in his pocket is a dirty piece of paper stating he was freed in Williamsburg Court years ago because he was descended from an Indian grandmother."

Old man Boyd shook his cane in Samuel's face and began a tirade about triflin' niggers who thought they were free, about Indians who were always the enemy, and about liars and cheaters who tried to pass as free people. Only today, one of Draper's niggers had said the same thing and Boyd had a fresh and local example to give to the crowd who began to gather around him.

Thomas took his father's arm and began to lead him away, when the Negro women in the kitchen stepped outside to join the crowd.

"There she is, there she is, that lyin' nigger. Says she is supposed to be free. Wanted me to help her with a freedom suit. Liars, liars, they are all liars!" he shouted.

Rachel turned to Melinda and Susannah and whispered, "He's talkin' 'bout me! I'm free, my grandmama was an Injun and I was freed in Williamsburg years and years ago. I'm not a liar. I'm not. Nobody will believe me. Nobody. And nobody will help me." Rachel began to sob. Judy put her arm around her mother's shoulder and urged her to come back inside.

"I want to shout it to the heavens, I'm free, free, free!" Rachel jerked away from Judy and flung her arms to the heavens. "The great spirit knows, he knows. My Grandmama Chance was an Injun from South Carolina, and I was freed 'cause of her. But then carried away and sold as a Negro."

The crowd that had gathered came in closer to hear her talk and while the old man continued his harangue, Rachel

145

continued her talk of freedom, both getting ever louder. Suddenly, silence! A shout came from Samuel, the man on the blanket, who had heard most of the arguments.

"Rachel Findlay, Rachel Findlay, answer me!"

"Rachel, Rachel, Rachel," his voice trailed off. Then in a solemn silent voice, he whispered, "My sister, Rachel."

Rachel turned and looked at the stranger who called her sister. She did not recognize the fifty-year-old man.

"You Samuel Findlay?" she asked.

"Yes, I am, and I believe you my sister. You look like Aunt Judy and your cousin Hannah. Now, tell me this. Did you have a child name Judy when you was a young girl?"

"Yes, I was only thirteen. Judy, come here." Rachel called to her daughter, now a mature mother herself.

Rachel and Judy stood before Samuel and asked Samuel the name of his grandmama.

"Her name was White Cloud in Injun language of the Catawbers of South Carolina. Henry Clay of Powhatan, catched her. He name her Chance."

Rachel's eyes went back into her head, her legs grew wobbly, and she collapsed to the ground with a thud. Judy pulled her toward her, and Melinda and Susannah came to help, bringing a cup of water from the nearby spring.

"Wake up, Mama, wake up. It's good news. It's your brother Samuel who sits here with his broke leg. It truly is him."

Rachel's eyes fluttered and as the water touched her lips and her face she began to awaken from the dream. Surely it was a dream. Over and over in her mind she had hoped that something would happen to bring her good news about her condition. Today it was her own brother. An answer to her dream.

"Samuel, Samuel," she murmured. "You come to help

me. Thank you, thank you, but how can we prove we is free?"

"Rachel, I have a piece of paper in my pocket that says I'm free, and how it all came about. The paper that Dr. Thomas read is for me so that I can travel around the state without any trouble. But I have another paper that will help you prove your are really free."

"What is it?"

"It is the court record which name me, you, and Judy, and is dated back more than twenty-five years ago. I show you."

"What's going on here?" interrupted Captain Draper. He and his wife, hearing the commotion and seeing the crowd that had gathered, made their way to the kitchen, and there saw Rachel and a Negro in conversation.

"Rachel, get back to work in the kitchen," ordered Captain Draper. "You know you are here to do the cooking, so get in there and get busy."

"Yes, Rachel, when Captain Draper says get to work, he means it," added Jane Draper in a sarcastic tone. "If you don't obey, you will be whipped again."

Rachel, Susannah and Melinda moved slowly toward the kitchen. Rachel turned to Samuel but said nothing. Her head held high, she knew that now she soon would be free, really free. Samuel would not be going anywhere soon, and he would help her. She was free, and she knew it, even if everyone else called her a liar.

"Capn' sir, I'm Samuel Findlay, the brother of your Rachel and the uncle of Judy."

"I think she told me one time she had a brother Samuel. Who's nigger are you, anyway? I never heard of any Samuel Findlay around here."

"I am a free man of color, as my grandmama was a

Injun. We, well that is, Rachel, Judy, me and all got our freedom in Williamsburg in 1773, and —"

The captain interrupted and in a loud voice exclaimed, "It's not possible. I have a paper that says Rachel and her daughter Judy were Negroes, when I bought them in 1774. You, nigger, are a liar, a liar for sure."

"No sir, I surely ain't, and if you look in my pocket you see the paper that say we free."

"Never mind, I don't believe you anyway, and I know they are Negroes on my bill of sale and that's all that matters." Captain Draper and his wife walked away before Samuel could say another word.

Doctor Thomas moved toward the blanket, opened his doctor's bag, and found the medicine, which he gave to the patient. Soon Samuel was asleep.

Chapter 13

SAMUEL MAKES A FRIEND

About mid-afternoon, the rafters went up, the hammers rang on the roof top, the floor was done, and the barn was complete enough for the frolic. The servants spread the tables with the wheat and cornbread, the ham and chicken, the corn, potatoes, the pies and cakes for all to enjoy. Some of the neighbors added their favorite dish to the display. The Negro men rolled the whiskey and wine barrels to a shaded spot under the oak tree, where the workers had lined up for their refreshment. Shady spots were chosen for everyone, the whites under one red oak tree, and the slaves under another.

After dinner, Will, Caesar and Peter went to the barn with its skeleton framing and newly laid floor and set up their three chairs. Caesar tuned up the fiddle, Will and Peter got their spoons, bones, drums, kettle, and banjo. The frolic would soon begin with such songs as "Possum Up the Gum Tree" and "Nigga Sick or Nigga Die, Nigga Long for Chicken Pie." The whole crowd would soon be whirling across the floor, to the reels and country dances.

The thrum of the banjo echoed over the hills. It was time for the Negroes to dance too. Cato and Judy led the crowd—she with a red ribbon in her hair, he in a clean linen shirt, and both with bare feet in the damp grass beside the barn. Others joined in, each holding hands with the others, skipping, trotting and keeping time to the music. When the tempo changed, the children began flipping arms and legs and holding their necks stiff like chickens do when they strut. Some of the others tried the cake walk. Sally, Melinda, James, Tom and Robbin picked up the beat and joined the laughing crowd. When the chicken strut came to an end, the children fell to the ground laughing.

Rachel, too, had joined the dancers, leaving her apron in the kitchen. Peter left the chair where he was making music and grabbed Rachel and swung her around and around. She's smiling, thought Peter, and it's the first time in months, no, probably years.

"You happy?" asked Peter.

"Yes, I see there may be hope for me and my children and grandchildren. Tonight I celebrate." Rachel smiled again.

Samuel Findlay was still on the blankets where he had been settled some hours before, and the laudanum had left him dazed and sleepy. He wanted some water and some food and needed to find Rachel. One of the little boys ran to the springhouse and Samuel summoned him on his return.

"Boy, could you find Rachel for me. She is Captain Draper's Rachel. And would you be so kind as to let me have a taste of that water?"

"Rachel is my grandmama," he said. He left the water behind for Samuel and ran looking for Rachel.

When the curly-haired boy, about ten or so, returned he reported, "Can't find her no place."

"Did you look in the kitchen?" asked Samuel.

"Didn't see nobody in there."

"Then try the big house. Did you look there?"

"No, but they don't 'low de chillun's in there. But maybe if I go there I find my mama and she look for her." And he ran off to the back of the big house.

An hour passed. The neighbors, friends, and relatives of the Boyds were enjoying the music and the dance. The whiskey was generously served to the crowd. But Samuel Findlay was still on the ground alone, hungry and thirsty. He dozed back to sleep.

"Wake up! Wake up!" shouted Dr. Boyd. "What did you say your name was? Samuel, I think."

"Yes, my name's Samuel Findlay."

"I came to see about the leg. Is it hurting much?" asked the doctor.

"Not so bad. Guess the laudanum keep the pain away some."

"Yes, and you probably need some more. But I have a question. Who is going to pay me for my services, and for the medicine?"

"I will pay," said Samuel. "I have a little money, and when I'm able I can work for you until all the bill is paid. I can fix up my wagon a little and deliver goods for you wherever you need me to take 'em."

"Fine, fine. Then I will prepare the medicine again for you. We'll see about the wagon and the work. In the meantime, you will need a place to stay. I have a little empty cabin over on my place, and you can have it until you are able to travel again. I want you to know that I do not think the same as my father. I can take you home when I leave. It will take a couple of weeks before you can stand up much on the leg, but we will worry about that later."

151

"I'm much obliged. I'll do anything I can to work for you, when I can. You believe me when I tell you I'm a free man of color?"

"Yes," answered Doctor Thomas, "and I want to hear more about your story. If Rachel is your sister I want to hear her story too. It sounds unbelievable!"

Samuel nodded and could not believe what he was hearing himself, from the tongue of the son of the man who called him a liar. "You sure are different kind of white man," said Samuel.

The doctor continued, "My wife and I have been to hear the Reverend Edward Morgan, a man of the cloth, a champion of the Methodists. They do not believe in slavery, and we are inclined to that belief as well. The Methodist bishop named Asbury will soon be coming to visit in Evansham, and we plan to hear him."

"I've heard of them Methodists, but ain't seen none around this part of Virginia."

"Well, there are only a few yet, but we have a lot of interest. Now, Samuel, here is the medicine to keep that pain away. I will be getting you after the frolic is over and will arrange to get your wagon and horses another time."

Samuel swallowed the dose handed to him and said his thanks to the doctor, then went back to sleep.

Samuel soon settled in the small cabin at Dr. Boyd's. He spent most of his time on the little straw bed the first few weeks, but now he was hobbling around using a tree limb specially cut and fastened together to act as a crutch. His pain had subsided and the swelling was now gone. Mrs. Boyd and her children had brought him food and water and he was mighty grateful for their kindness. So unusual in this day and time, thought Samuel.

When the leg had healed well enough, Samuel repaired his wagon and began to repay the family by going to the fort, or the town, or the lead mines on errands for the doctor. Once he had a trip to Staunton to get medical supplies and another time he went to Abingdon.

One morning he drove the Boyd family to Evansham to hear Bishop Asbury, who was staying at Johnston's Inn on Main Street. He heard Asbury say he was impressed with the town and mentioned that its twenty houses were neat, most of them new and many of them painted.

The Bishop lamented that there was no Methodist Church in the town. In fact, there was no church of any denomination. His sermon was given in the dining room of the inn. About thirty people were there, including Samuel. He had not been to a church service since he was a young man. The topic for the sermon was "To everything there is a season." He had heard the scripture verses before. There was a time to be born, a time to die, a time to weep and a time to laugh, a time to love and a time to hate, a time of war and a time of peace, and so forth. He wondered if the good book said there is a time to be in chains and a time to be free. He knew Rachel would believe it was time to be free.

The Boyds spoke privately with the bishop after the sermon and asked his assistance in regard to Rachel.

"Samuel," called Dr. Boyd. "Come here and meet the bishop. He is most anxious to help us."

"Sir, I am right proud to meet you," said Samuel with his head bowed to his chest.

Bishop placed his hand on his head and offered, "Bless you, my son. Let me see your face."

Samuel raised his head and the bishop smiled. "Now tell me about your sister."

Samuel told him, concluding, "She's been at the Drapers' ever since. She needs somebody to help her."

"My, my, that is quite a story. Never heard of any such thing myself."

Samuel reached in his pocket and thrust the dirty piece of paper in the Bishop's hands. "This is proof, sir."

The Bishop unfolded the wrinkled paper and read it to himself. "It certainly seems in order. Williamsburg, 1773, my, my. Never heard of such a thing, but as you know the Methodists do not favor slavery of any kind. I expect you need to find a lawyer for your sister. Likely you can find one while you are here today."

Dr. Boyd spoke up. "Samuel, let's go and see if we can find somebody right now." Giving their thanks and saying their goodbyes to the bishop, they left the inn and began walking down Main Street.

"Let's go to the courthouse first. We may find somebody there," offered Boyd.

They turned right at the next corner and walked up to the front door of the courthouse and went inside.

"No one here, Samuel. Let's walk down the street. There's Alexander Smyth's office. Let's see if he is about."

There was no one in the office except his clerk, who told them that Smyth was in Abingdon on court business. He also suggested that most of the lawyers who usually came to court in Evansham were also there as it was the court day for Washington County.

Samuel was disappointed and Boyd suggested that he come to town another day and then he could find someone. Samuel had paid his debt to the doctor and his family, and in November 1800 he had work offered him by the lead mines. He was to transport lead bars to Manchester in eastern Virginia. He said goodbye to the Boyds and left for the mines. It would be many years before Samuel returned to Evansham. It was not yet time.

Chapter 14

DISTURBING NEWS

Even though Rachel was not allowed to travel without the Drapers she still kept up with the news. By 1801 she knew that Gabriel had been tried, convicted and hanged. And she knew that twenty-seven of his associates were also put to death, although a few were acquitted and a few pardoned or given lesser sentences. No white person died as a result of his scheme, but the white people were afraid, including those in Southwestern Virginia where the number of Negro families were scarce. The talk now was of more restrictions. There were the patrollers, or as some called them, the "paddy-rollers," who could visit in the slave quarters or stop the Negroes on the street and ask where they were going and what they were doing. It was not a good time to talk of freedom.

Judy and Cato were now together and had five children. Rachel's youngest was six years old, and several of the others had been taken from her and given to the children of John Draper. Caesar had died and was buried in the field with the other slaves. Twenty-seven years had past Rachel and Judy arrived at Draper Mountain.

Judy came to the cabin door and called out, "Mama, you there?"

"Yes, child. Come in here."

Rachel was at the table mending socks and children's dresses. She looked up but continued to stitch the garments.

"I have some news," said Judy. "Just heard it from Melinda, who told Cato, who told me. Melinda heard it from James over at the Sayers place."

"What is it?" asked Rachel.

"A woman named Betsy, some called her Dilly, went to court in Evansham and got permission to bring her a freedom suit against her master." Judy pulled out the other chair and sat opposite her mother.

"That is good news. Who was the lawyer? I should find him and get his help," said Rachel.

"His name is Daniel Sheffey, a student of the famous General Alexander Smyth. His office is in Evansham," said Judy.

"Cato also told me that Sheffey has another case too. A man called Isaac, although some say his name is Jacob. He wanted to be free from his master too. And Cato says neither one of them had to pay and that if the masters tried to hurt them, the sheriff would protect them while the suit goes to the court."

"I wish I could go to Evansham," said Rachel in a dejected tone. "But I know I can't get away from here. I believe there is no hope for me to be free. Maybe you can go to Evansham and take my place," suggested Rachel.

"Mama, you've got to do it! You knows all the family lines and you know how we was brought out here and all. I was too little to remember much. I don't even remember Mitchell any more," said Judy.

"I've pondered over it a lot, Judy. Peter and me talk

158

about it, too. I reckon if I got free now I'd have to leave here, but Peter would have to stay. I can't do that."

"Mama, most of your children are gone in different directions. I get to stay here with some of my children, but one day they will be gone too. What can we do?"

"Judy, the time is not right." Rachel got up from the table and walked to the fireplace, stirred up the coals and added, "I tell you about Grandmama Chance and about the freedom suit in Williamsburg, and about the way the law says we have to do it. We have to have a lawyer and Evansham is twenty miles away. Maybe you can find one and you can tell them about our being sold as slaves. All these years I hoped I could get my freedom, but now I think it will never happen."

Rachel sat at the table and stared out the window. Judy left her to her thoughts.

In 1806 news came from Montgomery County that another slave named Rachel, Rachel Viney, sued her master, Henry Patton, for assault and battery, trespass and false imprisonment. This Rachel was asking for her freedom too, not only for herself but six of her children all held by Patton. Another son was in the possession of Samuel Patton, a son-in-law of John Draper. He had married Draper's daughter Nancy. They often came to Draper Mountain to visit and it was on one of these occasions that Rachel heard the story firsthand as she served the evening meal.

"What can we do, Mr. Draper?" asked Samuel Patton.

"You can delay it as long as possible. Your lawyer can help you there. Probably not much you can do except wait and see how the case comes out."

"We have Marcus Viney, but you gave us Rachel's daughter, Polly Findlay, when we got married," said Nancy to her father. "And Samuel's father has the rest of them to worry about."

Her brother John, sitting at the foot of the table asked, "How did this case get into court anyway?"

"Rachel Viney went to the county seat at Christiansburg with my father and some others and while he was at the tavern, she ran to the nearest lawyer and got his attention," said Samuel.

Rachel removed the plates and brought the cake and fruit tray. Judy brought the coffee and hovered nearby.

Nancy's voice was trembling and she announced to her brother, "Every one of them will be gone, and sooner or later, John, all yours will be gone too."

"Not ours," said John. "They will never go to the county seat anywhere. Not if I can help it."

"But you know that our Rachel has always said she was free."

"It's not true, Nancy. I have the bill of sale in Father's papers. It clearly says Rachel is a Negro."

Rachel came close to the head of the table where her master was sitting and in a loud voice said, "I am free. My Grandmama was an Injun, not a Negro. And I knows I is free."

"Rachel, leave the room," ordered the elder John Draper. "I don't want to hear another word about your freedom. I've listened to that nonsense too many years. Now leave us. Get out of here."

Rachel turned her back on the family group, put her head high in the air and stomped out like a strutting rooster.

160

"That's the first time I've heard Rachel talk about being free in years," said the younger John. "Of course, I am down at the Ingles Ferry so much now I don't see her often."

"She's probably too old to worry about it now anyhow," said Nancy. "We'll probably lose Marcus, and Mr. Patton will lose the others, but we still have lots of niggers on our place. And Polly will still be with us."

"We will be ruined if we lose all our niggers," said Samuel. "Who will do the work? I say we are looking at terrible losses ahead. One gets the idea of freedom, then another, and on and on. Even if they don't get free, they go to court and try."

"Yes, Samuel. I am sure your father is in a state of disbelief and worry. It puts all of us slaveowners in a state of shock. You know the basis for much our wealth is our niggers," said John.

Judy had heard enough. She cleared the dishes from the table. The men gathered by the fireplace with their pipes. The old man Draper shuffled to the chair near the hearth and flopped into it. His frame was beginning to show his seventy-six years. When he spoke his voice was no longer vibrant.

"What did the Vineys say in the court papers," asked John Draper.

"Rachel said she was the daughter of Sarah, a former slave of one named Thomas Smith of Northumberland County, in the far eastern part of Virginia. She also claimed to be of Indian, not of African extraction."

"That's what our Rachel claims too. How many is in her family, anyway?"

"Well, according to Rachel Viney, when Smith heard that she and nineteen members of her family had filed for

161

freedom, he sold her."

"He knew that if they were successful, he would lose everything," said Nancy. "I heard that her grandmother, Bess, was considered to be the original stock of the race of Vineys. She was an Indian who came into Virginia by ship when she was a young girl of twelve or thirteen years of age. She was said to be the granddaughter of Mary, who accompanied her. Is that what you heard?"

"Yes, that's what I heard too. When did Rachel Viney come to your father's place, Samuel?"

"I think she has been with us about fifteen years. She claims she was freed by the courts in 1791."

The captain's wife, Jane, who was now standing at her husband's side, whispered to the family.

"I am sure our future is doomed. Our Rachel, and Judy too, will not give up. We will lose them all. The only thing to do is delay the inevitable as long as possible."

Four years later, in 1810, Jane became ill. Alice, her daughter, cared for her for many weeks, before she passed into the land beyond. She was buried in the family grave-yard on the place beside Miss Bettie, the first Mrs. Draper.

Rachel watched as her old master mumbled to himself, asked for Jane over and over again, and cried and screamed when he thought no one was listening. Only a week ago she had joined the family to look for him. He was lost again in the mountain. At age eighty he could not remember the way home.

Young John and his family moved back home to take over the responsibility of running the farms acquired by the Drapers. Now it would be their turn to look after the old man.

John agreed to let his half-sister, Miss Alice Draper, live with them. She was born in 1783, never seemed interested in any of the local gentlemen, and at the age of twenty-seven was recognized in the neighborhood as a spinster unlikely ever to marry. She was deeply saddened by the loss of her mother. The way her father was acting disturbed her even more. Some days he would ask about Bettie, who had been dead many years. Other days, he would be crying "Attack, attack!" with his rifle over his shoulder.

Alice had one consolation. Her father gave her Jenny, the youngest daughter of Rachel, as her personal maid. Jenny was born in 1795, the eleventh child of Rachel born into slavery at Draper Mountain. Many of her brothers and sisters and some of her nieces and nephews were given away and were moved to other locations, some in the county and others to distant places. Some of them she would never see again.

Jenny, too, felt the loss of Jane Draper, but not in the same way. Jenny was relieved to see the old mistress buried in the family cemetery. She knew that her mother, Rachel, and her father, Peter, had suffered daily for many years because of her harsh and unyielding ways. Jenny too had felt the lash and had taken the abuse. She had heard her mother often cry and wail about her desperate need to be really free. At age fifteen Jenny often thought of freedom herself. If she could just have some money to buy a few pretties, or if she could just go to town sometime, or travel to the next plantation to meet some others her own age. But that had not happened.

163

Chapter 15

THE RUNAWAY

In the fall of 1810, Miss Alice received a letter from her married half-sister Mary, who was then living in Western Tennessee, extending to her an invitation to visit as soon as she could make arrangements.

"Jenny, where are you girl?" screamed Alice. "Come here this instant!"

Jenny shuffled into the bedroom on the second floor of the log house. She found Alice looking at her leather trunk and pulling at the brass clasp on the center of the lid. The more she pulled, the more of her brown hair fell over her reddened face. She raised her head and screamed again, "Get in here and help me, girl! Get this trunk open. We are going on a trip."

Jenny moved to the trunk, opened the clasps at either end and easily pulled the rounded top up against the foot of the bed. Jenny's blue skirt and oatmeal-colored shirt were covered with a dark blue apron. The shoes on her feet were old and worn and could hardly bear the nearly two hundred pounds which was spread over her tall frame. Her hair was pulled back and her red ribbon held it in place. A white mob cap covered her forehead.

"Where we goin', Miss Ally?"

Free in Chains

"Going to see Mary and David and their family down in Tennessee. We will get Jacob to drive us to the stage-coach and we will travel for many days to get there. We need to pack the trunk so we can stay awhile. You will need to pack your bags too."

"When we goin', Miss Ally?" asked Jenny, as she began to lay the clothes on the bed. One by one she unloaded the dresses, shawls, slippers, petticoats, blankets and sheets from the trunk so they could reach the bottom.

"In a week I suppose, if we can get ready. Now hurry downstairs and get me a piece of paper from the desk. I want to write Mary and tell her we are coming. I will look over the dresses and see what will go in the trunk. Go!"

One by one Alice picked up and held up to her narrow waist, two, three and four dresses, finally choosing the black dress, the dark gray, the lavender Sunday dress and the blue, her favorite. She put them aside when Jenny returned with the paper, sat at her desk, dipped the goose quill in the ink bottle, and began writing. She would send the letter on the stage announcing that she and Jenny would be leaving the Mountain in about a week.

"Pack those four dresses, Jenny. I'm going to take those. You find the petticoats and my undergarments to go with them. Don't forget to pack some warmer skirts, my shawl and my heavy shoes."

Jenny picked up the dresses Alice had selected, carefully folding each one and returning it to the trunk. She rustled through the pile of clothes on the bed and found the petticoats and some of the undergarments. She went to the hooks on the bedroom wall and selected a cranberry-colored shawl and a black wool skirt. She hung some of the clothes not chosen on the hooks and packed the sheets and blankets into the walnut cabinet on the opposite wall.

When Alice finished the letter she addressed it, sealed it with her own personal seal dipped in wax which made her initials AD in red on the back of the envelope.

"Take this to your sister Judy and tell her to take it to the road tomorrow morning and give it to the driver on the stage."

Jenny was disappointed. She wanted to be trusted to take the letter herself, but she knew that once Miss Ally made up her mind, she, fifteen-year-old Jenny, could not change it.

When the clothes were packed for the trip, Jenny found Miss Ally's shoes, her cape, and some nightclothes to carry in the smaller bag. They would be many nights on the road and would need things daily from the bags.

Jenny found her mother and Peter at the slave quarters. When she entered the batten door, she noticed that they were sorting the laundry for the family. Peter was no longer able to do heavy work in the field or even clean stalls in the barn. His torn straw hat was cock-eyed on his head and his work clothes had not been washed in a long time.

Rachel heard the door, but continued to fold the sheets, pillow shams and towels. "Who that?"

"Mama, Mama, guess what? Me and Miss Ally is goin' on a trip. We goin' to Tennessee."

Rachel turned sharply. "I don't believe it. How is it that you are going to be able to travel and I can't." Rachel sighed. "When you leaving, Jenny?"

"Soon as we can get ready. Maybe next week. We going to travel on the stagecoach for many days to go and visit Miss Mary and Marse David."

"Sit down, child. Your mother wants to talk to you."

167

Jenny pulled up a chair to the wooden table where some of the clothes were spread. Her mother and father stopped folding the clothes, and Rachel reached for Jenny's hand.

"For more than thirty years I been dreaming of being free, and now I'm nearly sixty years old and got to realize that the dream might not come true. But for you there might be a way to be free. Now listen closely."

Peter nodded, as Rachel continued. "When you go to Tennessee you might have a chance to meet some other Negroes, or some free Negroes. Keep your eyes open for a chance to escape and find your freedom, not alone, but with some of those new friends. If you run 'way you might make your escape clean from this life of slavery. You got lots of talents and can find work easy in a good home. You know the housekeeping, you know the weaving, you know the sewing. And you is good with the younger children. I am proud of you and I be saddened you ain't here. I know it's a great chance for freedom. Don't be scared to ask questions."

Rachel took the corner of her apron and wiped a tear from her left eye. Peter bowed his head and waited for someone to say something.

"Mama, how can I do that? I don't want to leave you and all the others and I wouldn't know what to do, tryin' to escape," said Jenny.

"Now, Jenny, this might be the only chance you got. Be free! Be free! If you do run, take clothes and food, and travel at night. Go with others who knows the way. Try to get to the closest city. If you can, git some papers that let you travel free. Remember, pack those new shoes Peter will fix for you. Know freedom is a most precious thing."

Rachel turned to Peter and asked, "You can fix this child

a pair of good sturdy walking shoes before she goes, can't you?"

Peter smiled. "Yes, I can. I'll do it right now." He pulled himself up from the chair, took his cane and hobbled to the doorway. Turning to Jenny, he said, "You'll have your shoes, and your freedom too."

The October morning was clear and crisp and the sky was sapphire blue. The droplets of dew were still on the grass and the rooftops glistened in the dawn's early sunlight. Alice and Jenny waited at the roadside for the stage to arrive and to take them to Evansham on the first leg of their journey. Their trunks and bags were in the wagon waiting the thunder of hoofs from Christiansburg to the east.

When the stage rolled up Cato helped them into the carriage, and stowed the baggage on the back and on the top. Their fellow passengers were sleepy and quiet. They stopped along the way to pick up people and let them off. They ate at the Marshall Inn in Evansham, where they heard Mr. Marshall talk about the famous Louis Phillippe who visited back a few years ago. He just had to tell every stranger that he entertained a prince and his entourage.

In Evansham they changed to the Tennessee stage. They traveled the stage road, or as some called it, the road to Kentucky. They saw old Tory Jacob Kettering on the porch of his inn, waving his hat in the air as he did so many times in the Revolutionary War. They noticed Straw's and Ingledove's taverns and stopped to spend the night at the Stone House. They ate at the famous early tavern, simply called "The Tavern," in Abingdon and after seven more days of bouncing and swinging along the rutted roads, they were at the doorstep of David Love's Tennessee plantation.

"How good to see you, Ally, come on in." Mary wrapped her arms around Alice and guided her up the front steps and into the two-story frame house set amidst the oak trees. Negro servants hovered nearby and a black boy in the yard came to claim the horses.

"Your nigger girl can sleep in the quarters, unless you need her in your room," added Mary.

"That's fine. If I need her I'll call for her." Turning to Jenny, Alice added, "Go along, Jenny. The boy will show you where. Take your things with you."

Jenny followed the young boy down the lane past the log kitchen and the stone springhouse. The boy stopped at the first cabin and hollered, "Chloe, she here!" When the door creaked open the boy left with the horses and headed for the barn farther down the lane.

"Come in. What your name?" asked Chloe.

"Name's Jenny." Jenny looked around the small room. A couple of small beds, a little table, a couple of broken chairs, a hook or two for clothes, and a small fireplace. Clean and tidy, thought Jenny.

"You can stay here with me," added Chloe. "Want somethin' to eat?"

"I'm tired and a little hungry, thank you."

"Bring your things over on this bed, and you can have those hooks for your clothes. I'll cut some bread and make some tea. You like tea?"

"Thank you, that's fine." Jenny moved to the bed in the corner, opened her bag and hung a couple of things on the hooks. She joined Chloe at the table.

"How long you been here?"

"All my life, 'bout twenty-five years. No place else to

170

go and if I don't bother nobody I can stay without gettin'
beat. My marse is a good one, and the mistress too. They
hardly gits mad and they treats us good. I works hard for
them, doing weaving, sewing, washing, looking after the
children, and most everything they asks."

Jenny was determined to take her mama's advice. The
words had spun around in her mind all the way from the
Mountain to Tennessee. "You ever want to be free?"

"I suppose I do sometimes, but I ain't tried to run away.
Now Barbara and Zack, they's always talkin' about being
free. You will meet them later." Chloe got up from the
table, turned to Jenny and said, "Now, I got to give the
children their meals. I'll be back soon."

"I'll clean up here and if I can help, you let me know.
Maybe I could visit with Barbara and Zack. Is they on this
lane someplace?"

"Barbara's over at the loom house, just 'cross the lane
and down a little. Zack is probably at the blacksmith shop."

After Chloe departed, Jenny fixed her hair, retied the
ribbon, put on her white cap, and picked out a clean apron
from her bag. After cleaning up the table and putting the
bread away, she ventured out the door and crossed the dusty
lane to the loom house. Her mother had told her to be free.
No use in wasting time.

Barbara had her back to the door but Jenny guessed she
was about twenty or so, pushing her feet and hands in the
rhythm of the loom. A coverlet in dark red and green was
about half done, as near as Jenny could see. The shuttles
were thrown back and forth across the threads with great
dexterity. Certainly, she had done this same thing many
times.

"You Barbara?" asked Jenny.

"Oh, I didn't hear you. Yes. Who is you?"

171

"My name's Jenny. I came here with Miss Alice from Virginia. Am staying with Chloe, but she got to go feed the children."

"Come in and watch if you want. I got to work on this for awhile. Wished I didn't have to, but Mistress Mary needs it as soon as I can fix it. She's been in a bad mood for days," said Barbara.

"Did ya ever think of running away, being free?" asked Jenny.

"Sure, ain't you?"

"Yes, but my mama more than me. One day we hope we can all be free."

"I don't see that coming, unless our marses frees us. I doubt they can give us up either. Nobody to do the work for them."

"That's true," said Jenny.

She moved closer to the loom and fingered the red and greens of the cloth Barbara had woven.

"Chloe say you and Zack talks about being free a lot. Do you think some day you'll try to run away?"

"Don't know. Maybe."

"I'm goin' now, so you can get back to work. I'm at Chloe's cabin, if'n you want to visit."

"Bye," said Barbara and continued with the rhythm of the shuttles.

Jenny wandered down the lane toward the blacksmith shop. She heard the clanging of the steel on the anvil and smelled the smoke from the fire inside the shop. The door was open and when she came near, she saw the figure of a giant of a man. He must have been six feet six or more and muscles like she had never seen before, sweating and glistening as the hammer rose and fell.

Zack stopped in mid-stroke as if he could not believe

that a young wench could be of such size. How old was she, he wondered. Was she really as tall as he was? He laid the hammer down and wiped his forehead with a dirty cloth he kept in his back pocket. Zack stepped outside.

"Well looka here. A young lady. Who are you?"

"Name's Jenny. Is you Zack?"

"Yes, that's me. Where'd you come from? I ain't seen you here before." Zack studied Jenny as he asked the questions and waited for her answer.

"I come from Virginia, rode the stage with Miss Alice Draper. We come here to visit for a spell. Not sure how long, but maybe till Christmas."

"Good, then we'll get to know each other. What'd you do in Virginia at the Drapers'?"

"I learned to spin and weave. Done some sewing and housekeeping. Helped Miss Alice tend her mother 'til she died awhile back. Left my mama there with old marse."

Jenny talked on and on like she had known Zack all her life. He smiled and nodded his head, finally interrupting Jenny.

"Where you stayin'?"

"I'm staying in the cabin with Chloe. How 'bout you?"

"I'm in the quarters down next to the end of the row. Now I got to get back to finishing this horseshoe. I'll try to see you later on." Zack smiled and turned back to the anvil and the heap of glowing charcoal.

Jenny walked slowly up the lane, knowing in her heart that Zack would help her. If anyone had asked her why she knew that, she would have said, "I just know it."

Several days went by before Jenny saw Zack again. Miss Alice needed her to help her with her clothes, besides giving her several jobs to do for Mary. Even later in the evening she and Chloe were left with the children when Mary and

Miss Alice went visiting. Marse David Love, Mary's husband, was called to the court and was gone several days.

The summer had returned and the early November Sunday was warm like June. Toward evening, Chloe and Jenny were sitting on the doorstep of the cabin, when Zack came strolling up the lane. Jenny wiped her face with her apron and brushed her hair from her forehead. Zack lifted his straw hat as he saw Jenny. He was grinning and his eyes were focused on Jenny.

"Nice evenin' ain't it?"

"Yeah, it is. Sit a spell?" asked Jenny.

Zack took his place beside Jenny. After some brief talk about the weather, Chloe began to fidget and finally walked down the lane to see Barbara, leaving the two alone to talk.

"I hear you was interested in bein' free," said Jenny, getting to the point at once. Hadn't her mother told her not to miss any opportunities?

"What you mean? I'm already free."

"Free? Really free?" asked Jenny, not believing what she was hearing.

"Yeah, been free for several years now. My marse was a Methodist preacher, and he didn't believe in slavery, so he set me free. I got my papers." He reached in his pocket, pulled out a worn yellow piece of paper and showed it to Jenny.

"Can't read it. What's it say?"

"It says I am now twenty-five years old, have been certified at the court and registered as a 'free person of colour,' that I am six feet six inches tall, and that I have a scar on my back, and that I was freed by a deed in 1805."

"What you doin' here then?" asked Jenny.

"I gets to work around the other plantations, doing smithy work and get my own pay. When work is through at one place I moves on to another. People around here knows me. Been doing this for 'bout five years or more."

"Was you born here?"

"No, I was born next to Nashville and you knows that is almost to Alabama where my mammy lives. Have you ever been to Nashville?"

"No, can't say as I have. I wasn't allowed to go nowhere when I lived in Virginia. This is the first time I been away."

"Any your folks free?" asked Zack.

"No, but my mama says we're entitled, not from our marse but because we are from an Injun grandmama. For years my mama has talked about getting her freedom, and she wants us all—all eleven of us—to be free. There is some grandchildren too, about thirty-some in all in our family now, but none free."

"You wanna be free?" asked Zack, studying her reaction closely.

"Don't everybody want freedom? I surely do, all my family do too. But how to get it is one thing we ain't been able to do. Not yet, anyhow."

"I can help," offered Zack.

"How can you do that? I hear you can get picked up by the patty-rollers if you help somebody do that."

"Well, there is ways," said Zack.

When Christmas time came to the slave quarters, there was extra meat, even some apple brandy from the master's still house. But most of all there was time away from the regular duties. The Love family followed the tradition and gave their slaves a week off.

Miss Alice talked about going back to the Mountain early in the new year, and Zack talked of moving back toward Nashville, probably before Christmas. Barbara was lying on the cot in the slave cabin next to Jenny's, alternately shivering and burning with fever. Chloe had been allowed to visit the next plantation where some of her children were being raised and where she hoped to find their father.

Over the past few weeks Zack had been busy, but on the day before Christmas, he came to the cabin and found Jenny alone.

"Jenny, we see each other most every day for the past weeks, and I think we sort of like each other. Don't you say so?" asked Zack in a whisper. He stared out the cabin window with his back half turned to Jenny and waited.

Jenny bent her head and stared at the floor. She mumbled a sort of "Yes, guess so."

"I want you to come with me when I leaves here, be my wife, and I'll help you to run away and be free."

Jenny stammered and stuttered. What? No one had ever offered to help her before, and no one had ever told her they liked her. She knew she was not like others; she was tall, big, and as she put it, "not much to look at." Here she had to make a decision on her own, away from everyone, a secret decision which could change her life.

"You know I wanna be free. How can I do that? Tell me!"

Zack reached in his pocket and pulled out a paper. "First of all, I got here a paper that says you free. Never mind how I gets it, but I gets it. And it says you got the same last name as me—Robertson. In other words, you my wife.

176

We can travel together until we get to Nashville or wherever we wants to go. I know folks there, and you can get settled right quick with a family. I can get a place to work in the city. The biggest risk is running away from here."

"Oh goodness, you make it sound so great 'til you get to the last part—running away," sighed Jenny.

"The way I figure it, we could leave at night and if we's lucky we'll have a little moon. We need to leave during this Christmas time when nobody is really looking for us. We can travel at night for a couple nights and be down the road a long ways before they misses us. They won't be looking for me nohow, cause they knows I'm ready to leave here. And they might not miss you for a couple of days. The biggest thing is, we can't tell anybody of the plan. What you say?"

"How we gonna eat and stay warm and find our way?" Jenny had so many questions.

"Don't worry 'bout any of that. I'll take care of all that. Just come with me, be my wife, and be free."

Jenny heard her mother's words again. Be free! Be free! Run away if you have to! She looked Zack Robertson in the eye and said, "Yes, yes, yes!"

Two days after Zack and Jenny left the Love plantation, Alice walked to the cabin where Chloe and Jenny had been living, but no one was there. When she called for Barbara, a low moan came from next door. Alice stuck her head inside and asked, "Where's Jenny?"

"Don't know. I been sleeping all day. Still have the fever." Barbara curled up in the blankets and turned her back to the door. Alice returned to the back porch where Mary was supervising the servants as they were washing some of the children's clothes.

"I can't find Jenny. Where has that child gone?"

Mary reassured her. "She's probably over at the neighbor's with Chloe. Remember, I told her she could go over there to see the children."

By dark it was clear to Alice that something had happened. She was not sure just what it was but her inner feelings told her it was something bad. If Jenny had run away, she surely could be caught. She knew nothing of the roads, or the places in Tennessee, and with her unusual appearance everyone would surely recognize her as a stranger.

The next morning David Love learned that Zack had left a day or so ago.

"Most likely those two left here together," said David. Now we must put an advertisement in the newspaper."

"Which one?" asked Alice.

"I reckon it has to be *The Democratic Clarion and Tennessee Gazette* in Nashville, the only one we got."

The two worded the offer of the reward for Jenny's return, and David wrote it for the newspaper.

> *$50 reward for runaway from her mistress*
> *Alice Draper, visiting near Nashville at*
> *the plantation of David Love, a large yellow*
> *girl, 15 years of age, tall, with delicate face,*
> *long straight black hair tied back with a red*
> *ribbon. Left about December 26. Goes by the*
> *name of Jenny. May be traveling with a black-*
> *smith by the name of Zack, six feet six inches*
> *tall. David Love, Wilson County, Tennessee.*

Weeks went by and no one responded to the ad. None

of the local folks had seen Jenny, and no one seemed to remember when they last saw Zack. The only thing Alice could find out was that she had asked Barbara and Chloe about being free and therefore had to conclude that Jenny, at least for the time being, was free.

Alice wrote her brother John, to give him the news and the reason for her delay in returning to Virginia.

As for her journey back to Virginia, Alice asked her niece, Molly, to come to the Mountain for a visit. In the early spring, the two left Tennessee and made the trip back to Virginia without any news of Jenny. It seemed she was gone forever.

On her return to the Mountain, Alice asked for some other slaves and this time her father gave her Milly and Anne, two of Rachel's grandchildren.

Chapter 16

GOOD NEWS AND BAD NEWS

News reached Rachel and Judy and the Draper family in the spring of 1811 that Mitchell Clay had passed on to the other world, leaving a large family, numerous slaves, and several large tracts of land along the New River in Giles County. His will had divided his wealth among the children and grandchildren. For nearly forty years he had been among the leading citizens of the western part of Virginia, his wealth having started with land he acquired by selling Rachel and daughter Judy to John Draper in 1774.

In 1812 the nation was plunged headlong into war with England. The Speaker of the House, and a major leader of the War Hawks, was none other than a Henry Clay of Kentucky, a descendant of old Henry Clay of Powhatan. The younger Clay was known as the "Harry of the West." These westerners had a major stake in the economy of a nation that had been forbidden to ship its goods across the sea. With a choice of war against France or England, they chose the Mother Country. British arms were being provided to the western Indians. Impressments and seizures of shipping off the eastern coast had been happening on a regular basis. Also, there was a choice prize to the north, the English colony of Canada.

In Wythe County, the local militia was called to supply troops to Norfolk, and Joseph and Samuel Draper, grandsons of the captain, were among the men of Captain Christopher Brown's Company. Young men in their teens, they were ready to defend their country against the English even if they had to serve in the eastern part of Virginia. The war news came regularly to the Draper household and the captain withdrew more each day, reliving his days at Point Pleasant and in North Carolina. He remembered them well. He took his rifle from the rack over the fireplace, put it over his shoulder and marched up and down outside the cabin door, shouting orders to his company, "Attack, attack, the enemy is coming!"

He trampled over the remnants of the summer's garden. Profanity flowed from his mouth like the water in the rivers he had crossed. He cursed the wars, the Indians, the Tories, and now the English. He loaded up his saddle bags, took his slave, Will, and moved with his few possessions to a small cabin ten miles away from the Mountain where he regularly marched in the field reliving the horrors of those distant battles.

Regularly the old man took his tomahawk from the shelf, polishing it until he could see the face of a wild-looking gray-haired soldier. He wielded it over his head, shrieking at the red-skinned brave he saw in his troubled mind.

He dreaded the news that one of his grandsons might be lost in the war, and he took little interest in what his son John was doing at home.

After the younger John moved his wife and family to the homestead at the Mountain, he immediately began planning for the new brick house. He chose a location near the spring-fed pond and put the slaves to work digging the clay, molding the bricks, and piling them in the sun to dry. Thousands would be needed.

In the meantime, Samuel Findlay was bringing supplies to the troops and, early in 1813, came again to the lead mines. Believing Rachel was in the vicinity, he made inquiries along the way, finally learning that she was still at Captain John Draper's. Samuel decided to risk a stop there.

Arriving about noon on a windy March day, Samuel pulled his team into the yard, hobbled them and walked to the slave quarters. He saw several people making bricks and asked for Rachel.

"She's in the kitchen out back," offered a young black boy about ten.

Samuel followed the aroma of baked bread to the door of the kitchen, stuck his head inside, and called, "Rachel, you here?"

Rachel wheeled about from the fireplace and ran to her brother.

"Samuel! I thought you was never coming back this way."

They embraced, drew back to look at each other, and embraced again.

"I'm on my way to the lead mines directly. I got to come and find you. I wants you to have this piece of paper." He reached in his pocket and drew out the tattered piece of paper. "Rachel, this is the record of our freedom in Williamsburg."

Rachel hugged the paper to her neck and mumbled her thanks.

"I tried to find you a lawyer in Evansham years ago,

183

but nobody was there and I had to leave again. Dr. Boyd tried to help us. So did Bishop Asbury. I'm sorry we did no good."

"I'm so old now I can hardly walk. I'm sixty years old in a few months, and I'm scared that if I don't do something right now I won't be able to do nothing. I'm troubled 'bout the children and grandchildren, you know, about forty of them now and all depending on me to set them free. What am I going to do?"

Samuel thought a minute and then replied, "Sister, dear sister. When the time is right it's gonna happen. The Good Book says there is a time for everything. You need a lawyer, though. Nobody else can really do it for you."

"I know, I know," sighed Rachel.

"I got to go, Rachel. I'm due at the mines. Got to haul lead to the east for the army where the fightin's going on. After I make this trip I'm thinkin' I can settle down in Powhatan or someplace there. I'm getting too old for these long trips any way."

The two embraced once again and Samuel was gone. Rachel took the piece of paper to the slave quarters immediately, took out her needle and thread, took a scrap of material and made herself a little case. She made loops with some flax threads and when the case was finished, she tucked the paper inside and put it around her neck, hiding the valuable document beneath her dress. Here it would stay until the right time.

In May 1813 Rachel's man, Peter, became ill. He was now about sixty-five years old and he had been with the Drapers since the 1770s, laboring in the fields, planting crops, harvesting corn, building and repairing buildings, cutting stumps, driving the teams, watering the horses, milking the cows, birthing the calves, tending the sheep, delivering the lambs, and trying to do whatever his master asked him to do, as best he could. Scars on his back were proof of his inadequacies, at least in Captain Draper's mind.

Rachel hovered over her man, watching carefully for improvements in his condition. None came. Dr. Smith visited but had little to offer, except bleeding, which was done three times. Peter felt weaker as time wore on. On May 18, with Rachel at his side, along with the children and grandchildren Peter took his last breath.

Cato offered to fetch the Reverend Edward Morgan and to pass the word to the Pattons at Thorn Spring and to the captain and his other children who were in the neighborhood. Abraham began to build the coffin. Rachel and Judy prepared Peter for burial, washing him carefully and placing small silver coins on his eyelids. They dressed him in his best clothes, ragged and torn though they were.

Through the long "sittin' up night" they stayed by his side. Grandchildren came and went, and at dawn Polly came from the Pattons. Miss Ally gave her slaves permission to come to the funeral. Tom, Robbin, and Rachel's children at George's and James' soon arrived. Tom and Robbin went to the field with their shovels and there near the fence line began to dig the grave. Neighbors, black and white, who knew Peter came to pay their respects. Peter was well liked by all and had served his master well. But Captain Draper was unable to walk too far and did not see his faithful slave laid to rest.

At five o'clock Edward Morgan rode up on his black stallion. After an evening meal, the procession crossed the field to the grave site, their figures silhouetted against the yellow twilight sky.

Morgan committed the body of Peter to the earth and his soul to Almighty God, reciting the familiar lines, "there is a time to be born and a time to die."

Rachel came to the coffin, raised her hands up to the sky, and began speaking.

"Peter, you goin' to sleep now. It's evenin' time. You was good for me. You give me many children, and most of them is here today. We all loved you."

"Amen, amen," came from the children like a rehearsed chorus.

"I know there is a time to be born and a time to die. But our time ain't come yet. We got much to do, much to do." Rachel looked up and down the line of children and grand-children nodding her head as if everyone understood what she was talking about.

Tom turned to Robbin and said, "What's Mama trying to say, anyway? Pappy's dead and gone and she talking about doin' something. Don't make no sense to me."

Robbin nodded as Rachel's hands relaxed from their raised position over her head. She tried to kneel to the ground and when Tom saw she could not do it without falling he took his mother's arm.

"Get me some of that earth, chile. I want Peter to be sent off good."

"Yes, Mama." Amelia picked up the copper-colored soil and handed it to her mother, who once again began to speak.

"We's like this here earth. But that don't mean we don't have somethin' special to do—and it don't mean that we ain't part of the world. We all got a special place to be, and a special somethin' to do. Right now we got to say goodbye to Peter who's done gone into the next world. This earth is like part of us going with him. We all got a spirit inside us that tells us what to do. Even though Peter's gone, his spirit is with us too. If we don't forget him, he be with us all the time. And he knows we is with him."

Gradually grains of dirt fell on the pine box as Rachel moved along the fence row. First Rachel, then each of the children and grandchildren took a handful of the earth and spread it over the wooden box as they filed past and began their walk to the slave quarters. Only Tom and Robbin would remain behind to shovel the dirt back into the hole. When they finished at the grave site, they placed two pieces of locust, one at the head and one at the foot, to mark the spot where Peter was buried.

Rachel hobbled along on the way back to the house. Morgan walked beside her. "Rachel," he began, "You have been on my mind a lot lately. I finally found someone who had heard of a case like yours. You know that Rachel Viney over at Pattons? Well, her case was like yours, and after many years in the courts, she finally got her freedom for herself and her children. She got a lawyer in Christiansburg to handle her case. You will have to find one in Evansham."

"I know," said Rachel. And in a determined voice she added, "I'll find one, I will."

When Rachel reached the entrance to the slave quarters, Judy took her arm and helped her up the steps. Soon all the family were together.

Rachel stood in the middle of the room and began to speak. The little room was hushed.

"Now's the time, my children. Peter is gone, some of my children is gone, some of my grandchildren is gone and all in slavery. You must—no, *we* must—all go to the courthouse, find a lawyer and get free."

Rachel wiped her eyes with her apron and continued as all eyes were fastened on her wrinkled face.

187

"Mama, you want to be free. Tom wants to be free." Robbin was interrupted.

"Mama, me and my children wants to be free too. We all wants to be free," added Judy. "All of us over at Miss Ally's wants to be free and them at Pattons want to be free."

Rachel smiled to herself. Yes, these children and grandchildren had the spirit. She began to speak again. "Peter and me talked this over. I told him I would never leave him, but when he was gone, I would get all of you together and we'd all go, all of us, together, to bring our cases. None of us gonna be alone. This is my plan, the family plan."

"As you knows, the Drapers don't want us to go no place. We ain't been able to get to the courthouse over in Evansham, either together or alone. We'll do this, we'll all do this," said Judy.

"This is the plan," Rachel continued. "I'll leave early one morning and walk to Evansham. No one will miss me until it's too late. And even if they do, they probably would never guess where I'm at. They don't bother me much these days. As for you boys, I done decided you should take a chance and run away. You can't leave together but we'll all leave, late at night or early morning. We can do it. And Judy and her children got to leave too. And we will meet you in Evansham at the courthouse."

All of the children and grandchildren huddled together around Rachel encouraging her, promising to help her, and promising to help each other. There were tears and hugs. They would decide on a date soon, and Tom and Robbin would spread the word.

"Get out of there, you niggers," shouted John Draper. "Get on the road. Go home! There'll be no nigger gathering here. The funeral is over, now get on out of here."

The slave cabin emptied quickly, and the group left the premises to return to their master's rule a few miles away. Judy went to the big house. Rachel rested on her cot, her head churning with ideas for getting rid of her chains.

"What's goin' on here? Rachel, get out here!" shouted the captain. "Get out here."

Rachel hobbled to the doorway, leaned against the frame and was surprised to see the captain standing at the foot of the steps, his rifle over his shoulder. When he saw Rachel, he charged up the stairs, grabbed her by her long graying hair and pulled her to the ground. He put his gun down in the dirt and picked up a switch which was sticking out from under the steps. "You will never be free, nigger, never, never, never!" Each word was accented with a thrust of the switch. Rachel's dress tore and blood came from the gashes on her back. She tried to raise her heavy frame from the ground, but each time she did, she was thrown back into the dust.

"I heard you and Bettie talking about getting your freedom. Bettie won't help you. I won't let her. Bettie, where are you?"

Rachel knew where Bettie was—asleep forever in the family cemetery in the field not far from the house. *The man has no mind—he can't remember she is gone. Been gone for years,* Rachel said to herself.

"Get up, get up, get up!" shouted the captain as he put the switch aside and picked up the gun.

"Don't you know they are ready to attack? Attack, men! Attack!" He shouted and screamed and began his ritual march. Rachel escaped into the house.

189

Chapter 17

RACHEL GOES TO COURT: 1813

Rachel Findlay's back was sore, the welts, bruises, and injuries not healed. Her wrists were stiff and scarred. She now was sixty years old, crippled in her knees and back, and carried too many pounds. Her black, Indian-colored braids were sprinkled with gray and hung down her back and over her stooped shoulders.

Rachel reviewed her life. It had not been easy, and it would be over soon. She had accomplished little, except responsibility for bringing into the world more than forty descendants who were still held in slavery illegally. Every time she had mentioned the possibility of freedom, she had felt the whip, endured the shackles, and suffered the starvation.

In June 1813 she and the family set the day. She was now ready to run away, to escape the torture of many years. If she died in the process, so what? No one cared about an old slave woman any more. No one would bother to come after her. No one would stop her from carrying out her plan. Her Peter was gone, laid to rest at the edge of the Draper field, and Judy, and her children and grandchildren were scattered.

She hoped her youngest daughter, Jenny, was free, somewhere in the South. But she had no idea where she was. Other children and grandchildren were given to Draper's daughters, Rhoda and Elizabeth, and when they moved West they were probably sold. She knew nothing about them either. But now, she had nothing to lose, except being ordered to remove herself from Virginia. It really didn't matter to her any more where she would go or what she would do. It was her children and grandchildren that she thought about. She wanted them to be free. And she had a plan. All would run away to get help.

Rachel was glad to learn that her oldest sons, Tom, Robbin and Peter, shared her longing to be free. They too had suffered, been beaten, whipped, and fastened to the wall. They were no longer young men, but heading toward forty. They would assist their mother in her journey. But they could not leave together. They promised to find each other near the courthouse when they arrived in Evansham. They all would be in great danger, traveling without permission and without papers. They would be called runaways if they were caught.

Rachel opened the log cabin door where she had spent most of her life. The slave quarters were dilapidated and sparsely furnished. She had nothing to take with her, except her cane, her red shawl, a few pieces of silver, some cornbread, and the precious paper carefully wrapped in the cloth bag around her neck. All else was left behind as she began her walk to the courthouse in Evansham. She smiled and her heart pounded with joy—she was walking to freedom.

The sun had not surfaced above the eastern sky, but the dim light was enough for her to see the road and begin her journey. The fog still lay peacefully in the valleys, its mist covering the creeks and ponds with an extra silky layer. The cane, stout and heavy, was Rachel Findlay's only support. Her shoes were worthless, so she walked barefoot along the Great Road heading West. She knew she would have to rest often and she knew it would take a very long time to get to the court, but June was to be an important month, if she could just get to town. Maybe she could arrive before the court adjourned and find a lawyer who would help her. And she would meet her sons and the others of her family.

As she limped along the dusty road, Rachel sang softly the little songs she used to sing to Judy and the children. She recited the verses from the Bible and talked to herself. Her breath was short and raspy. She stopped to rest at the Lithia Spring, sat on her shawl, and refreshed herself with the fine spring waters. She washed her face and after a bite of corn bread, she raised up and continued the westward path, determined to reach her goal.

Her ankles were swollen, her legs were aching and every bone in her body seemed to hate what she was doing. She stopped often to lean on her cane. She forced herself to walk on. But her body was worn, tired, and demanding too much. Rachel Findlay took a deep breath, her eyes rolled back, and she collapsed on the edge of the road, falling on top of her red shawl, near the roadside ditch. She had only made it the vicinity of Locust Hill, the home of the Grahams.

The elder Robert Graham had been proud of his sons and his two families. But his life had ended about two years ago, leaving his two families to wrangle over their legacies, slaves, land and other property. Samuel and James

Graham, his sons, had been set up in a mercantile business at their home on the Great Road. They named the place Locust Hill. Business had been brisk and there was much demand for their goods, especially now that the militia had been called to active duty. Samuel himself was subject to duty as the war in Eastern Virginia heated up with the English invasion. Today, though, the two merchants saddled bays and called upon their Negro slave, George, to hitch the gray horses to the wagon. They would leave shortly for Evansham where they hoped to get some news about the militia and about some legal matters that were pending. They would also purchase supplies.

The sun had risen and the dew on the grass began to evaporate. Early morning in June was a special treat, not too hot and not too cool. The blue mountains to the south, now fresh with tinges of light green maple leaves, and the peaks ahead created a perfect pastoral scene. In a few hours the Graham entourage would be at the courthouse.

The Great Road had come alive! Horses, wagons, carts, cattle, turkeys, and walkers, blacks and whites, crowded the road, most going West. Some would stop at court, others would be taking the longer road to Tennessee or Kentucky. All had to travel the same road. Some wagons were loaded with household goods, others with young children or elderly travelers and some with trade goods for court day. Some north-bound wagons were headed to Baltimore, Philadelphia and Richmond, or places in the Valley of Virginia.

"Samuel, what's this?" asked James. "I see something red there on the side of the road."

"Probably an old rag, not worth anything," said Samuel.

"Probably so, but you know me, curious to know what it is. I am going to stop a minute."

194

James climbed off his horse and walked toward the ditch where he saw more than a red shawl.

"Samuel, come here, help me." James moved toward the still figure, face down on the red shawl.

Samuel dismounted and joined his brother, and together they turned the elderly yellow woman over, believing her to be dead. But such was not the case, for as she was turned she fluttered her eyelids and opened her eyes.

"Nigger, what's the matter with you? Are you drunk or sick?" asked James.

"Neither, sir," muttered Rachel. "Just that this walkin' is too much for me. My breath was short, and I guess I just fell over. Walkin' to Evansham I am, but doesn't look like I can make it. I's just too weak."

James and Samuel helped her to her feet, retrieved her cane and shawl and watched while she dusted herself off, wrapped the shawl around her shoulders, and with cane in hand she began to resume her walk to Evansham.

James whispered to Samuel, "I don't think she can make it. Wanna' give her a ride?"

"George is right behind us and has an empty wagon. Why not? Those niggers can talk to each other all the way to town."

"What's your name, old woman?" asked James.

"It's Rachel, sir."

"Well, Rachel, our wagon will be coming along here directly. Our boy George is driving and can take you to town."

"Oh, sir, thank you. And who might you be?" asked Rachel.

"We're old man Graham's sons, Samuel and James."

"Thank you, thank you, thank you." Rachel kept repeating her thanks and was still mumbling to herself about how the Lord had looked after her when the wagon came alongside. The boys helped her into the wagon and she and George were soon settled and on their way to the courthouse.

When Rachel arrived in Evansham she thanked George and made her way across the street toward the brown and white courthouse, hoping to find her sons. She felt refreshed and revived. And thankful. She would never have been able to survive the walk to the courthouse.

The courthouse was a two-story frame structure. Cato, Judy's Cato, had often mentioned his visits to town when he saw the work going on. He had seen the carpenters, the masons, and the painters do their work. Rachel passed the small log jail and went up the steps to the double doors of the courthouse. She went inside looking for the boys. They were not in the hallway. She entered the blue courtroom and saw four Gentlemen Justices on the bench. She heard them speaking that language she did not understand. She would later know that they were Straw, Nye, Stanger, and Lindenberger. Her sons were not there either.

Rachel limped back to the door, down the steps and back to Main Street. The boys came out of the Marshall Inn and greeted her with good news.

"Mama, we done found you a lawyer, and he wants to see you as soon as you can. His name is Granville Henderson. His office is on Main Street just a little ways from here. Come on." Robbin, Tom and Peter helped her down Main Street to a small log building, where the scales of justice hung above the door. It was the office of Granville Henderson, Esquire.

"Mama, this lawyer, Henderson, everybody says he is

the lawyer for you. They say he is smart, and has a warm heart. He'll know what to do."

Henderson stood over six feet tall, and his penetrating blue eyes were the prominent feature of his youthful face. He appeared to be in his twenties. Rachel sat opposite him gazing at the blond hair and youthful features. Was this young man her key to freedom? It hardly seemed possible, but her sons had insisted he could do the job.

"Rachel, I have heard the details of your case from your sons here. All we have to do now is convince the court that you may have a case, and then I will be appointed to represent you. What I need from you is that piece of paper from Williamsburg," said Henderson holding out his hand.

Rachel reached in her bosom and from the small flannel bag she retrieved the document which gave her Grandmama Chance, Rachel, Samuel, and Judy their freedom in 1773.

"Here 'tis. She handed the wrinkled and creased piece of yellowing paper to her lawyer.

"Thank you, Rachel. Please wait here and I will return in a few minutes. I have to go to the courthouse to find a justice and to the jail to find the sheriff."

"The sheriff? What we need the sheriff for?" asked Rachel.

"When the court agrees to hear the case, you will be protected by the sheriff and kept in his care until your master can post a bond," explained Henderson. "He will find you a place to stay and contact Draper about the bond."

Rachel looked at Tom and Robbin questioningly. "It's the way it's done," said Tom. "There's no danger, Mama."

Henderson returned from the courthouse shortly with the Deputy Sheriff Reddick. "It is done, Rachel. Justice John Stanger has reviewed your paper and agreed that you might have a case, and the others on the bench concluded the same. They have given me the authority to file the papers, not only for you but for these boys too. Your Master Draper must sign a bond in the amount of five hundred dollars for each of you, promising that he will not maltreat you during the time the case is pending. If he does, he must pay the money. After he signs the bond you will go back to his place, but in the meantime, Deputy Reddick, our local gunsmith and also the jailer, will take you all to Marshall's where you will stay with their slaves until we hear from Draper. Your master will pay."

The four, Rachel, Robbin, Tom, and Peter, were en route to freedom. Now there was no turning back. Henderson had been successful in getting the case to be heard, and he was fortunate in that result. Seldom did the justices sitting on the court agree to hear such cases, although few had been proposed in their area. Many of the justices were slave owners, and not interested in freeing anyone. Today, Henderson had a panel of justices, all of whom were German-speaking, and who seldom had slaves. If they did, they had two or three or maybe four to help on their farms or at the mill or ordinary while the landowners tended to court business. There was none of this thirty, forty or fifty slaves in their neighborhoods. In general, they had no qualms about freedom for those who deserved it.

In the summer of 1813 Rachel and her sons returned to Draper Mountain. The captain had put up his bond promising not to interfere with her case. She was granted permission to travel to her former home on Swift Creek and get the depositions she needed for evidence.

Rachel was in the log kitchen at the Mountain preparing the corn bread for the evening meal. As Judy came in the door, she called out, "Mama, I got good news."

"What is it?" asked Rachel.

"I found a lawyer, a Mr. Henley Chapman, and he is our lawyer. You know, for me and my children, Lockey, Rhoda, Sam and Abram. We filed the same as you, for trespass, assault and battery and false imprisonment."

"What about my granddaughter, Milly, and her child, Harvey, and for Milly's girl, Anna, and her child Calvin?"

"Mama, they sued Miss Alice. They got Mr. Chapman too."

"I am so glad. Now, I can see that all of this depends on my trip to Swift Creek," said Rachel. "You can't be free unless I is free."

"That's right. And the captain, he gave us the bond too. And for Miss Alice too. But all of these court things takes time."

"I should go to find my witnesses tomorrow, but with the troops on the way to the east and the war going on, I reckon I best stay here until it is safe. I saw Captain Samuel Graham and his men pass this way a few days ago. They was going to Norfolk."

"Yes, Mama, be safe. You can ask the court again to get the depositions. Just think, when all thirty or forty of us gets free, the Drapers will have no help at all. They's goin' to fight us to the bitter end," said Judy.

"I reckon so," said Rachel.

The following summer, Rachel and Attorney Henderson traveled to Powhatan together, a distance of about two hundred miles. Rachel, heavy and uncomfortable, mounted and rode the horse as a man, day after day after day. No side saddle for her. On July 25, 1814, she and Henderson, John Draper, Jr., representing the family, and the witnesses met at the house of John Dean. There, George Radford, John Langsdon and Fanny Langsdon told what they knew about Rachel and her grandmother Chance.

The following spring at the March term of the Wythe County Court, Gentlemen Justices, Joseph Crockett, John Stanger, Hugh McGavock, James Devor and George W. Davis, were on the bench. Granville Henderson rose to his full height, cleared his throat, pushed his blond hair to the side and addressed the court.

"Gentlemen, on behalf of my client, Rachel, that is Rachel Findlay, standing here with me today, I respect-fully petition the court to set a date for the trial of Rachel and her children against John Draper, Sr. You are well acquainted with the facts, for the chief topic of conversation, as you know, for the past two years or so anywhere in the county has been Rachel's freedom suit."

No one was closer to the facts than Justice Joseph Crockett. His sister Jane was the wife of the younger John Draper. His cousin Hugh McGavock, also with a Crockett connection, knew every detail as well as Joseph or the Drapers did. And having it within their power to cast their vote against the hearing, and for the benefit of their family connections, they had no hesitation is saying, "I vote no."

Devor and Davis joined them, and said, "I vote no."

John Stanger, voting in Rachel's favor at the previous hearing, voted yes.

"The majority have denied the petition, Mr. Henderson. Case dismissed," said Justice Crockett.

Henderson had expected that decision. What else could Crockett and McGavock do? Certainly, family came before some Negro slaves who claimed to be descended from an Indian.

Henderson coughed, covered his mouth with his silk handkerchief, thanked the justices and left the courtroom, followed by Rachel. They returned quickly to his office on Main Street where they were soon joined by John P. Nye, one of the justices who knew Rachel's story well. He was on the bench the day her petition was filed two years ago. Henderson requested that he write her new petition.

Henderson turned to the door and said, "I will be back before long. I have another client waiting at the courthouse. Rachel, Mr. Nye will help you get the paper written."

Justice Nye sat at the walnut desk and began to write with his quill pen, dipping into the inkstand as needed. Rachel's petition was directed to the Honorable Peter Johnston, one of the judges of the General Court, living in Abingdon, Virginia. The document began with the usual formalities.

> *Your petitioner Rachel Findlay humbly represents that,many years ago the grandmother of your plaintiff was taken by a certain—Clay from the Indian nation and brought to the county of Powhatan in this state as your petitioner understood expects to prove—that her said grandmother was born an Indian and free. That your petitioner's mother was a daughter of said grandmother. That about 40 years ago your petitioner instituted a suit for her freedom against her then*

> *Master upon which she has understood and be-*
> *lieves a verdict and judgment was rendered in*
> *her favor of her title to freedom. But before the*
> *determination of said suit, a certain Mitchell*
> *Clay, a descendant of him above mentioned, fear-*
> *ing the result of said suit brought her from the*
> *county of Powhatan to New River where she was*
> *sold to a certain John Draper with whom she*
> *has since resided and who now claims her as his*
> *slave.*

Nye read what he had written to Rachel."Uh huh, that's it. That's right. Mitchell sold me to Marse Draper. Never thought he would, but he did," said Rachel. The tears came to her eyes as she said, "And so many years with Draper and the whip."

"In this next paragraph I will tell the judge about the delays, about your trip to Powhatan and then mention Crockett's connection and reason for the refusal of a court hearing," said Nye, again dipping his pen into the ink. The scratching on the paper began again.

> *That in the month of June in 1813 your peti-*
> *tioner instituted a suit against John Draper in*
> *the County Court of Wythe for her freedom, since*
> *which the said suit has remained upon the docket*
> *of said Court. Your petitioner would further state*
> *that in consequence of unjust and oppressive re-*
> *strictions imposed by the County Court upon*
> *those of her descendants that could aid her in*
> *traveling a journey, she being upwards of 60*
> *years of age, she was unable to go to the county*
> *of Powhatan until last summer where she could*

prove her title to freedom. That she there met with persons who knew her and whose deposi-tions have been taken and clearly prove your petitioner to be a descendant of an Indian through the female line.

Again, Henderson read the paragraph to Rachel, and she nodded her head in agreement. Was she really sixty years old? Had she been with Draper forty years?

Nye continued his writing,

That John Draper, Jr., intermarried with the sister of Captain Joseph Crockett of Wythe County, and it would be difficult to procure a court of justices that were no ways related to said Draper and your petitioner could not have a trial of her cause at the March Term, 1815, in consequence of some of the magistrates refus-ing to set for above mentioned reason.

"Rachel, how many descendants, you know, children and grandchildren do you have by now?" asked Nye.

"It's probably now between thirty and forty, and more on the way." Rachel smiled.

"Very well," said Nye, again picking up the quill and beginning to write.

Your petitioner has between thirty and forty descendants, children and grandchildren, the lib-erties of all of whom depend the determination of the suit and your petitioner is old and very infirm her living cannot be much longer calcu-lated upon and should she die previous to the

203

*decision the means of proving their right to free-
dom would be much lessened. Your petitioner
therefore humbly hopes and prays that Your
Honor will grant a certiorari for the purposes
of removing her said suit to the Superior Court
of Law holden for Wythe County especially since
it has been unnecessarily delayed, and as in duty
bound will ever pray.*

Justice Nye wrote the acknowledgment, added the date of March 10, 1815, and signed his name.

On March 22, 1815, Judge Peter Johnston granted the request and the case was transferred to the Wythe County Superior Court of Law. Now the case would be heard before long, thought Rachel. But it was not to be.

Further depositions were taken in the spring of 1816 when Rachel and her attorney Henderson once again had to travel to Powhatan County. Henderson hated to leave home now because after a year of marriage with Alexander Smyth's daughter, Darthula, he had a little daughter named Nancy Smyth Henderson.

In 1816 the case was transferred to Powhatan County for further action, primarily because Rachel's witnesses were too frail and elderly to make the long trip to Wythe County to testify in the court. Although the case was again scheduled for hearing in 1818, Mr. Henderson could not be there. In 1819 the case was continued several times, finally scheduled to begin on May 11, 1820.

Chapter 18

THE TRIAL BEGINS

On the morning of May 11, 1820, the Powhatan County crowd gathered early on the courthouse square. The newly formed celery-colored leaves on the maple trees provided shade. Smells of breakfast came from the nearby inn. Several of the men had crossed the road to the steps and entered the dining room from the long front porch. The court officials, attorneys, and members of the sheriff's team were busy at the courthouse door checking the names of each juryman as they arrived.

When Rachel, Mr. Nash, her Powhatan County attorney, and several of her cousins of Powhatan arrived, they walked slowly toward the four white columns and the portico. A crowd had gathered along the sidewalk and under the trees. Two whiskered ruffians tipped their flasks and danced around the group.

"Henry, I hear this nigger wants to be free," screamed Michael Pettyjohn. "You hear that? She wants to be free. She ain't gonna be free, no she ain't."

"Not this one, not any of 'em," shouted Henry Maxwell."We don't need any more free niggers 'round here."

Mr. Nash moved to one side, pushing Rachel along the

sidewalk, and calling to the sheriff.

"Sheriff, get these drunken sots out of our way."

The sheriff moved into the crowd as Pettyjohn and Maxwell stumbled toward the tavern.

Rachel hoped that entering the courthouse would change her life. Today she would taste freedom at last.

Rachel sat quietly with Mr. Nash to the left of the judge on the bench. Across the room were the Drapers, John, Jr., and his son, Joseph, and their attorney. Her old master, the captain, was too frail to make the trip.

The bailiff called the court to order. "Oyez, oyez, this court is now in session. Judge Peter Randolph presiding."

The clerk called the case, and jury selection began. After an hour or more the twelve who would decide the fate of the Findlay family were sworn in and the judge adjourned the court until the following morning at eleven. Rachel was disappointed. Her hopes had been certain of victory this day, but it did not happen. Nor did it happen the following day as the court was adjourned again. On May 13 Rachel once more entered the Powhatan courthouse for another taste of freedom.

The bailiff and Judge Randolph entered the courtroom to discover that it was full with standing room along the side walls. In the balcony the blacks, mulattoes, and free persons of color were seated together overlooking the crowded room. Judge Randolph took a seat, the bailiff banged the gavel on the desk and announced, "All rise." Feet shuffled and those seated struggled to the upright position while the bailiff continued.

"Oyez, oyez, oyez! Silence is commanded upon pain of imprisonment while the honorable Judge Peter Randolph of the Circuit Court of the County of Powhatan is now sitting. All persons having motions to make, pleas to enter, suits to prosecute, or other business before the court, come forward and they shall be heard. God save the Commonwealth and this honorable court."

After taking a deep breath, the bailiff added, "You may be seated."

The clerk announced the case to the spectators in the courtroom, Rachel Findlay versus John Draper, Sr., and asked the attorneys if they were ready to proceed. Both responded in the affirmative.

John Nash rose to his feet, twiddled with his watch chain, smoothed his black hair from his face and began his opening statement.

"Gentlemen of the Jury, I represent Rachel Findlay, the sixty-seven-year-old woman you now see before you. For the past forty-seven years she has been illegally held in slavery because of actions of the Clay family of this county. You will hear the story of her grandmother, Chance, who was captured by the Indian trader Henry Clay and his friend Peter Womack in South Carolina from a tribe known as the Catawbas. You will learn that in 1712 when she was brought to Virginia, not far from here, it was illegal to hold a person of Indian heritage in bondage, and yet it was done by the Clay family."

Nash moved closer to the jurors. "In 1770, Rachel, her daughter Judy, and her brother, Samuel, filed in the General Court in Williamsburg for their freedom, and on May 4, 1773, the court granted their request and they were declared free. You may well ask then what are we doing here today if she is free? That is a good question. We will show by our witnesses that Mitchell Clay deliberately took her and her young daughter from Powhatan County to the then frontier of the New River, more than two hundred miles

207

away. There he sold her and her daughter to Mr. John Draper, Sr., not as Indian slaves, but as Negro slaves. So the question to be decided today is this, is Rachel Findlay a Negro slave or an Indian slave and entitled to her freedom?"

Nash turned to face Judge Randolph and continued. "We will prove that the Rachel here before you is in fact the same Rachel who obtained her right to freedom in 1773. And that she is the same Rachel who was sold by Mitchell Clay to John Draper, Sr., who now claims her as his Negro slave. And we will show that she has been legally free from 1773 and yet held illegally by the Drapers for these many many years."

Turning to the jury again and in his loudest voice, he declared, "Rachel was free but held in chains. When you hear all of the evidence, we believe that you will decide that Rachel is entitled to her freedom again. Thank you."

Nash sat down, wiped his brow and threw his hair away from his face. He looked across the room as Draper's attorney rose to defend the comments just made. At the table sat John W. Jones watching as his senior partner and mentor, John Robertson, began his opening statement.

Robertson was elderly, stout, and commanding in his appearance. His six-foot frame was slightly bent, his shoulders stooped and his back arched. His gray hair met his black coat at the shoulders. He cleared his throat and began in a clear, loud voice.

"Gentlemen of the jury, today you will hear from several elderly people telling this court what they know of events that took place more than one hundred years ago. Obviously they were not there, and so instead of facts you will be listening to hearsay, to what others have told them, and to what they believe they remember. It is oral tradition and I want you gentlemen of the jury to remember that when you make your decision today."

Robertson waved a piece of paper at the jury and continued, "The Drapers, on the other hand, are not relying on tradition of many years ago, but on a document, this document, which you will see shortly, a signed document that records the names of Rachel and her daughter and informed Mr. Draper, and will inform you, that she and her daughter are Negroes."

Putting the document on the table, he approached the jury and added his final words.

"It is certain that when you listen to all the evidence and see the documents presented that you will decide that Rachel is a Negro woman and is not entitled to her freedom. Thank you."

Judge Randolph spoke to Mr. Nash. "You may call your first witness."

"I call John Langsdon, Your Honor."

The elderly Langsdon, now eighty-one years old, made his way slowly to the witness chair, his breathing labored and loud. After he had dropped himself into the chair, the clerk gave him the Bible and he promised to tell the truth. Mr. Nash began his questions.

"Mr. Langsdon, how old are you and where do you live?"

"I am eighty-one years old, and I was born and raised and still live in Powhatan County."

"Did you ever know William Clay?"

"Yes, I did, and I know he owned a slave named Rachel, the daughter of an Indian woman."

"Did any of the Indian woman's children ever recover their freedom?"

"Yes, they did. They filed lawsuits."

"Do you know a man named Sam or Samuel Findlay?"

"Yes, I do know Sam, a brother to Rachel, and I know he was one of those who obtained their freedom."

"Did you know a man named Mitchell Clay?"

"Yes, I did. He was the son of William Clay and I know that he conveyed Rachel away from here."

"Do you know why he did that?"

"It was the general belief in the neighborhood that he conveyed her away for the purpose of preventing her obtaining her freedom."

"Where did Mitchell Clay take her?"

"I understood that he took her to the back settlements."

"Do you see in this courtroom anyone you believe might be that Rachel that was carried off?"

"I do. She is the large yellow woman seated at your table. I believe she is identical to the Rachel carried off by Mitchell Clay."

"Thank you, Mr. Langsdon. Mr. Draper's attorney will now ask you some questions." Nash sat down at his table beside Rachel.

The towering Mr. Robertson stood in front of Mr. Langsdon and began his questioning.

"Did you know Rachel was a granddaughter of an Indian woman?"

"I heard the Clays themselves say so."

"Did you particularly know the mother of Rachel?"

"I did not know her."

"What children of the grandmother or mother of Rachel have recovered their freedom by suit?"

"I do not know."

"Were the four Indians reported to have been brought by Clay and Womack from the Catawba Indian nation males or females?"

"I have always understood from the Clay family that they were male and female."

"Do you know of your own knowledge that the grandmother of Rachel was brought from the Indian nation?"

"I do not."

"What did you understand became of the Indian man that was brought from the nation?"

"I don't know."

"That is all, Mr. Langsdon. I have no further questions at this time."

Mr. Langsdon returned to his seat in the courtroom and helped his wife, Fanny, to the witness chair as Mr. Nash had called her name to testify next. She walked with her cane to the front of the courtroom, took the oath and eased into the witness chair.

"You are Fanny Langsdon, the wife of John Langsdon?" asked Nash.

"Yes, I am."

"How old are you?"

"I am now seventy-five years old."

"Did you know William and Henry Clay?"

"Yes, I did. I was born and raised here in Powhatan County and have remained here all my life. They were near neighbors."

"Did the Clays own slaves that were descendants of Indians?"

"Yes, they did."

"Which one of them owned Rachel who is seated at my table?"

"William Clay owned Rachel."

"Did you know Rachel's mother and grandmother, the one who was taken from the Indian nation?"

"Yes, I did."

211

"Did any of the descendants ever recover their freedom?"

"Yes, descendants of both of them, except those conveyed away from here."

"Was Rachel one of those who was conveyed away?"

"Yes, she was taken by Mitchell Clay, under the pretext of making a crop in Mecklenburg, for the purpose of depriving her of an opportunity of suing for her freedom."

"What have you heard about Rachel other than that?"

"Nothing until I was called upon to give my depositions a few years ago."

"How was it you knew something of this matter?"

"I was a relative of William Clay and often visited the family, and I have a perfect recollection and personal knowledge of Rachel."

"You were raised in the family of William Clay?"

"Yes, I was."

"Did he own a colored woman named Nan?"

"Yes, he did. He said she was born of an Indian mother."

"Who was Nan in relation to Rachel seated at the table over there?"

"Nan had a daughter Rachel and I remember seeing her suckling her."

"When Henry Clay died, what happened to Rachel?"

"She was left to his son, William, who retained her in his possession until some Negroes in the same family sued for their freedom."

"What happened next?"

"Rachel was taken by Mitchell Clay, son of William, to Thomas Clay's under the pretense of making a crop."

"How long did she stay there?"

"I believe she stayed until she had a child and then was taken by Mitchell Clay."

"Did you ever see Mitchell Clay after that time?"

"Yes, I did, and he said he had carried Rachel and sold her on the other side of Kentucky."

"That's all for now. Please answer Mr. Robertson's questions."

Robertson again rose and faced Fanny Langsdon.

"Did you know Rachel's grandmother?"

"Yes, I did."

"How do you know she was Rachel's grandmother?"

"The family always told me she was and she was always there when I was there."

"How did you know she was an Indian?"

"I heard Henry Clay, father of William, say that he brought her from the Catawba nation of Indians himself."

"How do you know that descendants of Rachel's mother and her mother's mother have recovered their freedom?"

"I know that all the children of Judy, who was a sister to Rachel's mother, belonged to Henry Clay, and Judy's children did recover their freedom."

"Did you not understand that at the time Henry Clay and Peter Womack brought those Indians from Catawba Nation that they were considered at that time to be slaves."

"I did understand that they were considered as such."

"In what year was Rachel carried from Powhatan by Mitchell Clay?"

"To the best of my recollection, in the year 1761."

"Was Rachel with child at the time she was carried from Powhatan?"

"I heard from the family that she was."

"Was Samuel Findlay, who has recovered his freedom in the General Court, a brother to Rachel?"

"He was not."

"Did Rachel ever belong to Thomas Clay?"

"She never did."

"Do you know of your own knowledge that Nan was daughter of old Chance?"

"I do not but always understood that she was."

"How old do you suppose you were at the time you saw Rachel suckling her mother?"

"Not more than four or five."

"That is all the questions I have for this witness. Thank you."

"No questions, Your Honor," said Robertson.

"I call Mr. William S. Dance," announced Mr. Nash.

A middle-aged man of neat appearance, blond hair and slim figure approached the bench, took the oath and seated himself in the witness chair.

"Mr. Dance, what is your occupation?"

"I am Deputy Clerk of Court for Powhatan County."

"You are familiar with the records of the county?"

"Yes, I am."

"And in your capacity as clerk, did I ask you to locate any records pertaining to the Findlay family of Powhatan, and if so, what did you find, if anything?"

"I found that Bess Findlay brought suit against Elijah Clay in 1788 for trespass, assault and battery and false imprisonment, in a freedom suit."

"What else did you find?"

"I found that her brother, James Findlay, was given permission to prosecute the suit on her behalf."

"Were depositions requested?"

"Yes, there is a reference to the depositions of Lucy Marshall and Matthew Farley, but they were not in the file."

"What else was in the file?"

"There was a copy of the decree of the General Court

filed in the case."

"Is this the document you refer to?" asked Nash as he handed the paper to the clerk.

After a moment or two Mr. Dance announced, "It is."

"Would you please read this document for the court."

Dance began in his slow monotone voice,

> *Virginia: At a General Court held at the Capital in the City of Williamsburg the 4th day of May 1773. Samuel, Rachel and her child, Indians, plaintiffs against Thomas Clay, defendant, in trespass, assault and battery and false imprisonment. This day came the parties by their attornies and thereupon came a jury, (to wit), Alexander Boyd and others, who being tried and sworn the truth to speak upon the issue joined, upon their oath do say that the plaintiffs are free and not slaves as by replying they have alledged and they do assess the damages of the plaintiffs by the occasion in the declaration mentioned to five pounds besides their costs; Therefore it is considered by the court that the plaintiffs recover against the defendant, their damages aforesaid, in form aforesaid assessed and their costs by them about the suit in this behalf expended, and the said defendants may be taken, etc. A copy signed by John Brown, Clerk of the General Court.*

"If it please the court, please mark this as exhibit one in evidence for the plaintiff," requested Mr. Nash.

"I object to the copy being entered into the record,"

announced Mr. Robertson. "It is a copy and not the original."

"Your Honor," argued Mr. Nash, "it has already been accepted in the case, just mentioned by this court."

"Your objection is overruled. Please mark this as requested." The document was handed to the clerk for identification. "Proceed, Mr. Nash," said the judge.

"Mr. Dance, were there any other papers in the file?"

"Yes, there was an indenture between Lucy Marshall and the church wardens of Southam Parish of Cumberland County, now Powhatan."

"What was the date, please?"

"It was dated April 11, 1774, following an order of court dated October 25, 1773."

"Who were the parties bound to Lucy Marshall?"

"They were James, Bess, and Archer who were to have their freedom dues when they became of age."

"Was there anything else in the court records about Findlays?"

"Yes, there was a reference to a suit brought by James Findlay against Elijah Clay, but it was dismissed."

"Was any reason stated for its dismissal?"

"The papers stated that Elijah Clay came into court and acknowledged the freedom of James Findlay, and he was to be emancipated under the Act of the General Assembly which authorized the manumission of slaves."

"Would you please look over these papers, Mr. Dance, and tell me if these are the papers you have just referred to."

As he turned each page, Mr. Dance nodded his head, and finally announced to the court that they were the papers he had mentioned. Mr. Nash requested they be accepted as exhibits for the plaintiff. This time there was no

216

objection and the documents were filed as requested.

Mr. Robertson again said, "No questions."

"I would like to call Mr. George Radford next, please," said Mr. Nash while shuffling papers on the desk.

There was no response, and the bailiff called the name, "George Radford, please come forward."

Mr. Nash turned around and saw that Mr. Radford was sleeping in the back row of the courtroom. The bailiff noticed him about the same time and went to his side to wake him up.

"Mr. Radford, sir. You must come to the front," announced the bailiff.

"Eh? What is it?" asked Mr. Radford, holding his hand over his right ear.

The bailiff shouted, "Please come to the front."

Mr. Radford shuffled forward to the witness chair and stumbled as he fell into the wooden seat. The clerk presented him with the Bible and asked the usual question in a loud voice.

"I will tell the truth," he said.

"Mr. Radford," began Nash, "How old are you?"

"I am upwards of eighty-six at this time."

"Did you know any of the Clay families in this county?"

"Yes, I was born and raised in the neighborhood of several families of Clays. There was Henry and William, two brothers, and each of them raised several sons."

"Did any of them have slaves of Indian extraction?"

"Yes they did, several of them."

"Did any of these slaves recover their freedom in suits at law?" Nash continued, shouting close to the ear of the witness.

"Yes, all of the slaves that remained in this part of the country recovered their freedom in freedom suits."

217

"What about the ones conveyed away?"

"About the time the suits were pending several of the children, descendants of Indian mothers, were conveyed off by the sons of Henry and William and sold to prevent them from an opportunity of obtaining their freedom."

"Who owned Rachel?"

"Rachel was the daughter of an Indian mother and was owned by William Clay.

"Did you know that Samuel Findlay recovered his freedom in the General Court."

"Yes, I did."

"Do you know this person sitting at my table?"

"What?" he asked.

Nash raised his voice and pointed. "Do you know this person sitting at my table, over there?"

"Yes, I do, from her color and her features I know this is Rachel, a sister to the man Samuel who obtained his freedom."

"Isn't it possible that this person is not Rachel, the sister of Samuel?"

"I have made many inquiries of Rachel, and her answers have made it impossible for me to say that she is any other person than the sister to Samuel."

"Is this the same Rachel that came here for depositions in July and October 1814, and again in 1816?"

"I don't remember the dates but she was present when I gave my depositions."

"Do you believe Rachel is of Indian extraction?"

"I object to that question." Mr. Robertson was on his feet and asking the judge for a ruling.

"I will allow it. Proceed," said the judge.

"I will repeat the question for you, Mr. Radford. Do you believe Rachel is of Indian extraction?"

"Yes, I do. I asked her questions and as she is a large yellow woman and because of the answers she gave me, I believe she is of Indian extraction."

"That is all the questions I have, but Mr. Robertson will have some, I am sure."

Mr. Robertson rose and confronted the witness face to face and up close.

"Who did you hear say Rachel was born of an Indian mother?"

"It was the general report in the neighborhood but I heard Thomas Clay, Elijah Clay and Lucy Marshall, their mother, say she was of an Indian mother."

"Are Thomas Clay, Elijah Clay and Lucy Marshall now living?"

"Thomas and Lucy are dead, but I don't know about Elijah."

"Do you understand Samuel Findlay and Rachel were brother and sister."

"Yes, I understood so from the general report of the neighborhood."

"Do you know whether Rachel was ever in the possession of Thomas Clay?"

"I do not know."

"Do you know whether Rachel had a child before she was carried away from the county of Powhatan?"

"I do not know of my own knowledge that she had one, but it was the common report in the neighborhood they had carried Rachel and her child away."

"Did you know the mother of Rachel?"

"I knew a woman said to be the mother. Her name was Judy."

"Might not Sam and Rachel be children of an Indian father?"

"Objection, objection, Your Honor."

"Mr. Nash, what is your objection?" asked the judge.

"This case has nothing to do with whether the father is of Indian heritage. It is irrelevant, Your Honor."

"Overruled, your client may answer the question."

"Mr. Radford, might not Sam and Rachel be children of an Indian father?"

"I don't know."

"That's all, Mr. Radford."

"Gentlemen," said the judge. "We will now take time to get something to eat. We will return at 2 p.m. Court is adjourned." He pounded the gavel as he left the courtroom.

Rachel and Mr. Nash were among the last to leave the courtroom. They were met at the door by Maxwell and Pettyjohn, who stood with their hands on their hips and refused to let them pass.

"Get out of our way," said Mr. Nash in a stern voice. "Move away."

"We'll not move. Don't you know we don't want no more free niggers 'round here. Got enough of 'em," said Maxwell. He lifted his flask and swallowed a mouthful of whiskey. He turned to Rachel, spitting and spewing remnants of his drink in her face. "We don't want you, nigger."

The sheriff came to the door, forced the two out into the courtyard, and Mr. Nash and Rachel were free to pass.

Chapter 19

THE TRIAL CONTINUES

When the session resumed, Mr. Nash called Elijah Clay, who came to the front of the bench, swore the oath and took a seat in the witness chair.

"Mr. Clay, are you acquainted with my client, Rachel Findlay, who is at the table over there?"

"Yes, I am, I have known her for upwards of forty years."

"How old are you now, Mr. Clay?"

"I am upwards of sixty years of age."

"Do you also know Samuel Findlay?"

"Yes, I have known him for many years, too. Haven't I, Sam?" responded Elijah waving his hand toward the first row in the balcony where Samuel was seated. "Samuel belonged to my brother, Thomas Clay."

"Did Samuel ever obtain his freedom?"

"Yes, he did, and about the same time that Rachel got her freedom."

"At the time Rachel got her freedom where was she living?"

"She was taken from here to New River with her child Judy."

"Did you ever own any slaves, Mr. Clay?"

"I owned two slaves, James and Bess, which I got from

my father after I became of age, and after my father died."

"Were they of the same family as Rachel and Samuel, or a different family?"

"They were of the same family, descendants of Chance, an old Indian woman, and I heard my mother and brother say that Rachel was the daughter of Nan, a daughter of Chance."

"Did any of your slaves receive their freedom?"

"Yes, Bess Findlay and her four children were freed because of a suit filed by Bess against me. James Findlay also filed against me, but he agreed to dismiss the suit if I would emancipate him, which I did."

"Do you know what was the basis for their suit."

"Yes, they used as evidence the freedom of Samuel, Rachel and her child in 1773."

"Were there other Indians at your father's or grandfather's?"

"Yes, there was a boy named James who was brought in from the Catawba Nation at the same time as Chance."

"Did Nan have a sister."

"Yes, her sister was named Judy. She was the grandmother of Bess and James Findlay."

"That's all, Mr. Clay. Please answer Mr. Robertson's questions."

When Mr. Nash sat down, Robertson rose and faced Elijah Clay.

"Did not James and Bess enjoy their freedom before they recovered it from you?"

"No, they never engaged it by any suit before that I know of. I held them in slavery till they recovered it."

"Did you not of your own accord emancipate James, agreeable to the Act of Assembly?"

"He brought his suit against me in the county court of

Powhatan and being convinced that if the suit progressed to a trial he must recover, I agreed that if he would dismiss his suit I would go into court and emancipate him, which I did, but Bess recovered her freedom by regular suit at law."

"Did you hold them in slavery from the time they were infants?"

"They were given to me by my father."

"How long was it after you last saw Rachel in this part of the country before you again saw her in the western part of the state and when was that?"

"I cannot say the exact length of time. I first saw her in the road when I lived at New Dublin and knew her before she got within fifty yards of the house. I did not know she was in that part of the country."

"Was Lucy Marshall your mother, and were James and Bess bound to her?"

"She was my mother and I did not know that they ever were bound to her, but I myself was an orphan and my mother was my guardian and I received them from her when I became of age, they having been willed to me by my father."

"That's all, Mr. Clay. "

"No questions," Robertson mumbled.

Clay left the witness chair and moved to the back of the courtroom.

"Your Honor, Mr. Edward Moseley could not be here today but in October 1814 gave us a deposition. He was a magistrate when Mr. Radford gave his deposition. At this time I would like to have his deposition read into the record."

"I object, Your Honor," said Robertson as he rose to his feet. "I was not present at the taking of that deposition, and although my agent was present. I intended to be there, but the plaintiffs would not postpone the deposition, and I did not get an opportunity to cross-examine the witness. I had to be in other courts that week."

"Your Honor," continued Nash, "he had notice and his agent did appear."

"I repeat, I had no opportunity to cross-examine him," said Robertson.

"I will dismiss the jury temporarily, and hear the deposition and then make my final decision," said the judge.

The jury was dismissed and the judge continued, "Mr. Nash, please read the deposition."

"Yes, sir."

> *The deposition of Edward Moseley of lawful age taken at the house of John Dean this 12th day of October 1814, by consent of the plaintiffs and defendants agents, both being present. To be read as evidence in a suit now depending in Wythe County Court, between Rachel a woman of color, plaintiff and John Draper, Sr., defendant.*
>
> *This deponant sayeth that he acted as one of the magistrates on the 25th day of July last in pursuance of an order and commission from Wythe County Court in the taking of George Radford's deposition and others in a suit depending in which Rachel a woman of colour is plaintiff and John Draper, Senr. is defendant. This deponant further sayeth that the plaintiff Rachel was present and that she rode a sorrel horse and on a mans saddle. She was a large yellow woman and had the appearance of being of Indian extraction. She came to the place appointed for*

224

taking the aforesaid deposition in company with a free man of colour named James Findlay who was said to be a cousin of said Rachel's.

Question by plaintiff's agent: From your acquaintance with George Radford are you of the opinion that he is entitled to credit on his oath.

Answer: As any man in the state.

Question by the same: From your acquaintance with John Langsdon and Fanny Langsdon his wife, are you of the same opinion?

Answer: Yes, never having heard anything to the contrary.

Question by defendant's agent: Were you well acquainted with Elijah Clay and what do you know of the credibility or incredibility of the said Clay.

Answer: He did not stand high among people of the first respectability while he lived in this county, further he knows not.

Signed by the deponant the day and date above in presence of us Justices of the Peace for the county of Powhatan.

Judge Randolph reflected momentarily and announced, "Deposition of Edward Moseley is not to be read before the jury. Bailiff, please recall the jury."

"I object to this ruling, Your Honor," stated Robertson.

"So noted, Mr. Robertson."

Stepping away from the witness chair, and after reviewing his notes at this desk, Mr. Nash asked the bailiff to summon Susannah Clay. A tall, slender black-haired woman stepped briskly to the front, was sworn to tell the truth and seated herself stiffly in the witness chair with her head held high in the air.

Mr. Nash began his questions. "You are Susannah Clay? What is your relationship to the other Clays mentioned in this lawsuit?"

"I am the widow of Thomas Clay, who was the former owner of Samuel Findlay, who obtained his freedom."

"Did you know whether or not Samuel had any sisters?"

"I know that Rachel Findlay was his sister."

"Did your husband ever have Rachel in his possession?"

"Yes, he did. She was sent by William Clay to secure payment on a certain sum of money. My husband was security for Mitchell Clay, and it was Mitchell that carried her away to Pittsylvania County."

"How long did your husband hold possession of Rachel under this agreement?"

"About five years as well as I remember."

"To whom was Rachel delivered by your husband?"

"To Mitchell, son of William Clay."

"Did not Rachel carry with her a Negro girl by the name of Judah or Judy?"

"Yes, she did."

"Was Rachel in the possession of Thomas Clay at the time Samuel recovered his freedom in the General Court?"

"No, it was before that time as well as I remember though it has been a long while since."

"Did you or did you not ever hear William Clay, Mitchell Clay and your husband Thomas Clay, or either of them, ever say that Samuel and Rachel were brothers and sisters?"

"Yes, frequently, all of them, but particularly my husband and all the family that I ever heard speak of them."

"Is Rachel the mulatto woman now before you, the same woman whom you have just spoken of and who was carried off by Mitchell Clay?"

"Yes, she is the same woman, though much older now. I have no hesitation in declaring her the same. When in the early part of this spring she came over to Amelia to see me I was from home at Dr. Olphin's and in company of three other ladies. She knew me and pointed me out immediately when she saw me."

"Was it not your husband Thomas Clay from whom Samuel recovered his freedom and, if so, did he or did he not at any time have in his possession any other Negro woman by the name of Rachel other than the one spoken of?"

"It was my husband, Thomas Clay, from whom Samuel recovered his freedom and he never had at any time any other Negro in his possession of the same name."

"Did you ever hear who was the mother of Rachel?"

"I heard the family of my husband and his mother, but not Mitchell Clay or his father, say that her name was Nan."

"Who was said to be the mother of Nan?"

"I heard that her name was Chance, who was said to have been brought from the Indian Nation by Mr. Thomas Clay's grandfather, Henry Clay."

"Did Samuel and Rachel or did they not while in the possession of your husband call and acknowledge each other brother and sister?"

"They claimed each other as brother and sister."

"You may answer Mr. Robertson's questions," said Nash and sat again at his table with Rachel at his side.

Robertson began gruffly, "Did Rachel ever commence a suit against Thomas Clay for her freedom?"

"She did not."

"Can you say on your oath that Rachel, the present plaintiff, is a sister to Samuel who recovered his freedom from Thomas Clay?"

"I cannot."

"Did you know the mother of Rachel?"

"No, I did not."

"Were there men of Indian appearance among the slaves of the Clay family sixty or seventy years ago?"

"I was not acquainted with them at that time."

"Might not Rachel be the daughter of an Indian father for all what you know?"

Mr. Nash interrupted. "I object. Relevancy. This case is not about Indian fathers but Indian mothers."

Judge Randolph responded, "Overruled. You may answer the question."

"She might be or not for what I know."

"How many slaves recovered their freedom from the Clay family?"

"I know of but four, Sam belonging to Thomas Clay, Peter to John Clay, and James and Bess to Elijah Clay."

"Did you not understand that Rachel's mother was a slave?"

"I don't recollect that I ever heard any mention whatever made of her."

"What was the general character of Mitchell Clay as a man of truth and honesty?"

"I was not intimately acquainted with him but I know nothing to the contrary."

"Was Rachel the property of Thomas Clay or was she only in his possession as a pledge?"

"No more than I have before stated. She was put in his possession to secure a sum of money."

"How long were you acquainted with Thomas Clay

before your marriage with him?"

"I don't remember exactly, but one or two years."

"How many Negroes did your husband have before marriage and was he in the habit of buying and selling Negroes?"

"I think he had six or seven counting Rachel and her child, Judy, and was in the habit of buying but not selling."

"Were you acquainted with the slaves of the Clay family generally?"

"I was not particularly acquainted with any others except the Indian part of them. Nan and Judy were said to be sisters. Judy and her children were given by Henry Clay, the elder, to his son Henry Clay and his children, with the exception of Samuel, who was given by his grandfather to my husband. Nan and her children were given to William Clay and his children. I know Bess and James, the grandchildren of Judy, have recovered their freedom in Powhatan County Court."

"Were you personally acquainted with those two women Nan and Judy?"

"I was not. I only knew them by reputation."

"Were there whole Indian men among the slaves belonging to the Clay family?"

"There was one as I understood, brought from the Indian nation."

"Did Nan die in slavery?"

"She did, as I understood, as no suit had at that time been brought."

"Were the ladies at Dr. Olphin's young or old women?"

"They were much younger than myself, but I knew Rachel at some distance off."

"Would you know Rachel by sight if you had not heard

of her being in this part of the country?"

"I don't know that I would have known her at the distance mentioned but I think I would have known her if I had been with her."

"Where did Thomas Clay live at the time Rachel was carried away?"

"In this county about four miles from Jinnato Bridge."

"How long were you married to Thomas Clay?"

"About forty years."

"Thank you, that's all the questions I have, Mrs. Clay." Robertson returned to his table and consulted with John Draper, Jr., and his son, Joseph.

Mr. Nash whispered to Rachel and then announced to the court. "I call Rachel Findlay to the witness chair."

Rachel got up and began hobbling to the front of the courtroom. Her long hair was loosely braided and sprinkled with gray. On her shoulders was her red shawl.

"I object to the calling of this witness on the grounds that the law in this Commonwealth is that Negroes, mulattoes and Indian servants shall be incapable to be witnesses in any cases whatsoever. That has been the law in this Commonwealth since 1705," announced Mr. Robertson.

Rachel stopped, leaning heavily on her cane. She knew this might happen, but she waited for her attorney and the judge to decide.

"Your Honor," began Mr. Nash, "would you please look at the law of 1786, Chapter VIII, which has the following sentence, 'One being detained in slavery, and suing for his freedom, shall be tried in the same manner as a free man.' Isn't an exception allowing Rachel to testify?"

Judge Randolph thought for a minute and then asked Mr. Nash to read the whole chapter to him in case the law was passed in another context. After the reading was completed, the judge nodded and said, "You are correct, Mr. Nash. Rachel may testify."

"Thank you, Your Honor. Rachel please take the witness chair, and tell us your full name, please."

"My name is Rachel Findlay."

"How old are you?"

"I am sixty-seven years old."

"Where were you born?"

"I was born here, down on Swift Creek."

"Who was your grandmother?"

"Her name was given to her by ole' man Clay, Henry Clay, that is. He called her Chance, but her Indian name was White Cloud."

"Where did she come from before she lived in Virginia?"

"She lived in the Catawber Nation in South Carolina. She told me so."

"Is Samuel Findlay your brother?"

"Yes, he is, and he is right there." She pointed to the balcony where Samuel was seated.

"When did you leave Powhatan County?"

"I believe it was about 1773, some time after me and Samuel had filed for our freedom and with my daughter too."

"Who else was with you?"

"My daughter, Judy, was about six years old and me and Marse Mitchell Clay."

"Why did you leave?"

"I didn't want to leave, but Mitchell Clay took me to New River and on to the Bluestone which was then the frontier. A year or so later he sold me and my daughter to

Mr. John Draper, Sr. Sold me for some land."

"Did you believe that you had obtained your freedom."

"I thought that I had, but was not certain until I saw the paper Samuel gave me."

"You mean this piece of paper?" asked Mr. Nash. He showed her the yellow, wrinkled piece of paper, folded many times, the one she had given to Mr. Henderson seven years ago when he had filed her suit.

"I cannot read it, but the paper looks like one I carried with me for years. I gave it to Mr. Henderson, my lawyer in Wythe County."

"Did Samuel tell you what the paper said?"

"Yes, he read it to me. It said that Samuel, Judy and me all got our freedom in 1773."

"Did you hear the clerk read from a paper from the General Court about your case?"

"Yes, I did. Sounded like the same thing."

"Your Honor," said Nash. "Please accept this document in evidence for the plaintiff."

After Robertson read the document, he stated, "No objection."

Mr. Nash continued the questioning.

"Why did Mitchell Clay take you to the back country? Do you have any idea?"

"Yes, him and his family did not want me to know that I was freed."

"Did Mitchell Clay ever call you an Indian after you went to the New River?"

"No, he never did. He called me a nigger wench, sometimes a Negro woman."

"When he sold you to Draper, what did he tell him, do you know?"

"He told him I was a Negro."

"Where have you lived ever since you went to Mr. Draper's?"

"I lived with the Draper family at Draper's Mountain in Wythe County, first with Mr. Draper and his first wife, then with him and his second wife. And now with his son John."

"Did Mr. Draper ever whip you, beat you, or confine you in shackles?"

Rachel bowed her head, remembering all the times she suffered at the hands of Draper. "Yes, he did, many times, especially in January 1813 when I begged him to let me find a lawyer to bring my case for freedom. That askin' made him mad, so mad."

"How many children and grandchildren do you have?"

"It's between thirty and forty, maybe more."

"Do you ask this jury to grant you your freedom?"

"Yes, I do. I am a very old woman and weak as you can see. I probably don't have much longer to live. I have been whipped, starved, shackled and beaten. My freedom has always been in chains, but for my children and grandchildren it will mean a new life. Yes, I want the jury to free me, as the other jury did long ago."

"I have no further questions. Mr. Robertson may have some questions for you," said Nash.

Mr. Robertson cleared his throat and stood in front of Rachel.

"Rachel, what was your mama's name?"

"Her name was Nan."

"How do you know that?"

"My grandmother Chance told me."

"You don't remember your mother?"

233

"No sir, she was poisoned by some nigger men when I was a baby."

"How do you know that?"

"Grandmama Chance told me."

"Was your grandmother freed by the Clays?"

"Never heard she was. She had to file the suit like the others."

"Is your grandmother alive now?"

"No, she died several years ago, but after she got her freedom."

Mr. Robertson decided to give up. "I have no further questions. You may now sit with Mr. Nash."

Rachel moved slowly back to the desk and sat with her attorney, wondering what was next, when the judge interrupted her thoughts.

"Call your next witness."

"I have no other witnesses, Your Honor."

"Very well, we will take a brief recess. Then we will hear from Mr. Robertson and Mr. Jones."

The bailiff called, "All rise," as the judge left the courtroom. The crowd dispersed to the local inn, to their homes, or to the courthouse lawn.

When the case resumed the judge announced, "Mr. Robertson, you have the floor."

"Your Honor," said Robertson, facing the bench, "I would ask the court to dismiss this case at this time, because the evidence shows that Rachel never belonged to Thomas Clay, and even though a suit was filed against him for the freedom of a woman named Rachel, we suggest that this must be another Rachel and not the one before us today."

"Mr. Robertson, your motion is denied. There may be some controversy in the evidence, but it is the jury's duty to decide what is true and what is false. The case will continue."

Robertson returned to the table, shuffled the papers, and called on John Draper, Jr., to come forward. The clerk presented him with the Bible and he was sworn to tell the truth. He seated himself with ease in the witness chair. His graying hair was perfectly groomed, his silk cravat and black suit were of the latest style. Only a few wrinkles could be found on his sixty-year-old face.

Robertson began with the usual questions. Name, age, place of residence. Then he asked the more pertinent questions.

"Is Rachel, the woman seated over there, owned by your family?"

"Yes, she is owned by my father."

"How long have you known Rachel?"

"She came to my father's when I was about fourteen years old."

"How old is your father?"

"He is now over ninety years of age and so feeble he was not able to make the trip to appear in this case."

"I want you to look at this piece of paper," said Robertson, "and tell me what you know of it."

"My father gave me this piece of paper. It is the bill of sale for Judy and Rachel dated 1774."

"Does this paper refer to them as Indians or Negroes?"

"It refers to them as Negroes."

"Please read the entire document for the record."

John Draper hesitated, cleared his throat, and began to read:

235

> *To all to whom it may concern. Know ye that I Mitchell Clay for and in consideration of the sum of one hundred and twenty pounds current money to me in hand paid by John Draper (the receipt whereof I do hereby acknowledge) have bargained and sold & by these presents do bargain and sell to John Draper his heirs and assigns a Negro Woman named Rachel aged 20 years or thereabouts and a Negro girl name Jude age 7 years or thereabouts, the title of which Negroes I and my heirs will forever warrant & defend to the said John Draper & his heirs and assigns against the claim of all persons whatsoever. Witness my hand and seal this 25 April, 1774.*

"Who signed the paper?"

"It is signed by Mitchel Clay, who made his mark, and witnessed by W. Ingles, Jacob Harman and Vallentin Harman."

"May it please the court, I would ask that this document be entered into evidence as exhibit one for the defendant."

Presenting the paper to Mr. Nash, and then to the judge, he heard Nash report that there was no objection. The clerk accepted the bill of sale into the record.

"Did your father have claim to the property at Clover Bottom where Clay was living?"

"Yes, he did. I heard him talk about it many times and the record will show that it was true."

"Is Mitchell Clay living at this time?"

"No, he died before this suit began, around 1811, I believe," answered Draper.

"Was there any discussion that you heard as a youth or perhaps later that referred to Rachel and Judy as Indians."

"Not that I remember, that is, not until Rachel began asking about filing for her freedom. It was sometimes said that she had long black hair like an Indian, and was a light yellow color, but that she was a mulatto, or a Negro."

"Did your father ever participate in this discussion?"

"Occasionally he would, but each time he concluded that the bill of sale said they were Negroes and that was what they were."

"I have no other questions. Please answer Mr. Nash's questions."

When Robertson sat down, Nash come in front of John Draper and began his questions.

"You say that your father gave you the bill of sale. When was that?"

"When Rachel filed her suit in 1813," answered John.

"Where has this document been since 1813?"

"Mostly in possession of the attorneys, and in between times in my possession."

"Were you present when the document was signed?"

"No, I was not."

"Isn't it true that you have no way of knowing if this is the actual bill of sale or not?"

"I assume it is as my father gave it to me."

"No other questions, Mr. Draper. Thank you."

Both men returned to their seats. Robertson rose again to announce to the court that there were no other witnesses, but he asked again to have the case dismissed. The judge would not agree.

The judge then dismissed the jury to their jury room and looked to the attorneys for the instructions to the jury. Both huddled at the judge's bench, suggesting this one and that one, some being accepted, some not. They would soon be read to the jury, followed by the closing arguments. The day was nearly over.

When the jury returned to the box, the judge explained the role of the instructions to the jury.

"Gentlemen of the jury, these instructions are the law of Virginia at this time, and the attorneys and I have agreed that the law will be read to you now. It is your role to take the facts in the case, based on the evidence presented to you today, and decide this case in light of the law. Now here are the instructions.

"First instruction is as follows: No American Indian brought into Virginia since the year 1705 can under any circumstances be lawfully made a slave.

"All children born in this country shall be bond or free according to the condition of the mother.

"If you believe the bill of sale to be the one given to John Draper at the time of the sale, then you must consider that Rachel may be a Negro.

"If you believe that the document from the General Court dated 1773 relates to the woman named Rachel who has brought this suit, then you must consider that Rachel may be descended from an Indian woman.

"If you find that Rachel is descended from an Indian woman, then she will be entitled to her freedom and you must so find.

"If you find that Rachel is a Negro, then she will not be entitled to her freedom.

"If you believe Rachel and Samuel are brother and sister, then you must decide in favor of the plaintiff, Rachel Findlay.

"If you find that Rachel has been assaulted and has been falsely imprisoned then you are required to find damages on her behalf.

"The plaintiff, Rachel Findlay, in order to win the case, must have presented proof by preponderance of the evidence, and if you find that she has proved her case by the preponderance of the evidence, then you must find on her behalf.

"Preponderance of evidence means the weight, credit, and value of the aggregate evidence or the greater weight of credible evidence. It does not mean the mere numerical array of witnesses. Now, Gentlemen, we are ready for the closing arguments."

Mr. Nash went face to face to the jury." Gentlemen of the jury," he began, "in my opening statement I told you that the question you must decide today is whether Rachel Findlay is an Indian slave or a Negro slave. The court's instructions tell you what the law is, and it is up to you to sort out the truth of matter here, based on the evidence."

Moving closer to the men of the jury, he continued, "You first heard from John Langsdon, who knew the Clay family, knew Samuel Findlay, knew Samuel was the brother to Rachel, and knew Samuel had obtained his freedom. His wife, Fanny, also knew the Clays, and was raised in their household. She knew Rachel's mother Nan and saw Rachel at her mother's breast many years ago. She knew Rachel was taken away by Mitchell Clay. She heard Henry Clay say that Rachel's grandmother, Chance, was brought into Virginia by Henry Clay and Peter Womack from the Catawba Nation.

"You heard Mr. Dance, the county's deputy clerk, read the document used in the suit of Bess Findlay against Elijah Clay, and this court record tells us that Samuel, Rachel and her child were classified as Indians and that they recovered their freedom. He knew Samuel and Rachel were brother and sister.

"Elijah Clay knew Samuel Findlay well and knew that he had obtained his freedom and that he and Rachel were brother and sister. Elijah Clay inherited James and Bess, descendants of Chance, and told us that Bess won her freedom and that he emancipated James. What evidence did they use in this case? The document presented to you is from the General Court in 1773 whereby Samuel, Rachel and child obtained their freedom.

"Susannah Clay, widow of Thomas, who formerly owned Samuel, knew Rachel was his sister. She knew her husband never had any other Rachel in his possession.

"As for John Draper, Jr., he knows nothing of the facts. He presents only a bill of sale that he says was given to his father by Mitchell Clay. But John, Jr., was not there.

"And finally, you heard from Rachel Findlay herself. She told you of Mitchell Clay taking her to the back settlements and selling her to Mr. Draper. You heard her state that she was beaten, starved, shackled and kept in slavery from 1774 to the present. She knows her name appeared on the freedom papers with her brother Samuel's.

"In summary, we have six witnesses who testified that Samuel had been freed and five who knew that he and the Rachel sitting here were brother and sister. Four of these witnesses knew that Mitchell Clay took Rachel away. The evidence is overwhelming that Rachel was descended in her maternal line from an Indian held illegally in slavery. I ask you to find that Rachel is free and award her damages accordingly."

John W. Jones, Robertson's assistant, had been preparing his notes for the final argument all day. This sandy-haired young man was full of confidence and walked briskly to the jury and began in a loud voice.

"Rachel Findlay is not, I say not, entitled to her freedom. Although five witnesses have given us much information about her, four of them are over seventy years of age, and their stories do not agree. One says Rachel went to Kentucky, one said Rachel of the Clays went to Pittsylvania County and another said she was taken to Mecklenberg County. That leads us to believe that there were other Rachels. How do we know that this sixty-seven-year-old woman here is, in fact, the baby at the breast or indeed the one carried to New River. We don't know that. None of these witnesses knew.

"Fanny Langsdon told us that Rachel was taken from here in 1761, expecting a child. Rachel according to her petition filed in this case, and according to the bill of sale, was born in 1754 and would only be seven years of age in 1761, and obviously not with child.

"As for Mr. Dance we don't have all the papers pertaining to the case of Bess Findlay, and we have nothing in evidence to tell us what her suit was based on. Also, no one has established when the Indian woman, Chance, was brought into Virginia."

"It is also clear that the Rachel here was never owned by Thomas Clay, the person she supposedly obtained her freedom from in 1773. Based on all of this evidence you must consider that this was another person named Rachel. And Rachel herself was listening to the words and statements of her grandmother. She did not know her mother, and as Rachel stated, her grandmother did become free. She was telling Rachel all the details to put the idea of freedom in her head.

"Over and over again you heard the witnesses say that 'according to the general report in the neighborhood' or 'according to what they understood' telling us they were

241

not present, they were not there. But Mr. John Draper, Sr., was there on the New River in 1774 and Rachel before you was then sold to him as a Negro. The bill of sale is your proof.

"Notice, too, that Rachel's mother was Nan one place and Judy another, another clear indication that there was more than one Rachel.

"When you consider all of these discrepancies in the plaintiff's case you will, I am certain, decide that this Rachel before you is NOT entitled to her freedom because she is a Negro. Thank you."

The judge gave his final words, "Gentlemen of the jury, you have heard the law given to you in the instructions and you have heard the evidence presented from the witness chair. Now it is your turn to deliberate. You may adjourn to the jury room."

After each one filed out, Rachel and Mr. Nash and the crowd in the courtroom adjourned to the outside. It was after five in the afternoon. Men, women and children scattered in different directions. Around Rachel her Findlay relatives, James, Bess, Archer, Samuel, her brother, her sister Judy and some of her grandchildren, formed a circle.

Hours went by. No one understood why the decision had not been made before dark. The jurors seemed to be intelligent land-holders and the story of Rachel surely was not new to them. Others in Powhatan had been given their freedom in the court. Finally, Rachel and the gentlemen of the jury were called back to the courtroom.

"All rise," commanded the bailiff as the judge and jurors returned to their specified locations. "You may now be seated," droned the bailiff.

Rachel held her breath and her palms began to perspire. A trickle of water from her hairline came down her face.

She reached for the blue handkerchief and mopped her brow and patted her hands on the damp material.

The judge spoke again. "Gentlemen of the jury have you made your decision."

"Yes, we have," responded George Smith.

"Please tell the court."

"We the jury do find that Rachel Findlay, the plaintiff in this suit is entitled to her freedom and—"

Cheers arose from the balcony. Boos came from the back row of the courtroom where several drunken white men were seated. They had eyes as wild as mountain cats and hair as unkempt as a bear skin. None of them had shaved in weeks, and their clothes were wrinkled and smelly. In their midst were Henry Maxwell and Michael Pettyjohn.

Rachel sobbed, and the judge banged his gavel, ordering silence in the courtroom. "Please continue."

"We find that Rachel Findlay, the plaintiff in this suit, is entitled to her freedom, believing that she is descended from an Indian named Chance, and that her damages are one cent."

"Rachel, you are free. Just remember you must register at the courthouse soon. The court is dismissed. Thank you, gentlemen." As the judge left the bench and jurors their box, Rachel hurried as best she could to her family who were waiting outside. She thanked Mr. Nash and with head high, red shawl on her shoulders, she took her cane and pounded the floor of the courtroom, marching to the door and to freedom. The chains had fallen.

Rachel could not believe that she was finally legally free. Free now to go where she wanted to, free to live her own life, and free to pass her legacy on to her children and grandchildren. The chains had finally disappeared and she was sixty-seven years old!

Her cousin, James Findlay, met her at the door and took her arm. Together they walked a few hundred yards up the street to the west where he had a small house. All the relatives and friends had gathered to help her celebrate. As they entered the front door of the Findlay home, there were cheers, hugs, laughter, and tears.

Over in one corner of the living room, Ole Mose made the fiddle sing and Jerome kept time with his banjo. Dancing began. James took Rachel in his arms and walked her around floor, moving slowly at first, but as the music continued, Rachel seemed to be able to go faster and faster. Everyone cheered. More couples joined the dance. Singles tapped their feet and the children ran around the living room in time to the music.

When the front door opened, Rachel had no reason to turn her head for she knew there were more people coming to help her celebrate, but loud voices prompted her to turn around.

"We don't want no more free niggers round here. We done told you that. We don't want you here at all, Rachel Findlay," shouted Michael Pettyjohn.

"No, we don't want no more free niggers," chanted his courthouse friend, Henry Maxwell. The music stopped abruptly and the crowd shuffled to the sides of the room, leaving Rachel standing with James near the center.

"Get out of the way, man," shouted Pettyjohn. He brought his right hand out of his pocket and pointed the gun at Rachel. He staggered toward James.

"Move, move, nigger."

As James moved to the side, silence filled the room. The women hugged the little children and hid their faces in their skirts. Ole Mose dropped the bow to the floor, and

244

Jerome pulled the banjo to his side.

"Now we will have no more free niggers here," he screamed. He cocked the pistol and fired.

Rachel fell to the floor. The two men scrambled for the street.

James hollered to Jerome, "Go out the back door and get the doctor, get the sheriff! Hurry!"

Bess and James held Rachel quietly as her life's blood drained away. She closed her eyes and whispered, "I am free, fully free."

Rachel was freed in Powhatan on May 13, 1820, but enjoyed her freedom for only a few hours. Her friends and relatives, stricken to their hearts, arranged the funeral and Samuel insisted that Mose and Jerome bring their music. The next day the funeral procession marched down the street, past the tavern where the Drapers stood silently, past the courthouse, and past the mercantile establishment on the corner. There was no sound except the shuffling of the feet along the sandy road. Rachel's red shawl was the only adornment on the pine box that was her coffin.

The turn to the right led them into the countryside, past the log houses, past the plowed fields, and past the Clay plantation house. The entourage proceeded to the field where Fox Boy, Chance, Nan, and others of the Clay slaves were buried. There were no stones, only little wooden crosses, weathered in the wind. Samuel had carved the markers and had cleared the grass from the gravesites. The hole in the ground was ready for Rachel. Her cousins lowered the box into the hole.

A preacher, a free man and a friend of Samuel's, said the words and read from the Bible. "There is a time to live, and a time to die..."

They were wailing, sobbing, and swinging back and forth with the humming of the hymns. Finally Mose and Jerome took the fiddle and banjo and played a lively tune. To them it was a celebration of her life. She was free. Now she was truly free. Forty-two members of her family would be free too.

Chapter 20

MORE TRIALS

When young Joseph Draper and his father realized their family had lost their case in the courtroom, they were trying to decide how they would tell the captain. How would they be able to tell Judy and all the others that Rachel obtained her freedom, but she was now dead. On their return ride to Draper Mountain, Joseph and John, Jr., had plenty of time to think about it all.

"You know, Father, it is not likely Grandfather will realize what has happened. But we must tell him," said Joseph.

"Aye, that we must do, but it will be just a formality. The more difficult thing to do will be telling Judy and her children and the others over at Pattons."

"But the worst, Father, will be telling Alice that she must give up all those slaves she has had for so many years."

"You know, I wonder where the others are. Father gave Elizabeth and Rhoda some of Rachel's family too. Then they decided to move off to Illinois. I think I heard they sold the slaves before they left to go West."

"What about Jenny?" asked Joseph.

"She's probably somewhere in Tennessee, and she may never learn that she is free. Of course, she could be dead by now, for all we know."

"Just imagine, forty-two in all, hard to believe."

"And then we must realize that when all of these slaves are free, we will have no help at all, except Will, and he is too old to do much work. We'll have to think about buying some more slaves, this time *real* niggers."

"Father, I think it would be a good idea to start suit against the Clay's executors. Even though Mitchell is dead, his estate should be liable to us for damages they have done to us, you know so much per slave. Mitchell knew Rachel and Judy were free and were of Indian blood and never said a word. He signed that bill of sale and called them Negroes. That sounds to me like a good case of fraud," offered Joseph.

"Yes, we will do that as soon as we can. I believe General Smyth would be a good one to handle that case. What do you think?"

"Yes, indeed. He has had a lot more experience than I have had."

"When will the others get their case heard, do you think?

"Mr. Nash told me he would get the records copied at next month's court session and send them to me. I suppose by the time we file them in Wythe another month or two will go by. But one thing is certain, by fall we will not have any slaves of Rachel's family."

On August 9, 1820, Rachel's sons, Tom, Robbin and Peter and her daughter, Judy, and several of her children gathered at the courthouse in Evansham. Each case was to be heard before a jury.

Tom and Judy talked quietly at the bottom of the steps of the new three-story courthouse, waiting for news.

"I just cannot believe that Mama is gone," said Judy. "She wanted so much to be free. Not just for herself, but for us too."

"I saw her cry many times. She tried to get so many different people to help her and no one really would," said Tom.

"She lost Bettie. I know she would have helped her if she had lived. But old Justice Boyd, he hated all of us and would do nothing. If it wasn't for Sam bringing her the papers she would never have been free," Judy said.

"Those preacher men wanted to help her but didn't really know what to do. And one sure thing, no one at the Draper house would lift a hand, especially the captain's wife."

"That's right. Every time Mama mentioned freedom she was beaten and chained and yet she kept trying. She never gave up." Judy took Tom by the arm.

"You know, Tom, it all came down to family. Sam and Mama, Mama and Sam. They done it for all of us."

"Sure did. Mama was over sixty years old and could hardly walk, but she set out for Evansham anyhow." Tom patted her hand.

"What we gonna do when we gits free?" asked Judy.

Tom shrugged his shoulders and wiped his face. He was feeling the August heat as the time wore on." Guess we should go up North somewhere. I hear Ohio would be a good place. But how do we git there?"

""We'll find a way. If Mama found a way to her—our—freedom we can surely find a way to get away from here."

"One thing we have to do is register as free people, or we will be brought in by the patty-rollers," said Tom.

"We can do that, and when we gits our papers then we can go, go where we wants to go. We will be free forever."

249

"If Mama was here she would go with us and—

The deputy sheriff interrupted. "Get in here. Jury's back."

They all climbed the steps and entered the courtroom, standing near the front tables. The jury announced that Tom, Robbin, and Peter were free. Damages granted to them were one cent. The next announcment came for Judy and her children, Locky, Rhoda, Sam, Abram and Charlotte, and a granddaughter, Lucinda. Now ten of Rachel's family were free.

Judy hugged her children and her brothers. Peter picked up little Lucinda and they marched outside to freedom.

Also in August a jury in Montgomery County brought freedom to Rachel's daughter Polly and her six children, Lucy, Lockey, Rachel, Harvey, Sally and Maria. Now seven more of Rachel's family were free.

Two years later, Milly, Judy's daughter, and her child Harvey, and another daughter, Anne, and her children, Melinda, Eliza, Randal and Franklin, brought their suit against Miss Alice Draper. Little Franklin had died before freedom came and Anne had another child named John. Another seven free.

More lawsuits were to come, this time for the Clays in 1821. The Drapers sought out the expertise of General Alexander Smyth, at his office in Evansham. After discussing the case with the Drapers, the general filed suit against Mitchell Clay's administrators and securities, Mitchell Clay, Jr., Henry Clay, William Clay, George N. Pearis and William Smith, all of Giles County, Virginia.

The charge was fraud in the sale of Rachel and Judy in 1774. Joseph Draper, as the administrator of the estate, carried the suit against the Clays through successfully to the final decision on June 7, 1828. The court awarded a substantial sum to the Draper family, causing the losers to go bankrupt.

John Draper's long life had brought him through the frontier days when Shawnee Indians took his wife Bettie and his sister Mary. They had killed his mother, and although no one knew what happened to his father, he was probably a victim of those same Indians. John Draper could have retreated to the east and to safety, but he chose to raise his seven children on the frontier with his wife Bettie, who was recovered from her captivity after several years. He had gained large tracts of land at the foot of the mountain which took his name. He was proud of his son John and his lawyer grandson, Joseph.

But his wartime experiences at Point Pleasant and in the Carolinas deeply affected his life. He would never be the same. And he would never be the same after the loss of Bettie, and later his second wife, Jane.

He never expected to be sued by Rachel and her family. Hadn't he fed them, clothed them, and given them shelter? Hadn't he watched over them when they were sick? And as for the Clays and their deception, the Drapers vowed they would pay for their losses. Hadn't Mitchell Clay cheated him, defrauded him and outright lied to him?

But the old captain did not live to see the result of the fraud trial. In 1824 John Draper died at the age of ninety-four. Joseph, his grandson, tended to his minimal estate. There was not much left to administer as the captain had given most of his property to John Draper, Jr., in return for his support and maintenance until his death. He did have two beds and coverlets, his gun and shot pouch and its contents. The beds were sold for twenty dollars and the gun for a little more. Slaves Peter, Dave, Peggy, and Marlborough were claimed by John, Jr. Dave filed suit against the younger Draper for his freedom, but died before the case was decided. This accounted for thirty of Rachel's descendants.

In 1824 news of the freedom of Rachel and her children and the death of the captain reached Franklin County, Tennessee, where Sarah Foster now lived. She had known the Drapers and Rachel when she lived in Draper Valley. On a recent trip to Huntsville she saw Rachel's daughter, Jenny, on the street.

"Are you Jenny from Draper's?" asked Sarah.

"Yes, ma'am,"

"Did you know your family got their freedom?"

"Oh, no! I did not know. I am so glad," exclaimed Jenny. "I know Mama must be so happy. Have you seen her?"

"Jenny, child, I am so sorry. The day your mother got her freedom in Powhatan County, a white man came to the celebration and shot and killed her. He and his friends were later hanged for this terrible deed."

Jenny began to sob. "That's all Mama ever wanted, was to be free of her chains. Free of chains. Not for herself, but for all of us. She knew none of us could be free like the eagles unless she done it. And she done it."

"What I heard from the Mountain is that your mother's case can be used as proof for the others. Several of your brothers and sisters are also free now. You can be too, and

I will help you," offered Sarah.

"What should I do?" asked Jenny, wiping her face with a corner of her apron.

"I suppose you will need the papers from Powhatan for the court. Can someone, perhaps a lawyer here, write for you?"

"I guess so. Zack will help me," said Jenny.

"Who is Zack?"

"Zack helped me escape from Miss Alice when I visited the Loves in Tennessee. We have been together ever since. He is a free man. We have one child, a girl. Could she be free too?"

"Yes, I suppose so." Sarah continued, "Did you know old John Draper died a few months ago?"

"No, I hadn't heard. He must have been a very old man."

"Yes, about ninety-four. But what I want to know, Jenny, is how did you find your way here?" asked Sarah.

"We stayed in Nashville a long time and we both found work. Zack, he's a blacksmith, and I worked in several nice homes. One of the places I worked at was the McGavocks'. You know, the ole man at Fort Chiswell? Well, his sons moved there. Then Zack wanted to see his mama and she lived here in Huntsville, so we came here."

Sarah reached in her bag, opened the silver case and gave Jenny her calling card. "When you are ready, let me know and I will give my deposition for you. Just let me know when," offered Sarah.

"Thank you ma'am, thank you."

"I am sorry to bring you sad news about your mother. But her life was successful because it was her goal to be free and to give that same freedom to her children and grandchildren. She was a very determined person. She never gave up. Good-bye Jenny."

253

"Good-bye."

Jenny rushed to her little house and found Zack out back working at the forge.

"Zack, Zack, I can be free for sure. Mama got her freedom and Judy and the others too. I can be free."

"What you talkin' 'bout, girl?"

"I saw Sarah Foster who lived in Draper Valley. She told me. She's goin' to help me."

"Well, you is already free. Those papers I fixed for you says you is free."

"I know, but I want it legal like. Have to find a lawyer to git those papers from Virginia."

"Jenny, I's glad for you. Did Sarah Foster see your mama?"

The tears began again and Jenny tried to get the words out. They stuck in her throat. "Mama, Mama, she's dead,"

"What? How is that? I thought you said she was free."

"She got her freedom but a white man shot her the very same day. She died a few hours after."

"Sorry, girl," said Zack, reaching for her shoulders. He held her till the sobbing ended.

"Now off to find a lawyer. We got some money, and here's a little more." Zack reached in his apron pocket and gave her several dollars.

"Thank you, Zack."

In 1826 the Powhatan records were copied and sent to Alabama where they sat without action for many years. Finally on April 24, 1835, Sarah Foster gave her deposition, describing Jenny as a black woman about forty years of age, with a large "risin' on her neck." She was further depicted as a woman larger than ordinary whose mother Rachel Findlay was a yellow woman, said to be part Indian. Sarah added that she knew her mother obtained her freedom from John Draper. Finally Jenny was legally free. She and her little daughter would be the last of Rachel's family to obtain their freedom. This would bring the number to thirty-two. Some day, perhaps, others would also be free.

BACKGROUND ABOUT THE FAMILIES

The story of Rachel Findlay and her family is based on facts obtained from official records in Wythe and Powhatan counties, Virginia. Her children are correctly named, the dates of the various lawsuits are accurate and the results are well documented. Rachel and others brought their suits for assault and battery and false imprisonment requesting certain amounts of money in damages. The order of the birth of her children is speculative except for the first child, Judy. There is no documented evidence regarding the father of any of the children.

Because Rachel's story covers the period of her sixty-seven years, it became necessary to try to build her life in light of historic events which took place in Virginia during her lifetime. Because there are no records to tell us what she was thinking at specific times, her conversations had to be fictionalized but with certain criteria in mind. Many of the events that occurred, such as a measles epidemic on the wagon train did in fact occur, but at a different date than used here. The slaves Bob and Sam were actually hanged for killing their master, but again not on the date mentioned in this book. Rachel's attorney in Wythe County was in fact an attorney in Evansham (now Wytheville) at the time mentioned. Her thoughts, conversations and ideas, are composites of what might have occurred in light of the slavery situation in Virginia at the time, her geographic location, and the other people involved in her life, and are therefore fictionalized. Her death in May 1820 is fictional.

The story of Samuel Findlay, her brother, is based on the fact that he obtained his freedom. The rest of the story is fictionalized to meet the demands of the story. Hannah Findlay (Fender) was an actual cousin who lived in Henry County. Bess and James Findlay, of Powhatan, were in fact, Rachel's relatives. Jenny, a daughter of Rachel, did obtain her freedom in Alabama according to the records in Madison County. How she found her way there was a creation of the author's imagination. The information about Rachel Viney was from actual records in Montgomery County, Virginia.

The existence of Indian slavery, although not well known, is not a fiction and occurred in all the Southern states in Colonial times. The laws of Virginia have been cited as accurately as possible as they relate to Rachel's case. The evidence given in her trial is based on the depositions filed in several cases relating to the family. In addition, the instructions of the judge to the jury are extant and proved to be very helpful for the portraying the final arguments in the trial.

Not all of the forty-two descendants mentioned by Rachel and the Draper family have been identified by name. Because some members of the Draper family moved away and took some slaves with them, their names are not recorded locally.

As for the Draper family, their name is well known in Southwest Virginia history and has been for more than two hundred years. The names of the children mentioned in this story are accurately given, but in the absence of a family Bible, the order of their births is speculative. Their actions and reactions to Rachel and her family were generally created by the author, but using as a background the various

258

lawsuits in which they were involved. The author suspected that Bettie Draper probably died earlier than the date given in this story, but for purposes of the novel she remained in the life of Rachel until the 1780s. It is known that Bettie was alive in 1775.

The Clays were well known in eastern Virginia, with the center of their activities located in what is now Powhatan County. They did own Negroes, mulattoes, and Indian slaves, a fact well known to researchers. Their family history is well documented, although dates are not always available. Mitchell Clay's stay on the New River is also a matter of record.

Rachel was often referred to by her first name only, but there are numerous references to her surname, Findlay. Her cousins also used the name. Why the name was chosen was never mentioned in any record consulted by the author. Rachel was also referred to as "a free woman of colour" and occasionally as "Rachel, an Indian." For more information about Rachel Findlay, *see* an upcoming article in *The Virginia Cavalcade*.

It has not been the intention or desire of the author to take sides with Rachel, the Clays or the Drapers. The lawsuits give us the proper perspective at the time. The language used, possibly offensive to some today, was, as much as possible, the language that would have been used before 1820. The actions taken by any of the whites were usually in line with the times mentioned in this book, and therefore the story should be read in view of the conditions at the time, not in view of our notions today.

259

BIBLIOGRAPHY

The following references are a small sample of available literature dealing with Indian and Negro slavery. In addition, numerous lawsuits consulted in the *Virginia Reports* are not listed here.

Ball, Edward. *Slaves in the Family*. New York: Ballantine Books, 1999.

Barton, R. T., ed. *Virginia Colonial Decisions, the Reports of Sir John Randolph and by Edward Barradall of Decision of the General Court of Virginia, 1728-1741,* Boston: The Boston Book Company, 1909.

Blumer, Thomas J. comp. and annotated. *Bibliography of the Catawba*. Metuchen, N.J. Scarecrow Press, 1987.

Campbell, Edward D.C., Jr., ed. With Kym S. Rice. *Before Freedom Came, African-Amerian Life in the Antebellum South*. Richmond: The Museum of the Confederacy and the University Press of Virginia, Charlottesville, 1991.

Carbone, Elisa. *Stealing Freedom*. New York: Alfred A. Knopf, 1998.

Catterall, Helen Tunnicliff, ed. *Judicial Cases Concerning American Slavery and the Negro*. Vol. 1, New York: Octagon Books, Inc. 1968.

Couture, Richard T. *Powhatan: A Bicentennial History*. Richmond, Virginia: The Dietz Press, Incorporated, 1980.

Egerton, Douglas. *Gabriel's Rebellion*. Chapel Hill: University of North Carolina Press, 1993.

Flanigan, Daniel J. "Criminal Procedure in Slave Trials," *Journal of Southern History* Vol. 40 (November 1974), 537-564.

Franklin, John Hope, and Loren Schweninger, *Runaway Slaves, Rebels on the Plantation.* New York, Oxford Press, 1999.

Guild, June Purcell. *Black Laws of Virginia. A Summary of the Legislative Acts of Virginia Concerning Negroes from Earliest Times to the Present.* Repr. Lovettsville, Virginia: Willow Bend Books, 1996.

Hall, Everard. *A Digested Index to the Virginia Reports...from Washington to Third Leigh.* Richmond: P. Cotton, 1825-1835.

Heinegg, Paul. *Free African Americans of North Carolina and Virginia.* 3d ed. Balitmore: Clearfield for Genealogical Publishing Company, 1997.

Hume, Ivor Noel. *1775: Another Part of the Field.* New York: Alfred A. Knopf, 1966.

Hurmence, Belinda, ed. *Before Freedom:. When I Just Can Remember.* Winston-Salem: John F. Blair, 1989, reprint 2000.

Johnston, David E. *A History of the Middle New River Settlements & Contiguous Territory.* Huntington, W.Va: Standard Ptg. & Pub. Co., 1906.

Kegley, Mary B. *Early Adventurers on the Western Waters,* Vol. 2, Orange, Virginia: Green Publishers, Inc., 1982.

_____. *Early Adventurers in the Town of Evansham, the County Seat of Wythe County, Virginia, 1790-1839.* Volume 4 in the *Early Adventurers* Series. Wytheville, VA: Kegley Books, 1998.

Killen, Linda. *A History of Slaves and Freedmen in Nineteenth Century Pulaski County, Virginia.* Radford, Virginia: Radford University, 1996.

Lasky, Kathryn. *True North.* New York: Scholastic Inc., 1996.

Lauber, Almon Wheeler, *Indian Slavery in Colonial times Within the Present Limits of the United States.* New York: Columbia University, 1913.

Lebsock, Suzanne. *Free Women of Petersburg: Status and Culture in a Southern Town, 1784-1860.* New York: W.W. Norton & Company, 1984.

Lyons, Mary E. *Letters from a Slave Girl: The Story of Harriett Jacobs.* New York: Charles Scribner's Sons, 1992.

Meaders, Daniel. *Advertisements for Runaway Slaves in Virginia, 1801-1820.* New York: Garland Publishing, Inc., 1997.

Merrell, James H. "Indians New World: The Catawba Experience," *Material Life in America, 1600-1860,* Northwestern University Press, 1988, pp. 95-112.

_____. *The Catawbas.* New York: Chelsea House Publishers, 1979.

McLaurin, Melton A. *Celia, a Slave.* Athens, GA: University of Georgia Press, 1991.

McLeRoy, Sherrie S. and William R. McLeRoy, *Strangers in Their Midst, The Free Black Population of Amherst County, Virginia,* Bowie, Maryland, Heritage Books, 1993.

Peacock, Peggy Carswell. *Choctaws in Virginia in 1712!"* *The Virginia Genealogist,* Vol. 29, No. 1 (Jan.-March, 1985), pp. 3-8.

Perdue, Charles L., Jr., Thomas E. Barden, Robert K. Phillips. *Weevils in the Wheat, Interviews with Ex-Slaves*. Charlottesville, University of Virginia, 1976.

Peterson, Harold L. *The Book of the Continental Soldier*. Harrisburg, PA: Stackpole, 1968.

Reports of Cases Argued and Determined in the Court of Appeals of Virginia [1821-1828] by Peyton Randolph. Richmond: P. Cotton, 1823-1929.

Robertson, David. *Denmark Vesey, the Buried History of American's Largest Slave Rebellion and the Man Who Led it*. New York: Alfred A. Knopf, 1999.

Rouse-Riboud, Barbara. *Sally Hemings*. New York: Ballantine Books, 1979, 1994.

Schmidt, Frederika Teute, and Barbara Ripel Whilhelm, eds. "Early Proslavery Petitions in Virginia." *William and Mary Quarterly* 30 (1973), 145.

Schwarz, Philip J. *Twice Condemned: Slaves and the Criminal Laws of Virginia, 1705-1865*. Baton Rouge, Louisiana State University Press, 1988.

Savitt, Todd L. *Medicine and Slavery. The Diseases and Health Care of Blacks in Antebellum Virginia*. Chicago: University of Illinois Press, 1978.

St. George, Robert Blair, ed. *Material Life in America, 1600-1860*. Boston: Northeastern University Press. 1988.

Snell, William Robert, "Indian Slavery in Colonial South Carolina, 1671-1795." Dissertation. The University of Alabama, 1972.

Tobin, Jacqueline and Raymond G. Dobard. *Hidden in Plain View, the Secret Story of Quilts and the Underground Railroad*. New York: Doubleday, 1999.

Walsh, Lorena S. *From Calabar to Carter's Grove, The History of a Virginia Slave Community,* Charlottesville: University Press of Virginia, 1997.

Wiencek, Henry. *The Hairstons, An American Family in Black and White.* New York: St. Martin's Press, 1999.

COURT RECORDS

Wythe County:

Chancery Cases:

Rachel Findlay, a woman of color vs. John Draper, Sr., 1818-01-SC.

Juda vs. John Draper, 1822-49.

Joseph Draper admr. of John Draper dec'd vs. Mitchell Clay, Henry Clay and William Clay, execs. of Mitchell Clay, dec'd et al. 1828-39-SC.

Samuel Patton and wife vs. Joseph Draper's Exors. & etc., 1844-13-CC.

Tom and Robbin [Findlay] vs. John Draper, Jr., 1820-60.

Court Orders dated June 10, 1813, August 11, 1813, November 10, 1813, August 9, 1820, February 13, 1822, March 13, 1822 and July 13, 1824. *See also* five volumes by Mary B. Kegley, *Abstracts of the Court Orders of Wythe County, Virginia.*

Henry County, Virginia, from the Library of Virginia, *Fender vs. Marr,* Loose Papers, Determined Cases, 1788-1789, folder 66.

Powhatan County, Virginia:
Order Book 3, Reel 22, Library of Virginia, pp. 319, 370,
419, 451, 477, 514, 545, 583, 613; Order Book
15, p. 174.
Chancery, *Rachel vs. John Draper, Sr.,* Decided May Term,
1820, Chancery Box 12.

Chesterfield County, Virginia:
Will Book 1, pp. 544-546, will of Henry Clay, Senior.
Will Book 2, pp. 350a-353, inventory of the late deceased
Henry Clay, Senior.

Montgomery County, Virginia:
Superior Court Order Book 1, pp. 270, 293, 305, 306:
Order Book 2, pp. 67, 68, regarding Rachel Viney.
County Order Book 1813-1815, Book 18, pp. 330, 331,
332; Order Book 20, pp. 66, 86, 111, 151, 195,
221; Book 21, pp. 9, 42, 79, 95, 96, regarding
Rachel Viney's family
Chancery, *Rachel Viney vs. Henry Patton*, Chancery File 185.

Giles County, Virginia:
Will Book A, p. 71, will of Mitchell Clay, Sr.1811.

Madison County, Alabama, Deed Book P, pp. 270-275.